MOBY DICK

Herman Melville

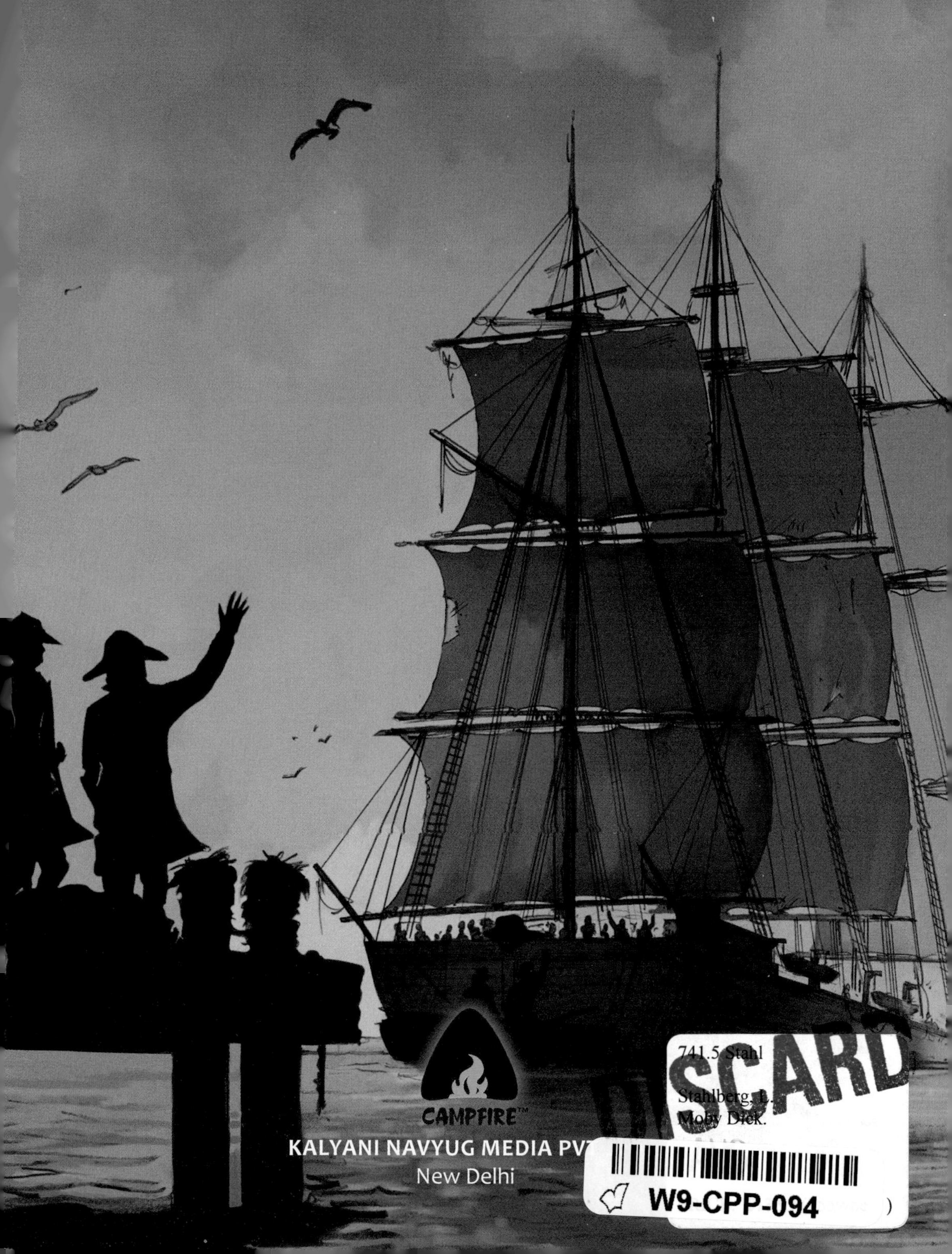

CAMPFIRE™

KALYANI NAVYUG MEDIA PVT

New Delhi

Sitting around the Campfire, telling the story, were:

Wordsmith	:	Lance Stahlberg
Illustrator	:	Lalit Kumar Singh
Illustrations Editor	:	Jayshree Das
Colorist	:	Ajo Kurian
Letterers	:	Bhavnath Chaudhary
		Vishal Sharma
Editors	:	Eman Chowdhary
		Mark Jones
Research Editor	:	Pushpanjali Borooah

Cover Artists:

Illustrator	:	Lalit Kumar Singh
Colorist	:	Ajo Kurian
Designer	:	Pushpa Verma

Published by Kalyani Navyug Media Pvt Ltd
101 C, Shiv House, Hari Nagar Ashram
New Delhi 110014
India
www.campfire.co.in

ISBN: 978-93-80028-22-4

Printed in India at Rave India

About the Author

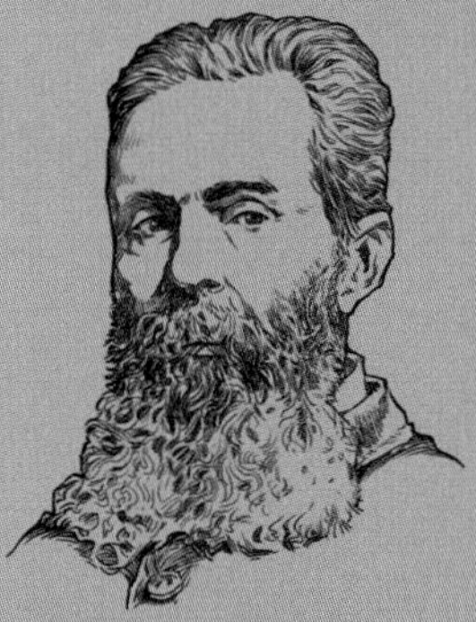

Born on August 1, 1819 in New York City, USA, Herman Melville was a novelist, poet and short story writer.

From an early age, Melville was fascinated with words and stories. Even though a bout of scarlet fever left him with impaired eyesight, he continued to be a voracious reader and writer throughout his life.

Early in his working life he trained to be a surveyor and considered undertaking that profession as a career. However, the canal project he had been hoping to work on never transpired. Although, at the time, this appeared to be a setback for Melville, it was quite probably a blessing in disguise. Instead of working on a canal, he ended up as a cabin boy on board a merchant ship. This eventually led to him taking a job on a whaling vessel which traveled to the south seas.

As his sailing career continued, Melville wrote his first novel, *Typee*, in 1856. It was inspired by his life on the seas and contains many scenes plucked from his own experiences.

Melville's life was certainly just as full of drama and excitement as his novels. In 1847, he joined a mutiny on a ship where the crew were arguing with the owners over their share of the profits. For this, Melville was thrown into a jail in Tahiti. He escaped from the prison without too much difficulty and was later able to use the experience to write the novel entitled *Omoo*.

By this point in his literary career, Melville had enjoyed moderate praise for the novels he had authored. Then, in 1850, he published *Moby Dick*, which was sadly met with little enthusiasm at first. However, its popularity has increased greatly over time, particularly after his death, and is now regarded as one of the best-loved classics.

In his later years, Melville suffered due to ill health and the loss of two sons. As a consequence of these two hardships, he died in April 1891. His life had been a difficult one and his literary merits had reaped him little profit. Nowadays, however, he is widely considered to be one of the greatest American writers of all time.

QUEEQUEG

CAPTAIN AHAB

ISHMAEL

STARBUCK

STUBB

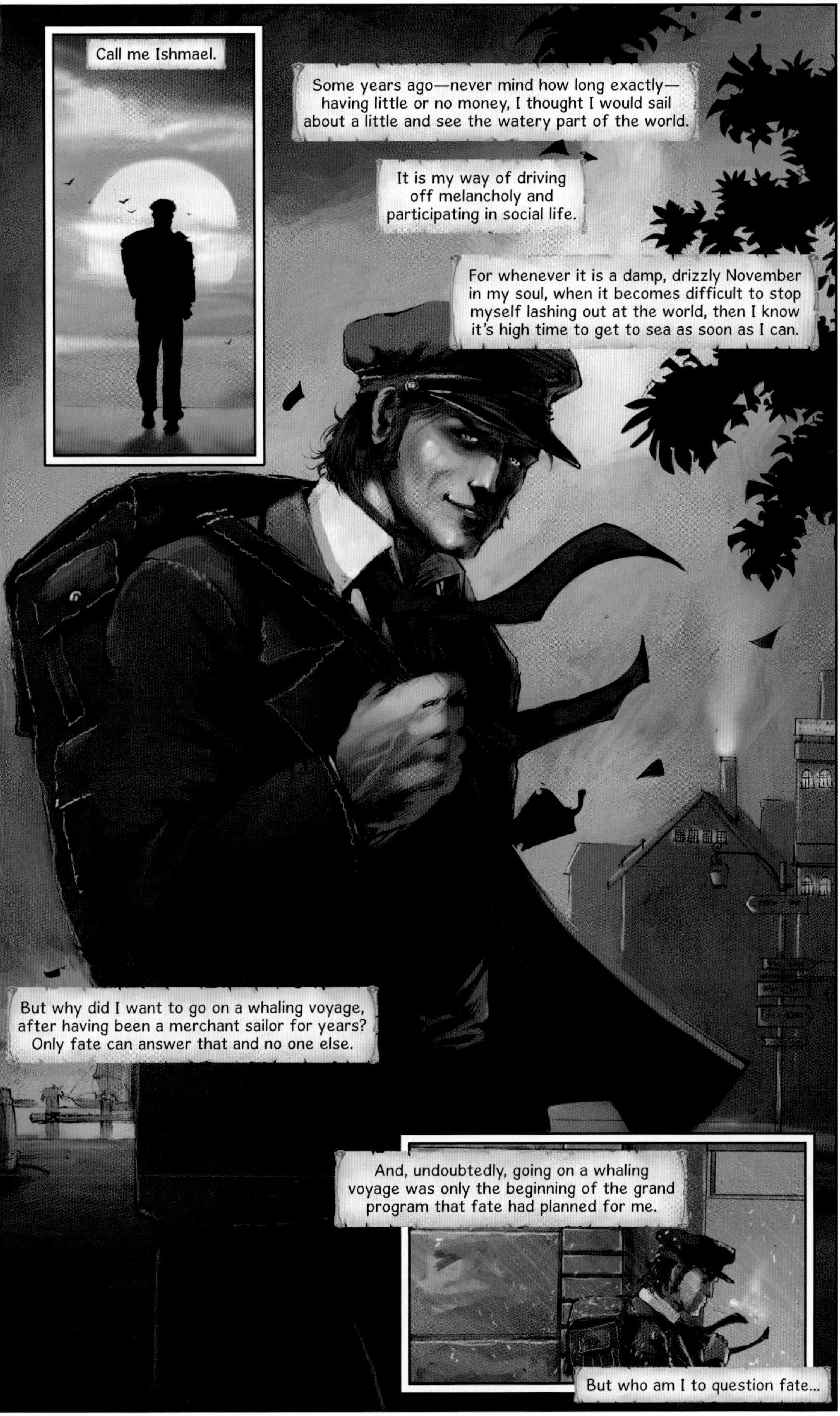

Call me Ishmael.
Some years ago—never mind how long exactly—having little or no money, I thought I would sail about a little and see the watery part of the world.
It is my way of driving off melancholy and participating in social life.
For whenever it is a damp, drizzly November in my soul, when it becomes difficult to stop myself lashing out at the world, then I know it's high time to get to sea as soon as I can.
But why did I want to go on a whaling voyage, after having been a merchant sailor for years? Only fate can answer that and no one else.
And, undoubtedly, going on a whaling voyage was only the beginning of the grand program that fate had planned for me.
But who am I to question fate...

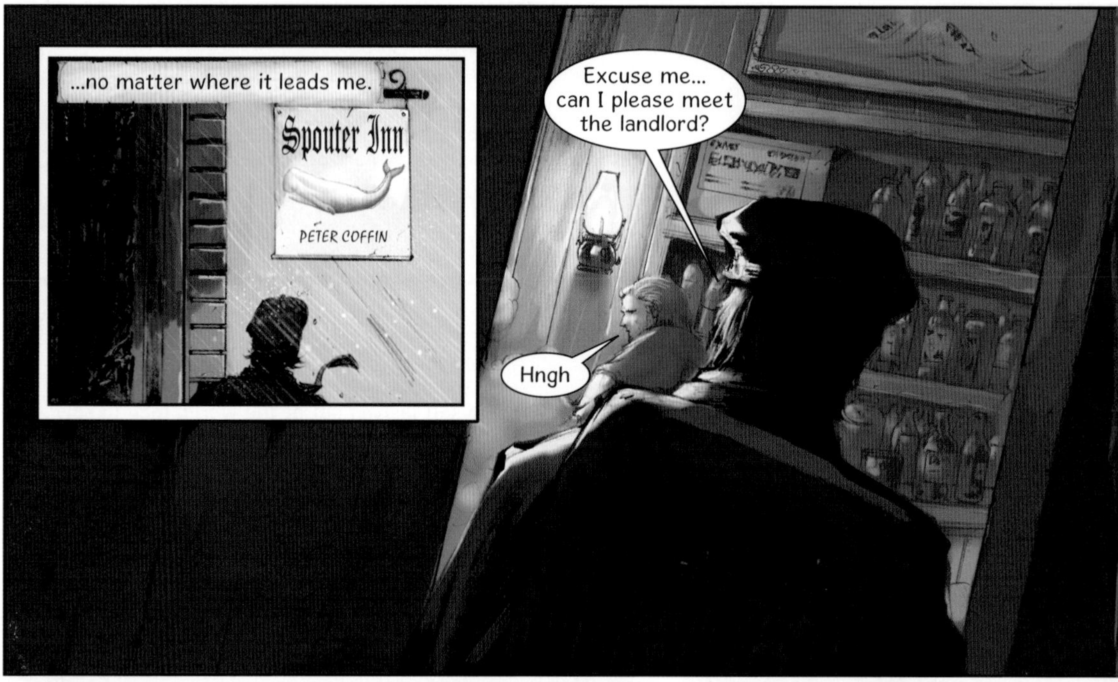
...no matter where it leads me.
Spouter Inn
PETER COFFIN
Excuse me... can I please meet the landlord?
Hngh

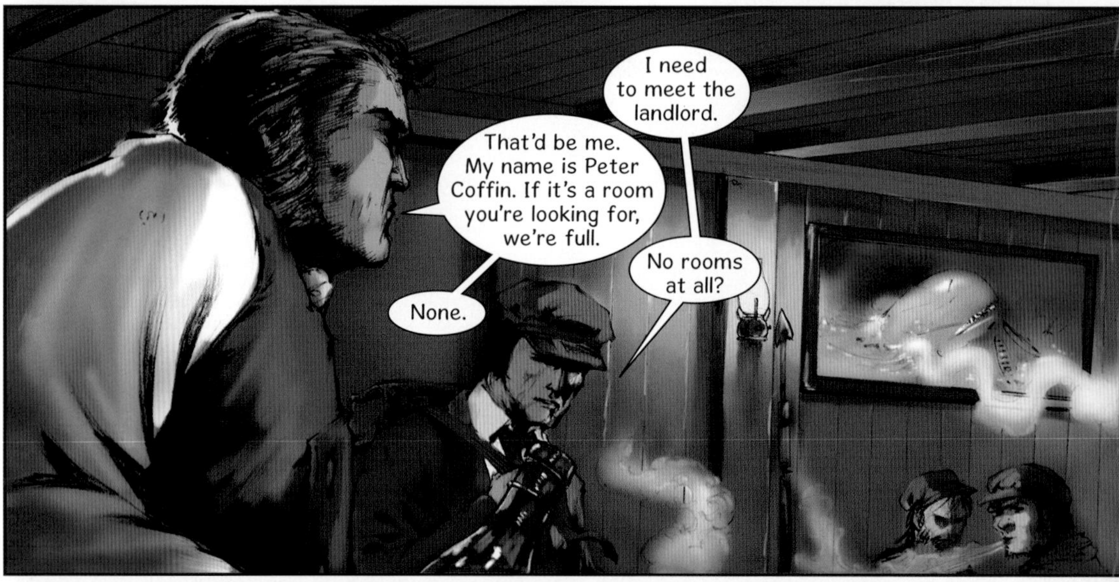
I need to meet the landlord.
That'd be me. My name is Peter Coffin. If it's a room you're looking for, we're full.
No rooms at all?
None.

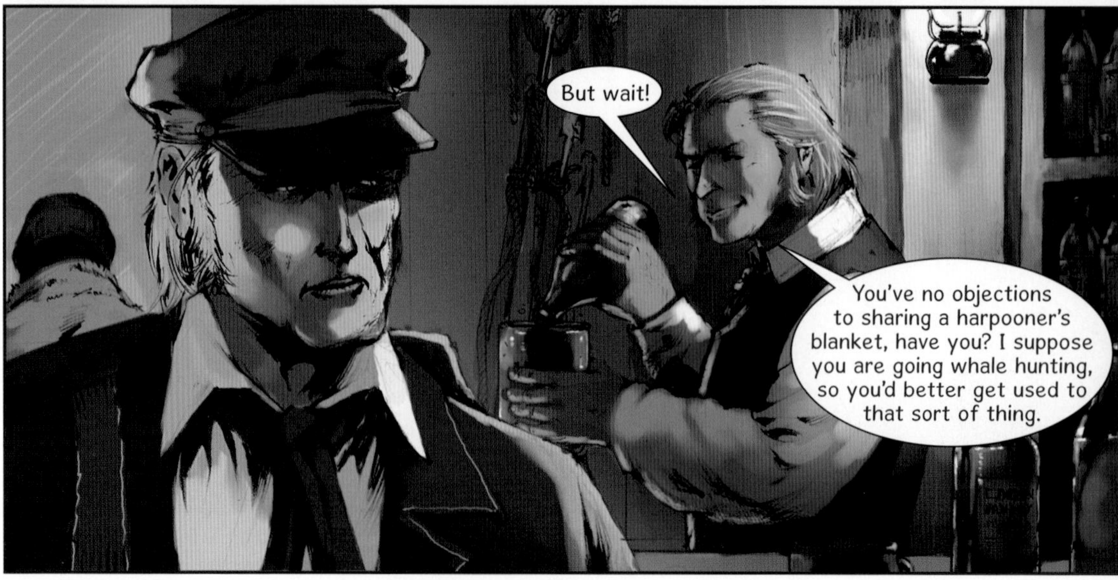
But wait!
You've no objections to sharing a harpooner's blanket, have you? I suppose you are going whale hunting, so you'd better get used to that sort of thing.

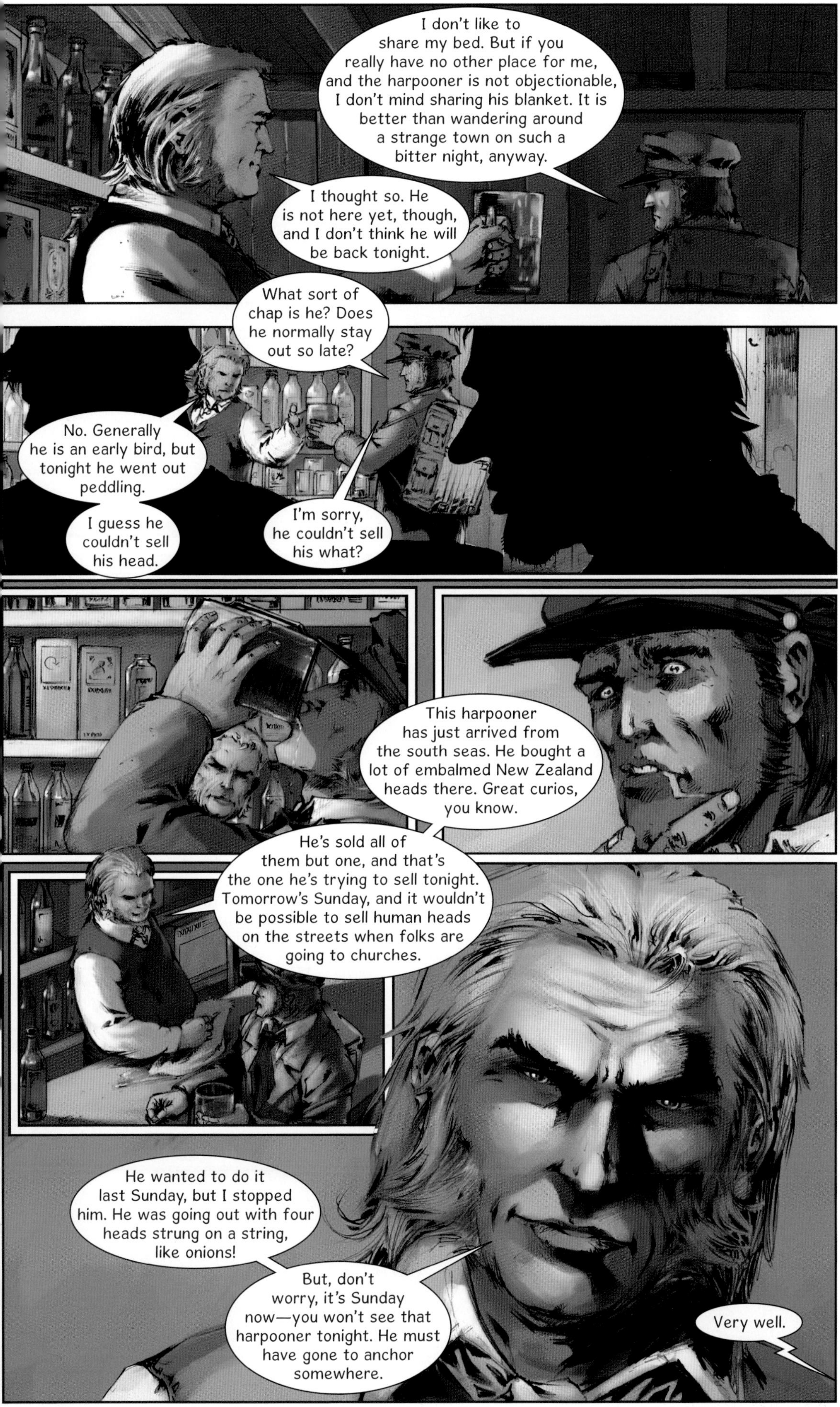
I don't like to share my bed. But if you really have no other place for me, and the harpooner is not objectionable, I don't mind sharing his blanket. It is better than wandering around a strange town on such a bitter night, anyway.
I thought so. He is not here yet, though, and I don't think he will be back tonight.
What sort of chap is he? Does he normally stay out so late?
No. Generally he is an early bird, but tonight he went out peddling.
I guess he couldn't sell his head.
I'm sorry, he couldn't sell his what?
This harpooner has just arrived from the south seas. He bought a lot of embalmed New Zealand heads there. Great curios, you know.
He's sold all of them but one, and that's the one he's trying to sell tonight. Tomorrow's Sunday, and it wouldn't be possible to sell human heads on the streets when folks are going to churches.
He wanted to do it last Sunday, but I stopped him. He was going out with four heads strung on a string, like onions!
But, don't worry, it's Sunday now—you won't see that harpooner tonight. He must have gone to anchor somewhere.
Very well.

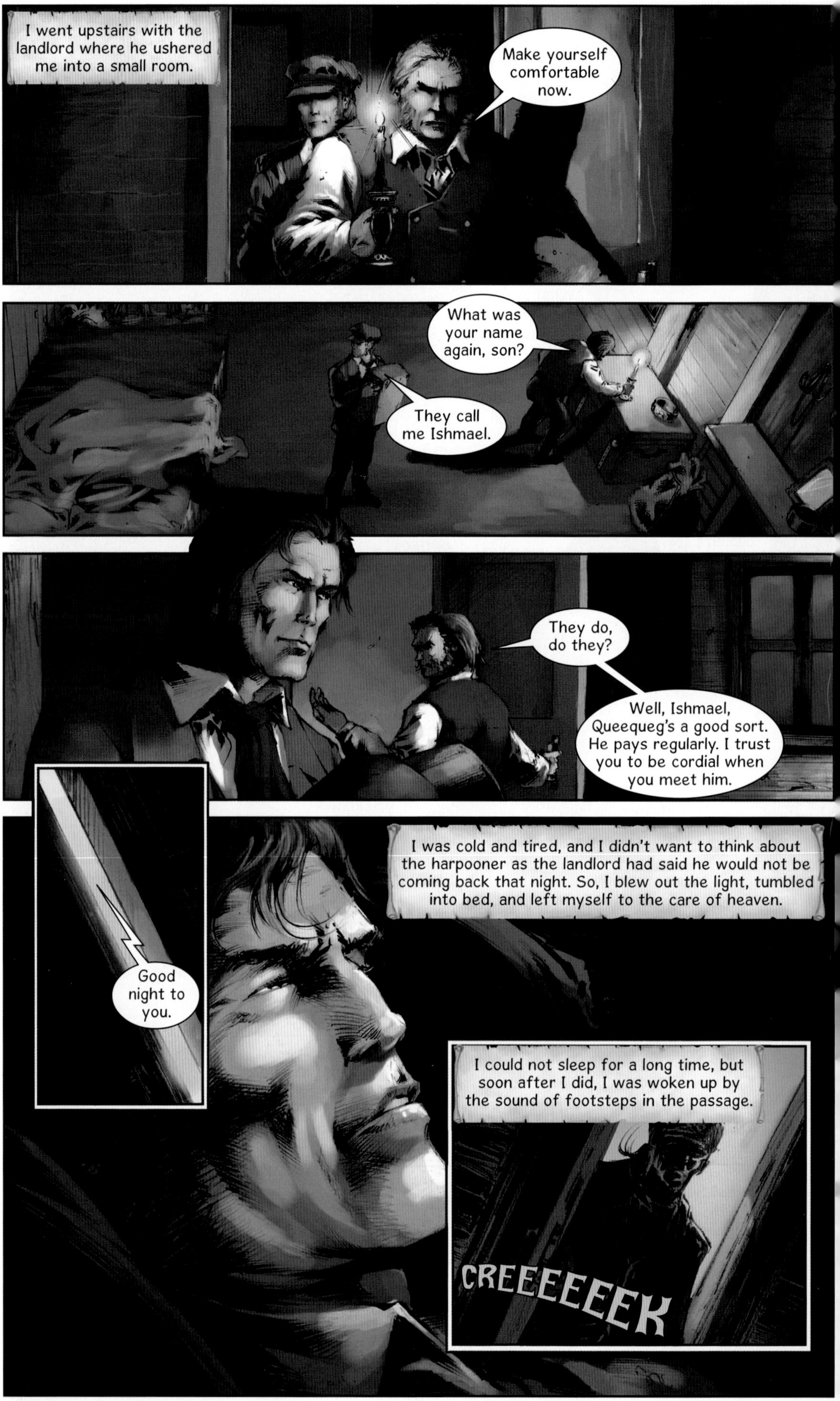
I went upstairs with the landlord where he ushered me into a small room.
Make yourself comfortable now.
What was your name again, son?
They call me Ishmael.
They do, do they?
Well, Ishmael, Queequeg's a good sort. He pays regularly. I trust you to be cordial when you meet him.
Good night to you.
I was cold and tired, and I didn't want to think about the harpooner as the landlord had said he would not be coming back that night. So, I blew out the light, tumbled into bed, and left myself to the care of heaven.
I could not sleep for a long time, but soon after I did, I was woken up by the sound of footsteps in the passage.
CREEEEEEEK

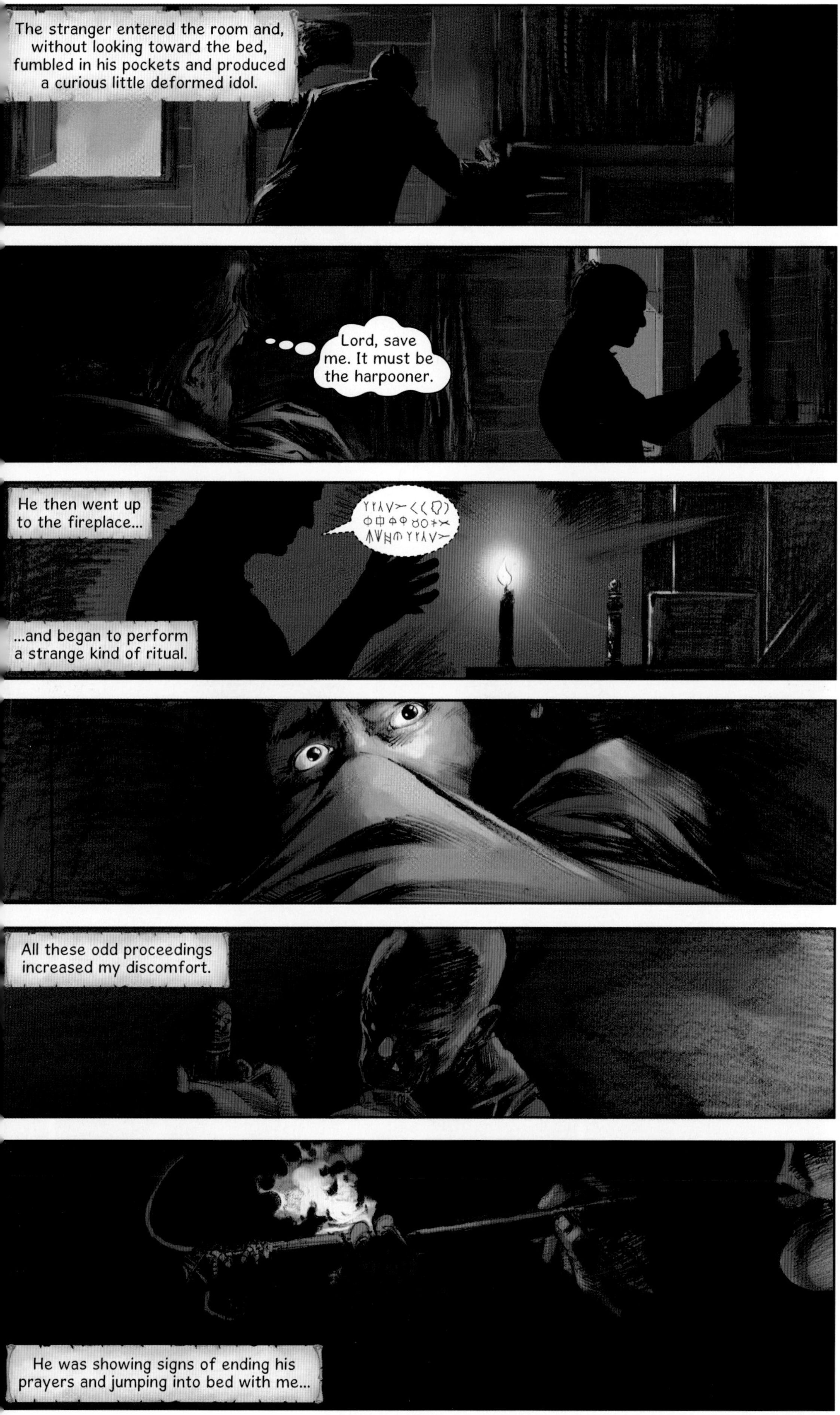
The stranger entered the room and, without looking toward the bed, fumbled in his pockets and produced a curious little deformed idol.
Lord, save me. It must be the harpooner.
He then went up to the fireplace...
...and began to perform a strange kind of ritual.
All these odd proceedings increased my discomfort.
He was showing signs of ending his prayers and jumping into bed with me...

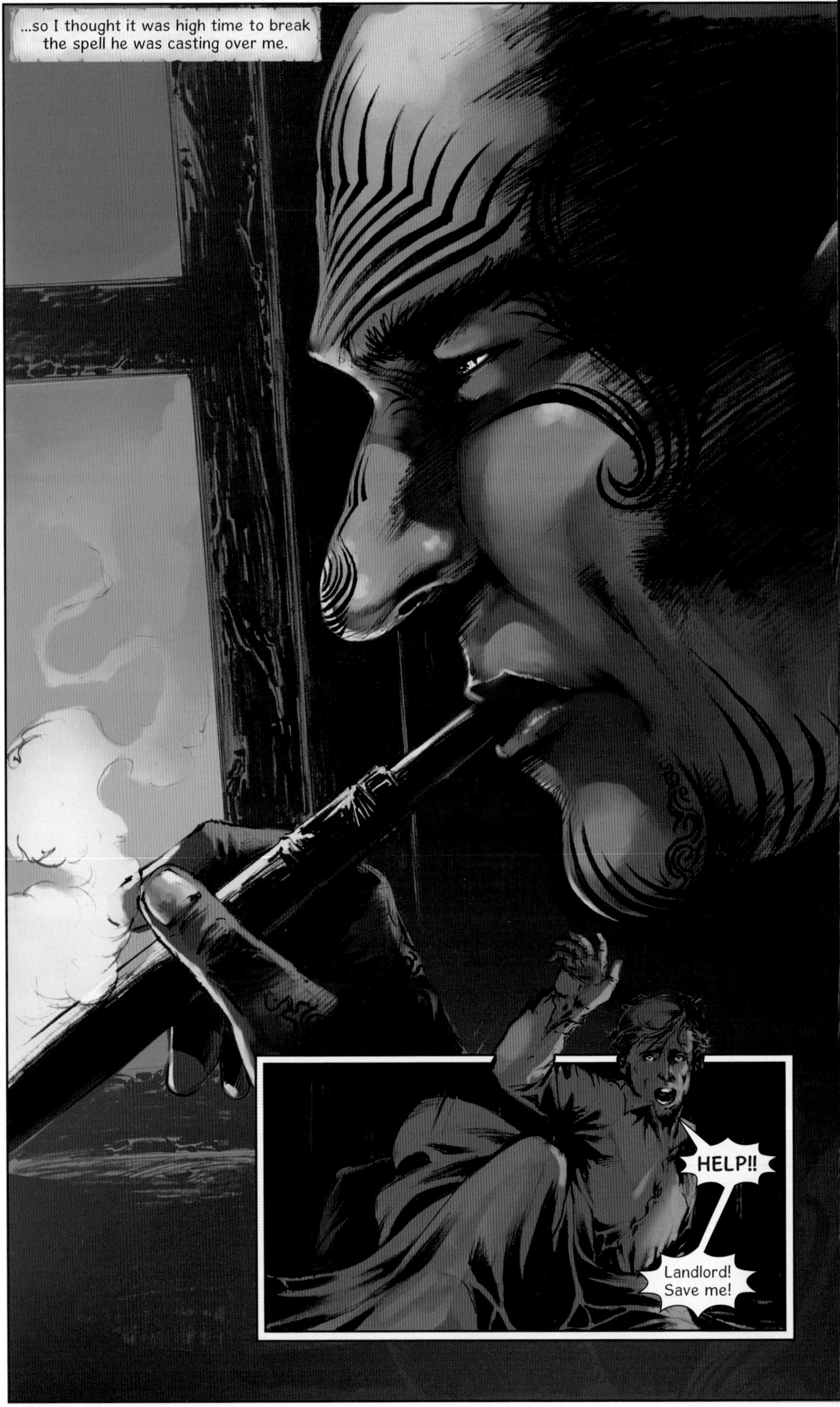

...so I thought it was high time to break the spell he was casting over me.
HELP!!
Landlord! Save me!

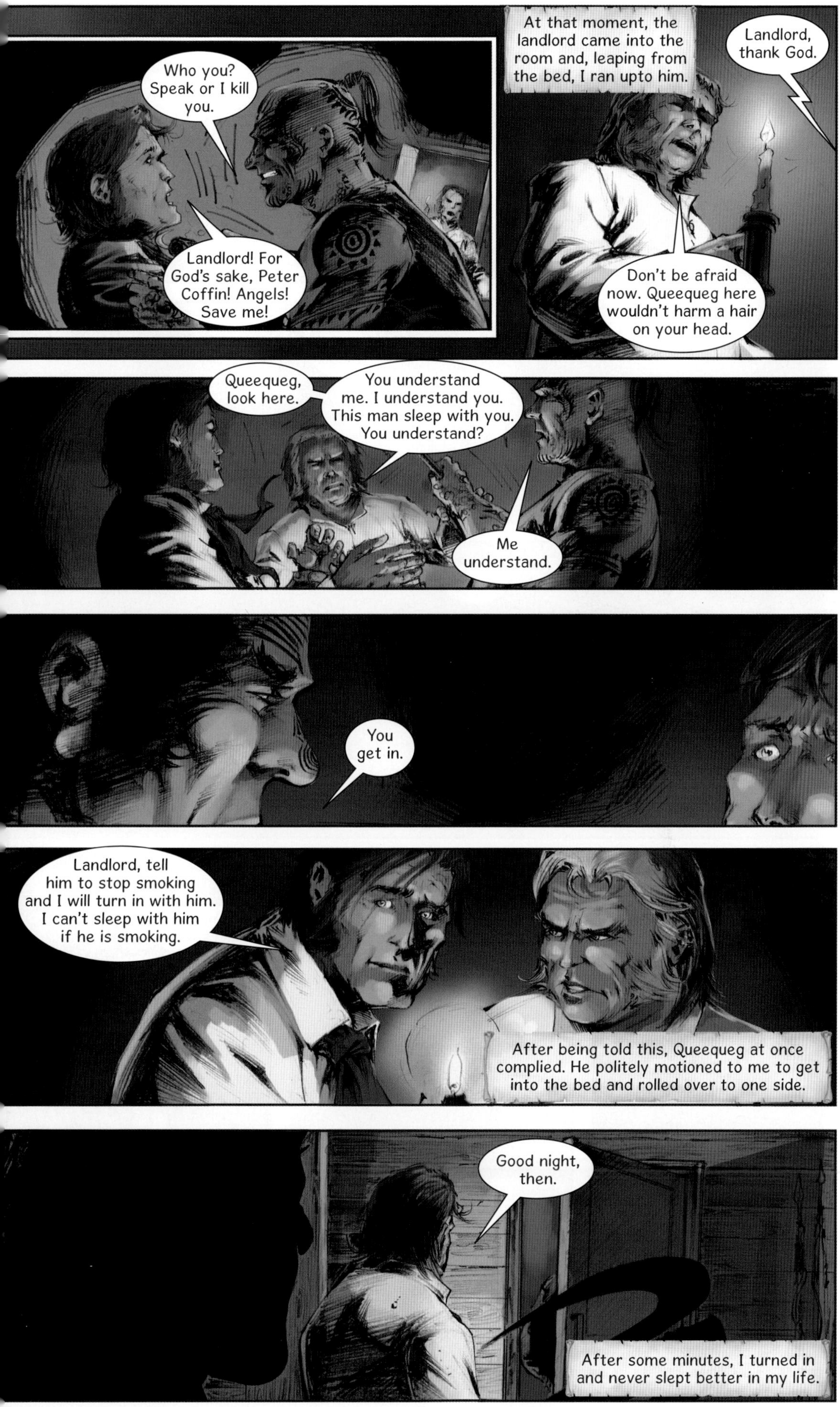
Who you? Speak or I kill you.
Landlord! For God's sake, Peter Coffin! Angels! Save me!
At that moment, the landlord came into the room and, leaping from the bed, I ran upto him.
Landlord, thank God.
Don't be afraid now. Queequeg here wouldn't harm a hair on your head.
Queequeg, look here.
You understand me. I understand you. This man sleep with you. You understand?
Me understand.
You get in.
Landlord, tell him to stop smoking and I will turn in with him. I can't sleep with him if he is smoking.
After being told this, Queequeg at once complied. He politely motioned to me to get into the bed and rolled over to one side.
Good night, then.
After some minutes, I turned in and never slept better in my life.

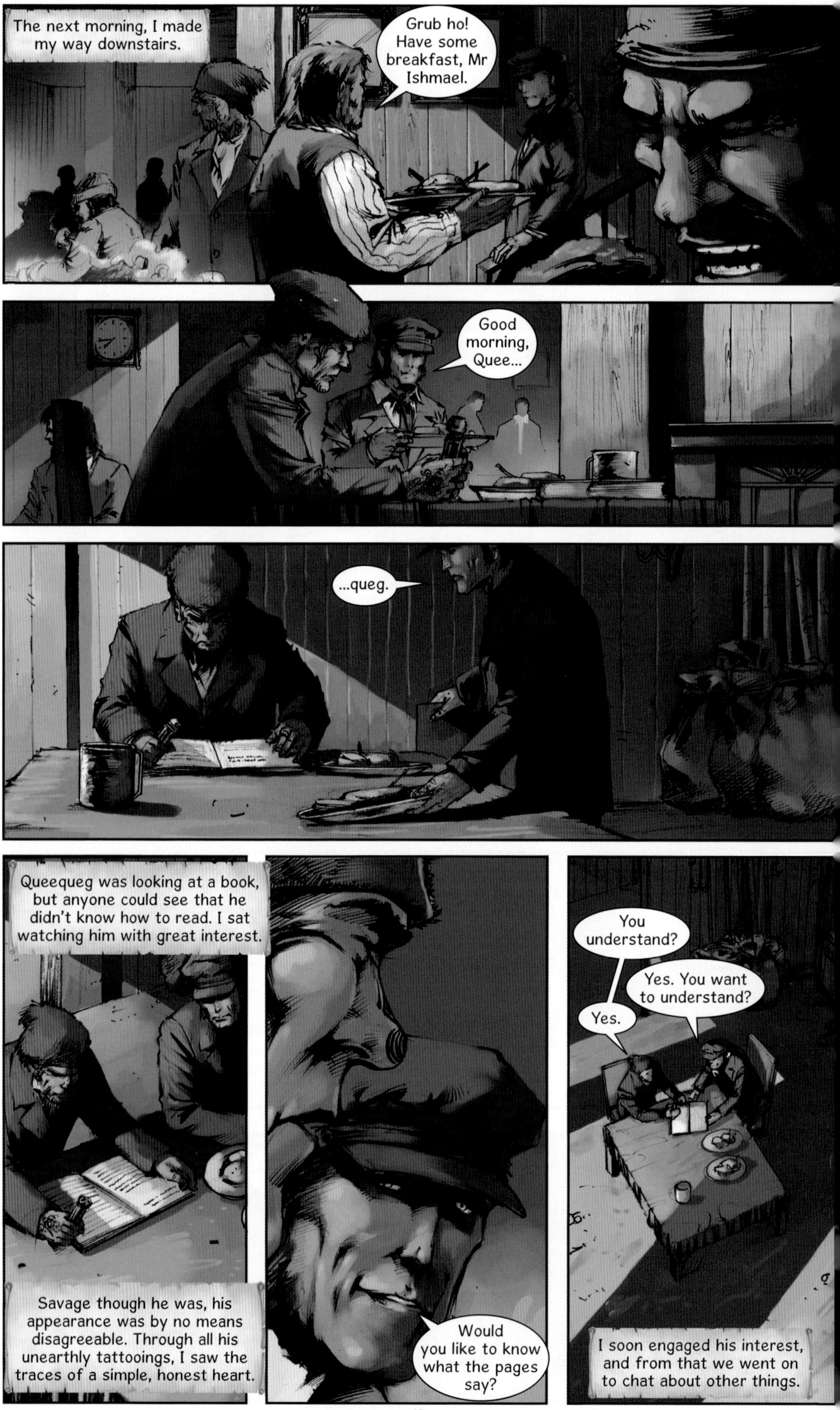
The next morning, I made my way downstairs.
Grub ho! Have some breakfast, Mr Ishmael.
Good morning, Quee...
...queg.
Queequeg was looking at a book, but anyone could see that he didn't know how to read. I sat watching him with great interest.
Savage though he was, his appearance was by no means disagreeable. Through all his unearthly tattooings, I saw the traces of a simple, honest heart.
Would you like to know what the pages say?
You understand?
Yes. You want to understand?
Yes.
I soon engaged his interest, and from that we went on to chat about other things.

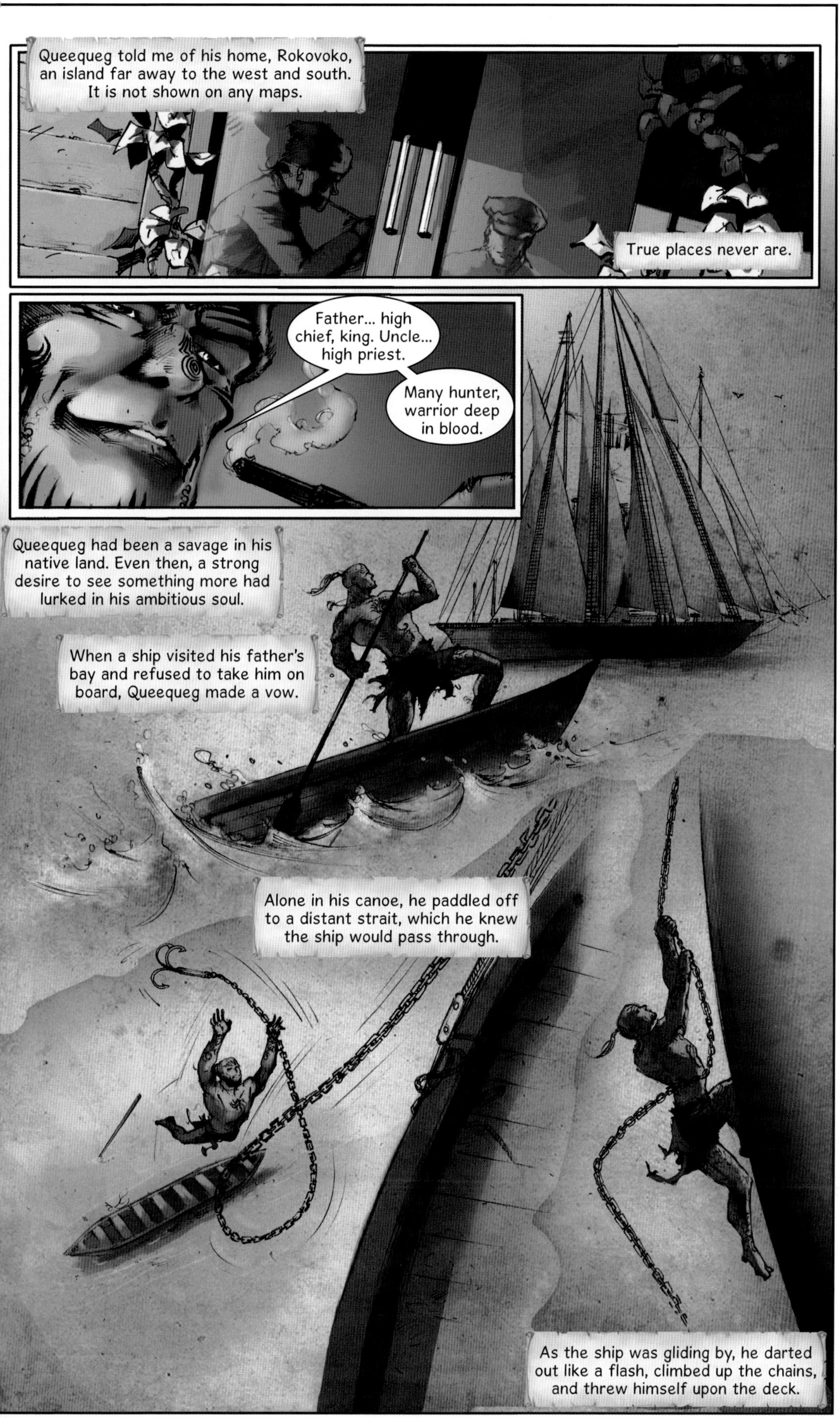
Queequeg told me of his home, Rokovoko, an island far away to the west and south. It is not shown on any maps.
True places never are.
Father... high chief, king. Uncle... high priest.
Many hunter, warrior deep in blood.
Queequeg had been a savage in his native land. Even then, a strong desire to see something more had lurked in his ambitious soul.
When a ship visited his father's bay and refused to take him on board, Queequeg made a vow.
Alone in his canoe, he paddled off to a distant strait, which he knew the ship would pass through.
As the ship was gliding by, he darted out like a flash, climbed up the chains, and threw himself upon the deck.

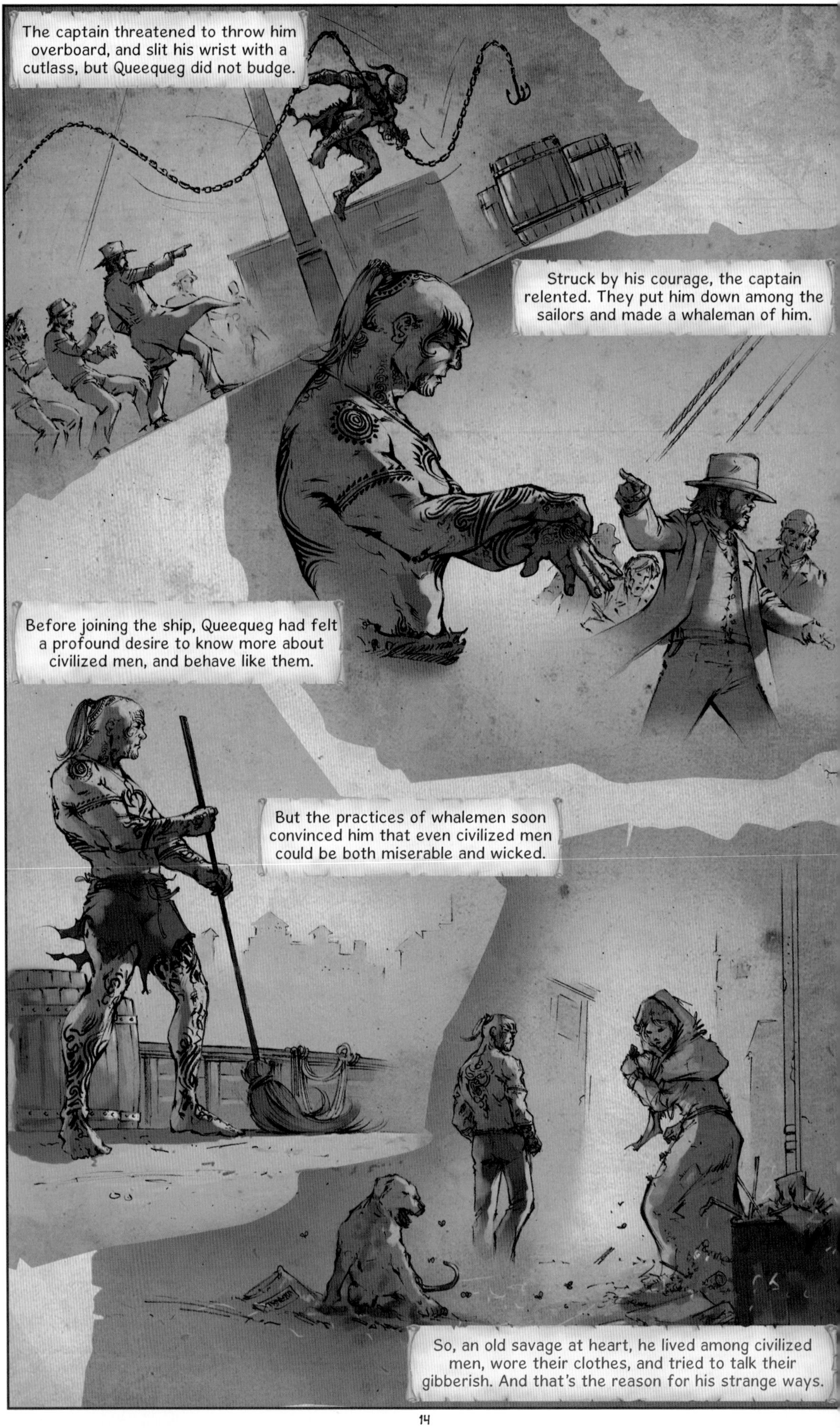

The captain threatened to throw him overboard, and slit his wrist with a cutlass, but Queequeg did not budge.
Struck by his courage, the captain relented. They put him down among the sailors and made a whaleman of him.
Before joining the ship, Queequeg had felt a profound desire to know more about civilized men, and behave like them.
But the practices of whalemen soon convinced him that even civilized men could be both miserable and wicked.
So, an old savage at heart, he lived among civilized men, wore their clothes, and tried to talk their gibberish. And that's the reason for his strange ways.

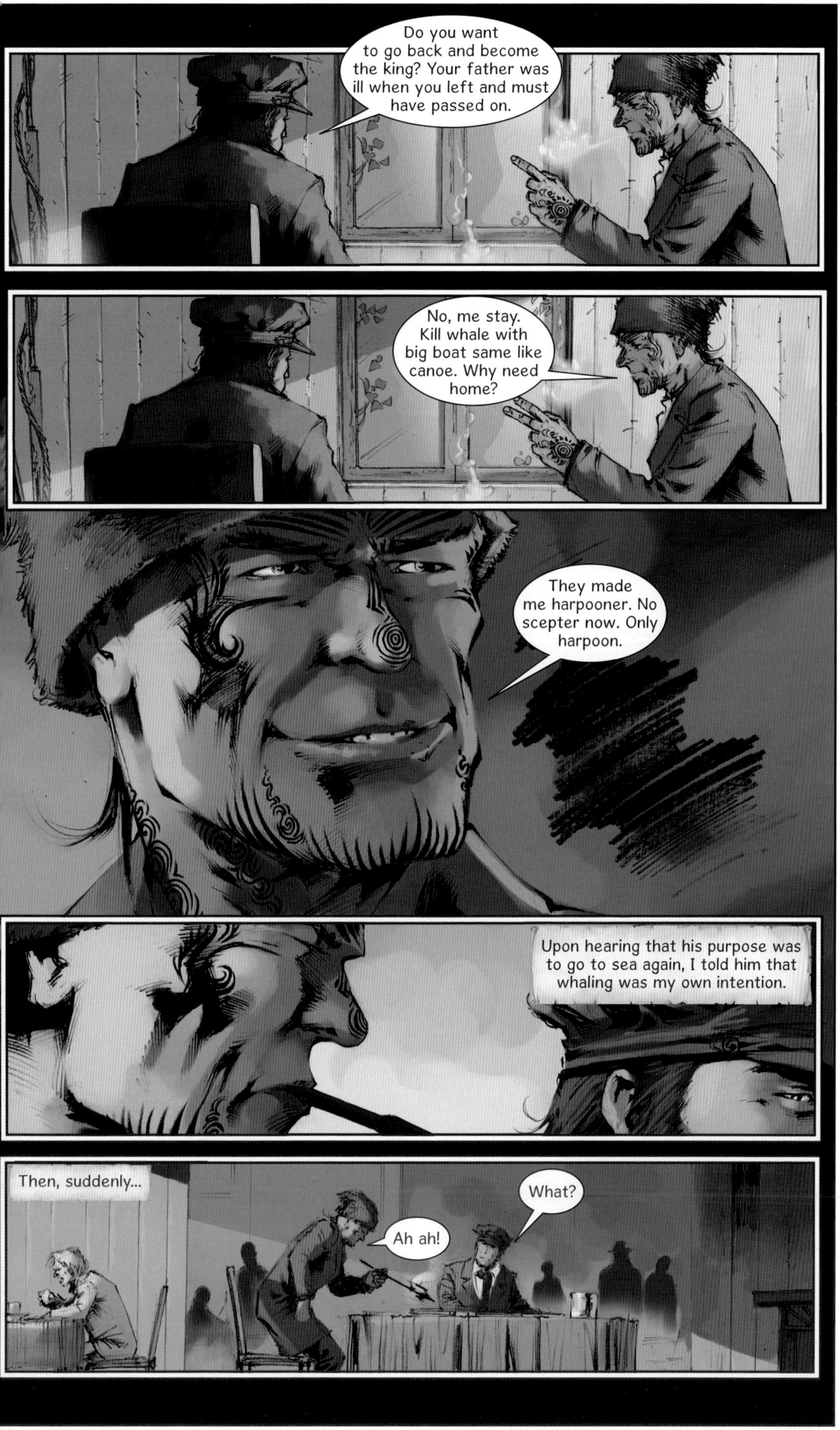
Do you want to go back and become the king? Your father was ill when you left and must have passed on.
No, me stay. Kill whale with big boat same like canoe. Why need home?
They made me harpooner. No scepter now. Only harpoon.
Upon hearing that his purpose was to go to sea again, I told him that whaling was my own intention.
Then, suddenly...
What?
Ah ah!

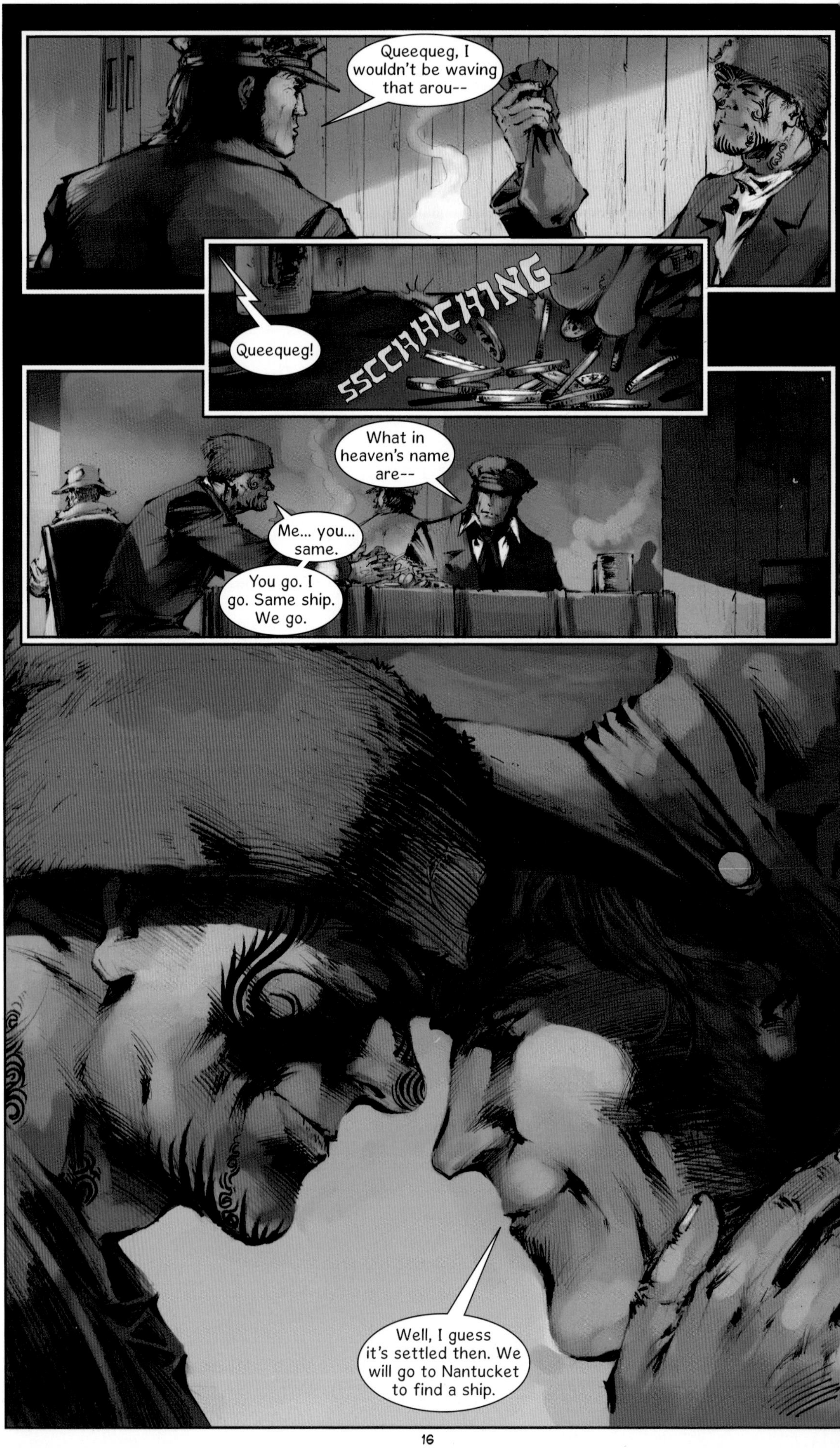
Queequeg, I wouldn't be waving that arou--
Queequeg!
SSCCHCHING
What in heaven's name are--
Me... you... same.
You go. I go. Same ship. We go.
Well, I guess it's settled then. We will go to Nantucket to find a ship.

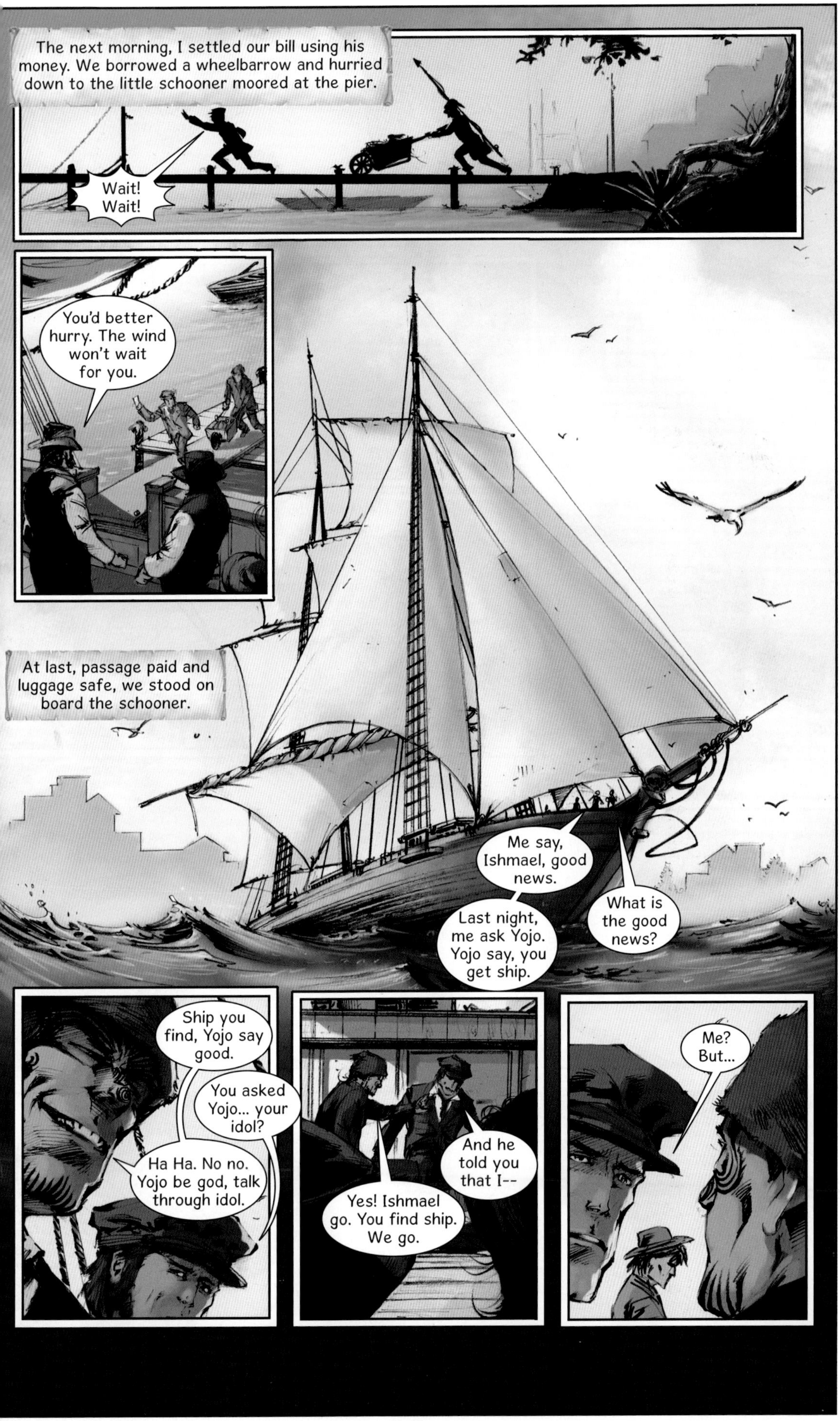
The next morning, I settled our bill using his money. We borrowed a wheelbarrow and hurried down to the little schooner moored at the pier.
Wait! Wait!
You'd better hurry. The wind won't wait for you.
At last, passage paid and luggage safe, we stood on board the schooner.
Me say, Ishmael, good news.
What is the good news?
Last night, me ask Yojo. Yojo say, you get ship.
Ship you find, Yojo say good.
You asked Yojo... your idol?
Ha Ha. No no. Yojo be god, talk through idol.
And he told you that I--
Yes! Ishmael go. You find ship. We go.
Me? But...

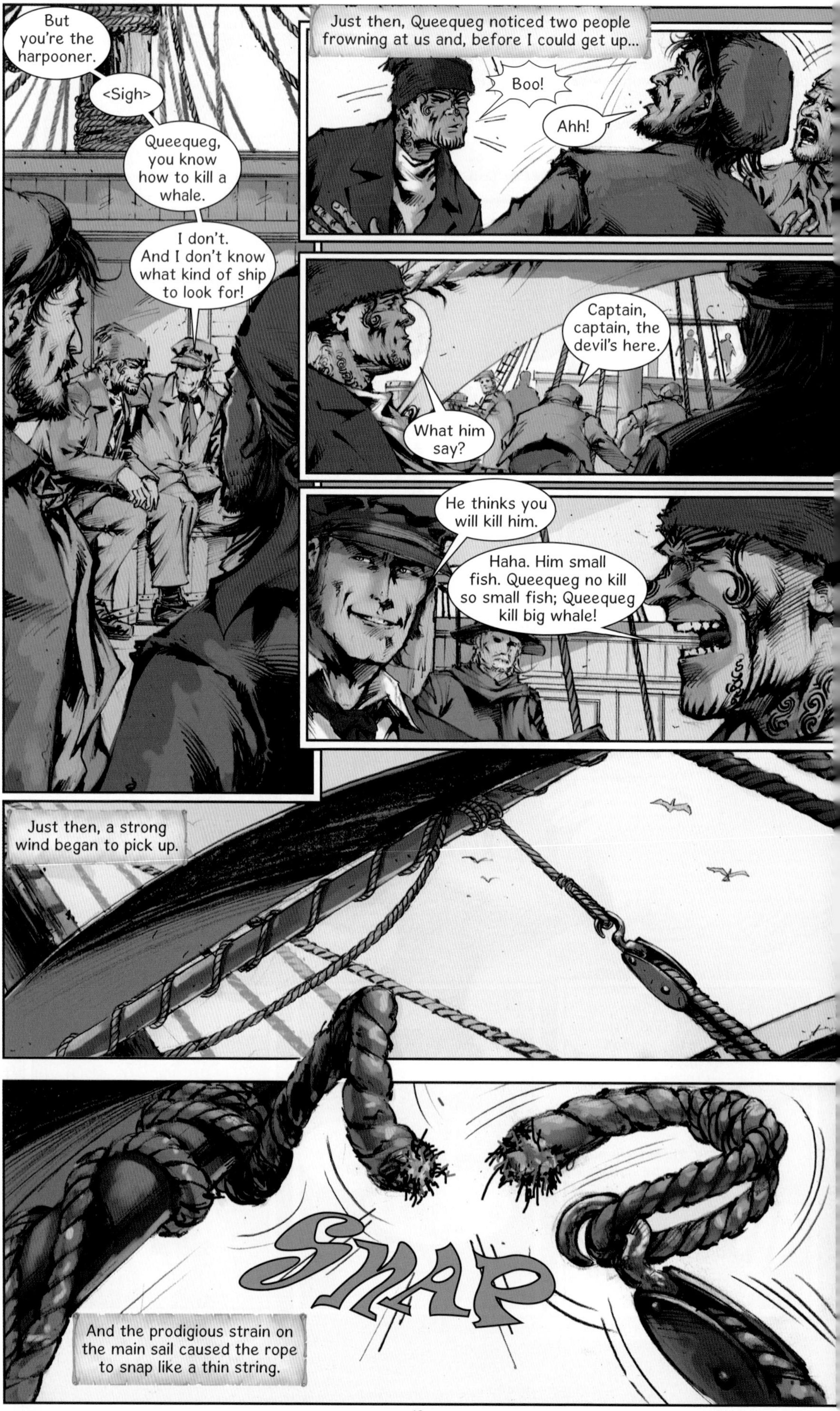
But you're the harpooner.
<Sigh>
Queequeg, you know how to kill a whale.
I don't. And I don't know what kind of ship to look for!
Just then, Queequeg noticed two people frowning at us and, before I could get up...
Boo!
Ahh!
Captain, captain, the devil's here.
What him say?
He thinks you will kill him.
Haha. Him small fish. Queequeg no kill so small fish; Queequeg kill big whale!
Just then, a strong wind began to pick up.
SNAP
And the prodigious strain on the main sail caused the rope to snap like a thin string.

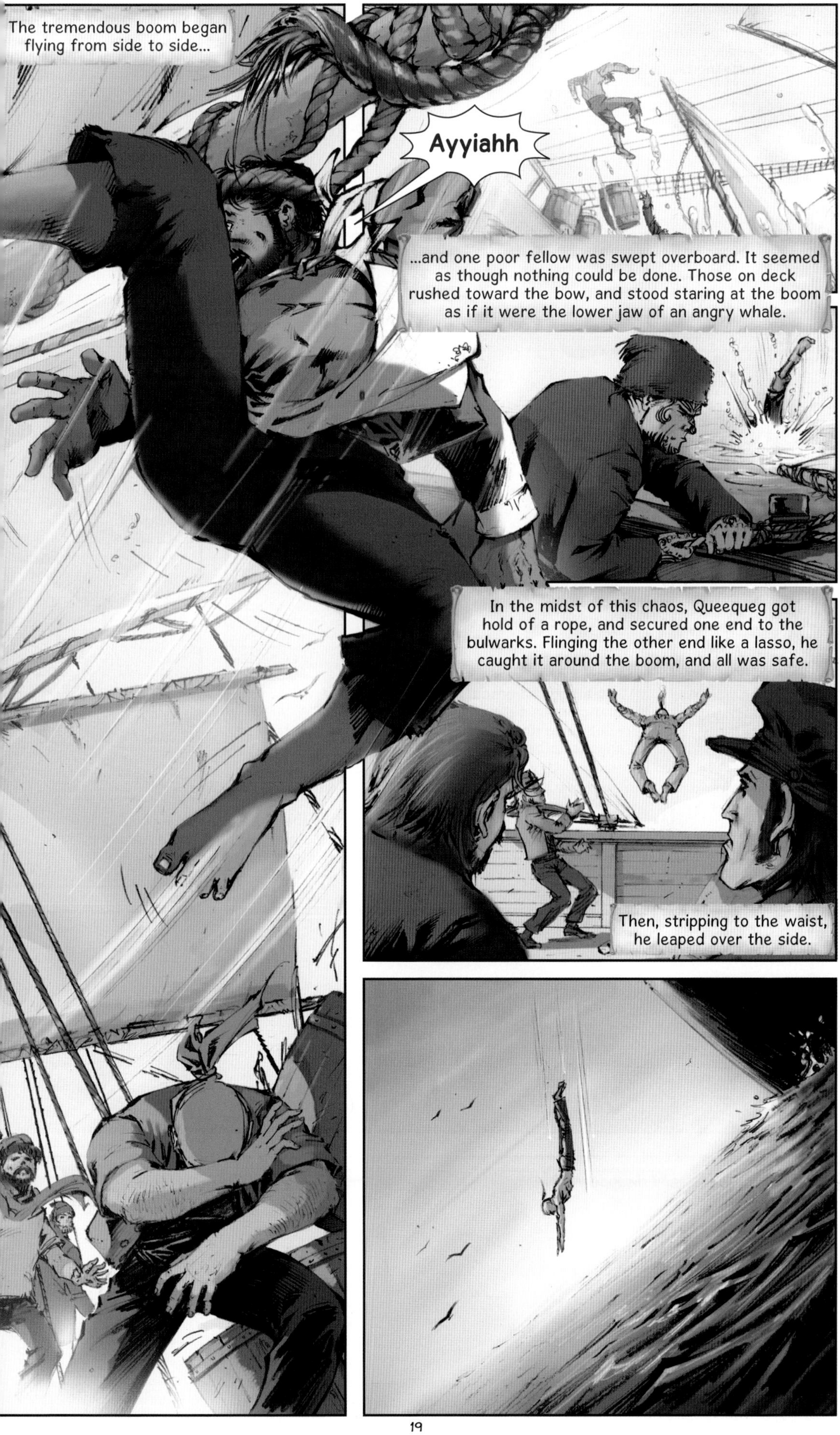

The tremendous boom began flying from side to side...
Ayyiahh
...and one poor fellow was swept overboard. It seemed as though nothing could be done. Those on deck rushed toward the bow, and stood staring at the boom as if it were the lower jaw of an angry whale.
In the midst of this chaos, Queequeg got hold of a rope, and secured one end to the bulwarks. Flinging the other end like a lasso, he caught it around the boom, and all was safe.
Then, stripping to the waist, he leaped over the side.

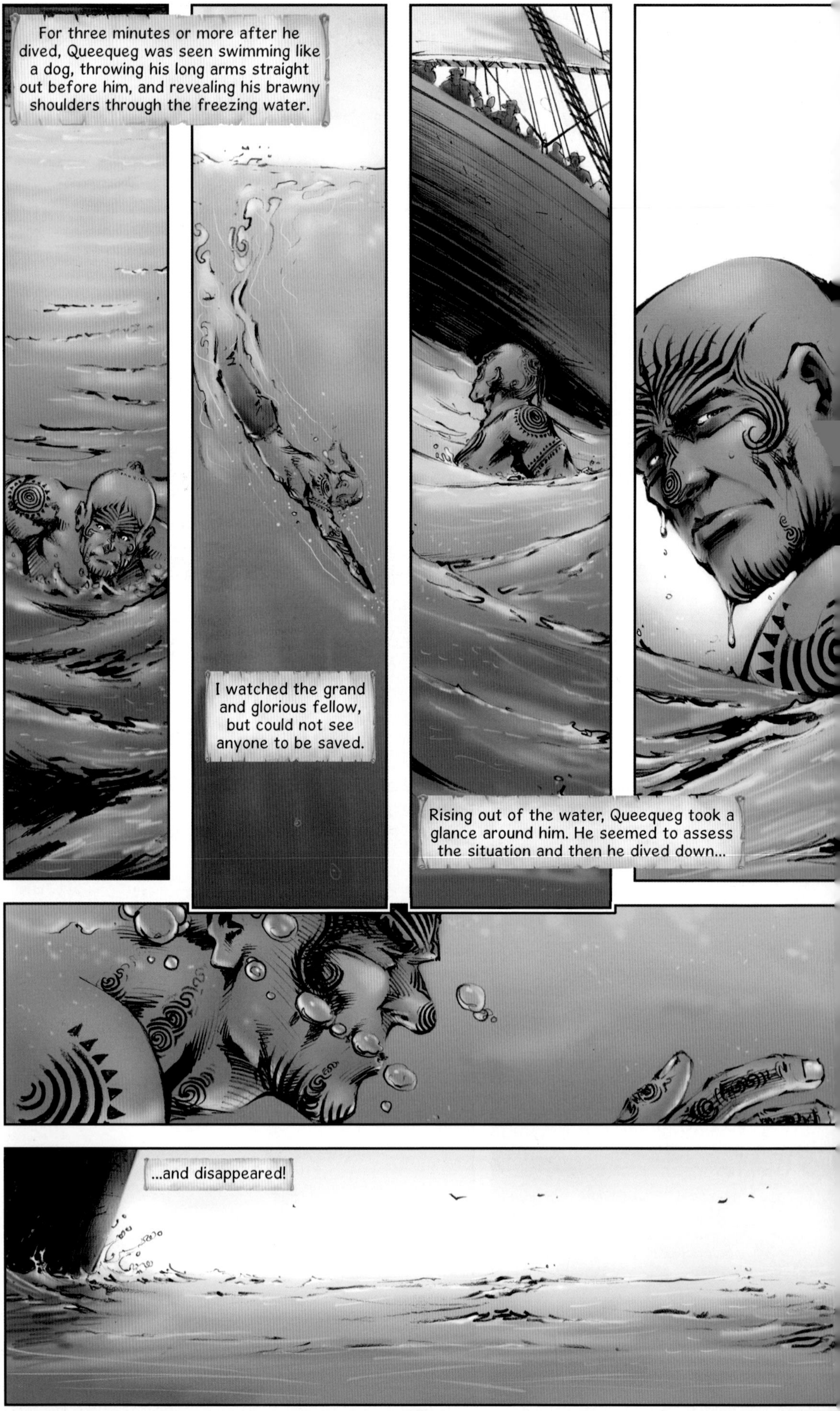
For three minutes or more after he dived, Queequeg was seen swimming like a dog, throwing his long arms straight out before him, and revealing his brawny shoulders through the freezing water.
I watched the grand and glorious fellow, but could not see anyone to be saved.
Rising out of the water, Queequeg took a glance around him. He seemed to assess the situation and then he dived down...
...and disappeared!

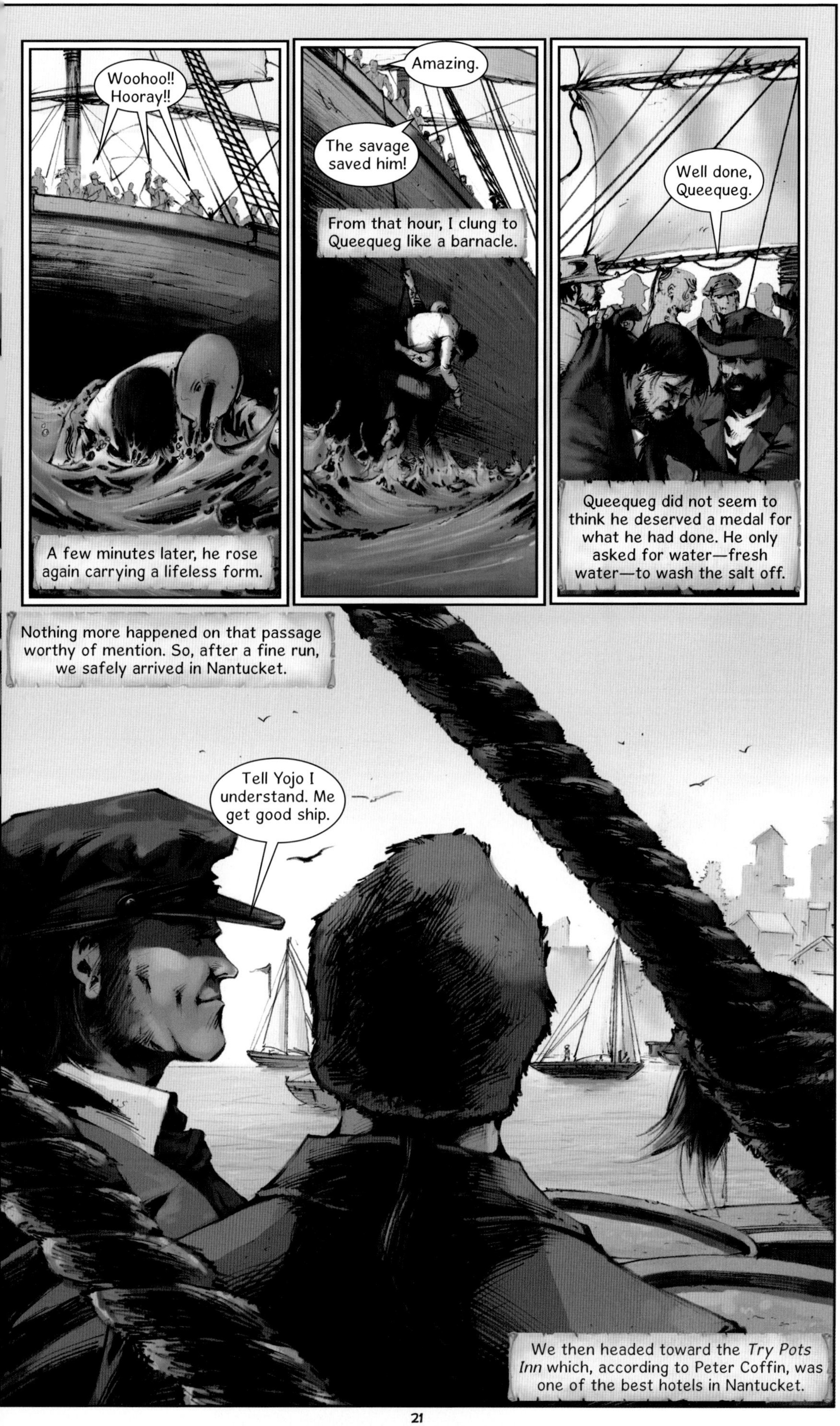
Woohoo!! Hooray!!
A few minutes later, he rose again carrying a lifeless form.
Amazing.
The savage saved him!
From that hour, I clung to Queequeg like a barnacle.
Well done, Queequeg.
Queequeg did not seem to think he deserved a medal for what he had done. He only asked for water—fresh water—to wash the salt off.
Nothing more happened on that passage worthy of mention. So, after a fine run, we safely arrived in Nantucket.
Tell Yojo I understand. Me get good ship.
We then headed toward the *Try Pots Inn* which, according to Peter Coffin, was one of the best hotels in Nantucket.

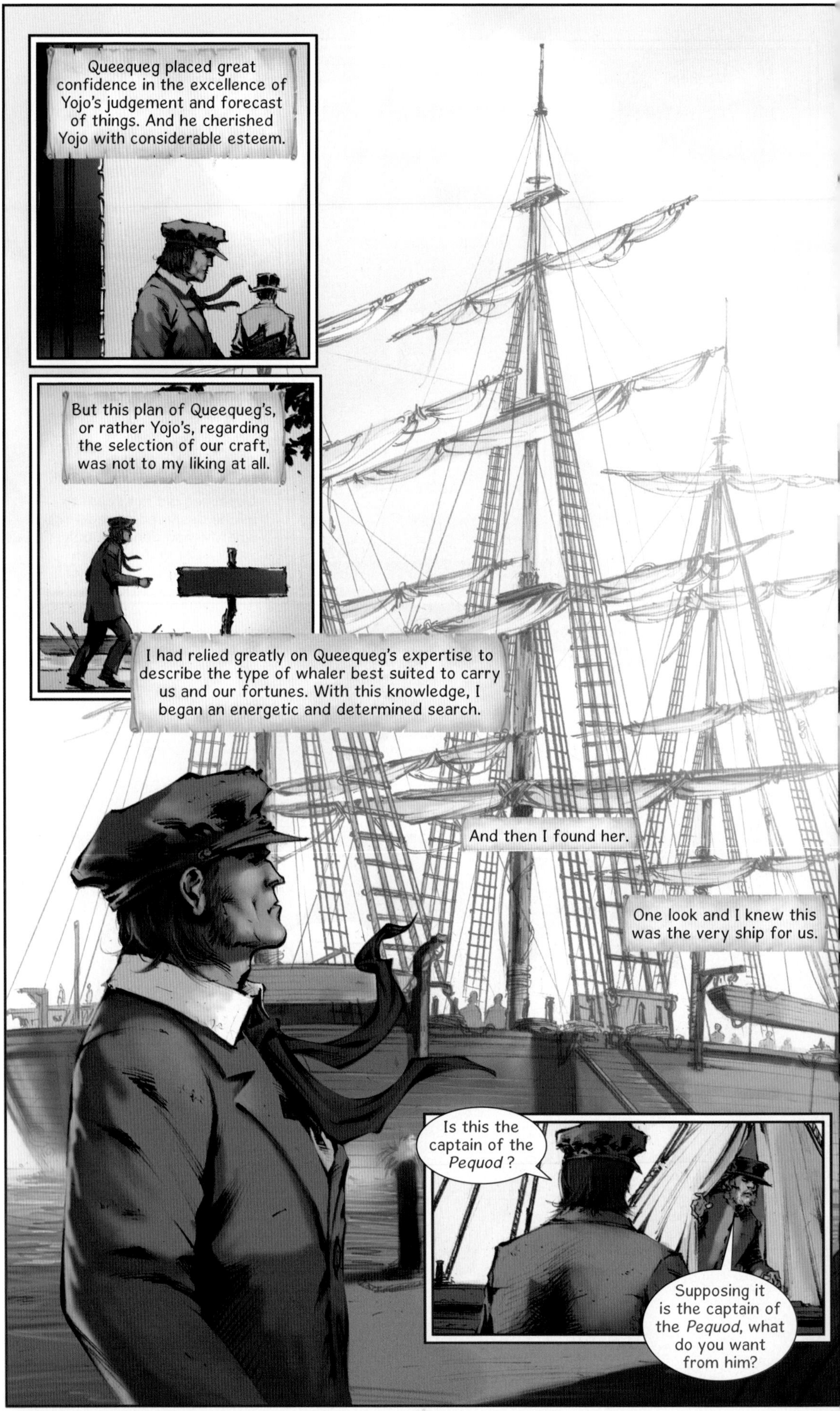

Queequeg placed great confidence in the excellence of Yojo's judgement and forecast of things. And he cherished Yojo with considerable esteem.
But this plan of Queequeg's, or rather Yojo's, regarding the selection of our craft, was not to my liking at all.
I had relied greatly on Queequeg's expertise to describe the type of whaler best suited to carry us and our fortunes. With this knowledge, I began an energetic and determined search.
And then I found her.
One look and I knew this was the very ship for us.
Is this the captain of the *Pequod*?
Supposing it is the captain of the *Pequod*, what do you want from him?

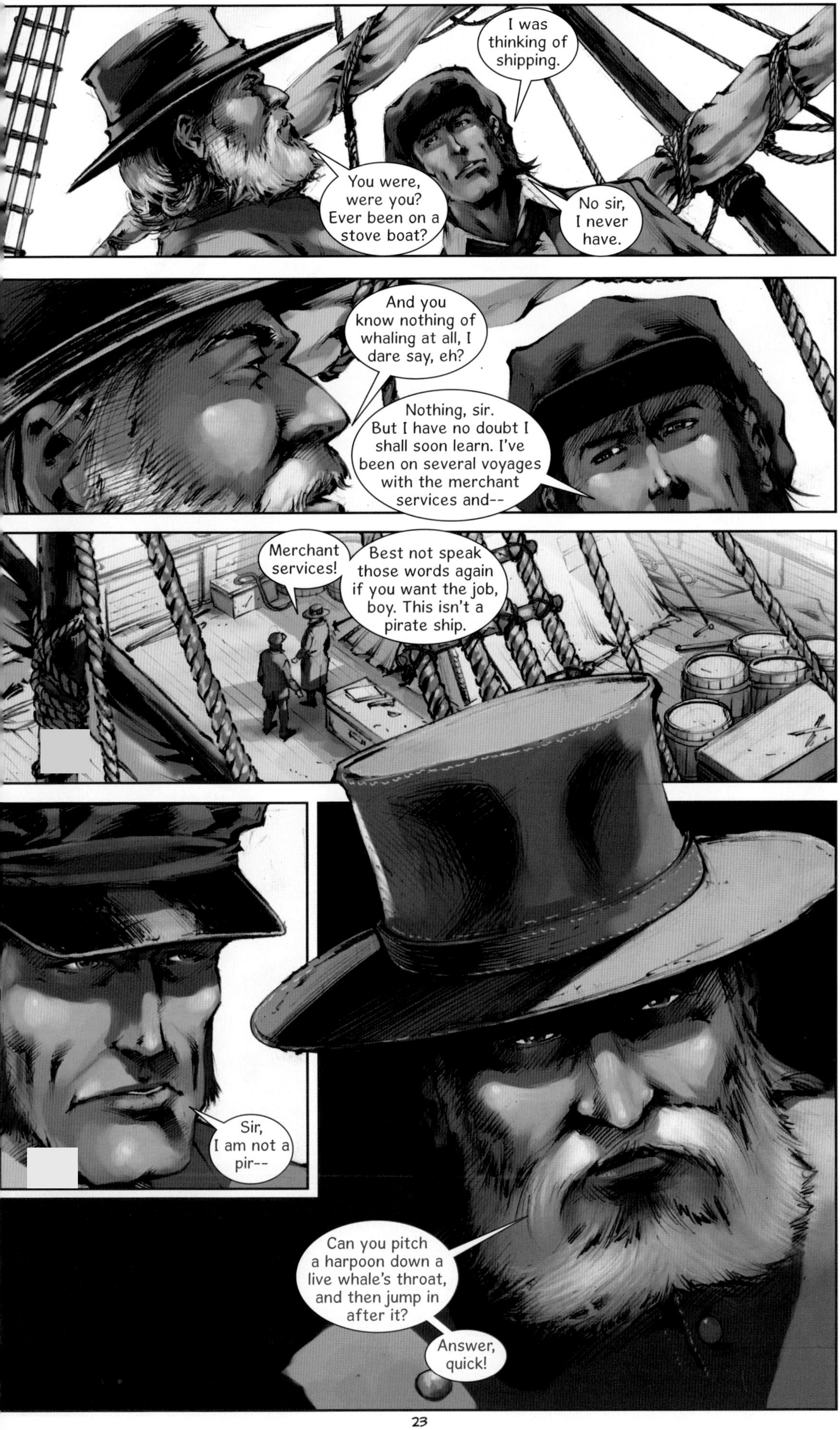
I was thinking of shipping.
You were, were you? Ever been on a stove boat?
No sir, I never have.
And you know nothing of whaling at all, I dare say, eh?
Nothing, sir. But I have no doubt I shall soon learn. I've been on several voyages with the merchant services and--
Merchant services!
Best not speak those words again if you want the job, boy. This isn't a pirate ship.
Sir, I am not a pir--
Can you pitch a harpoon down a live whale's throat, and then jump in after it?
Answer, quick!

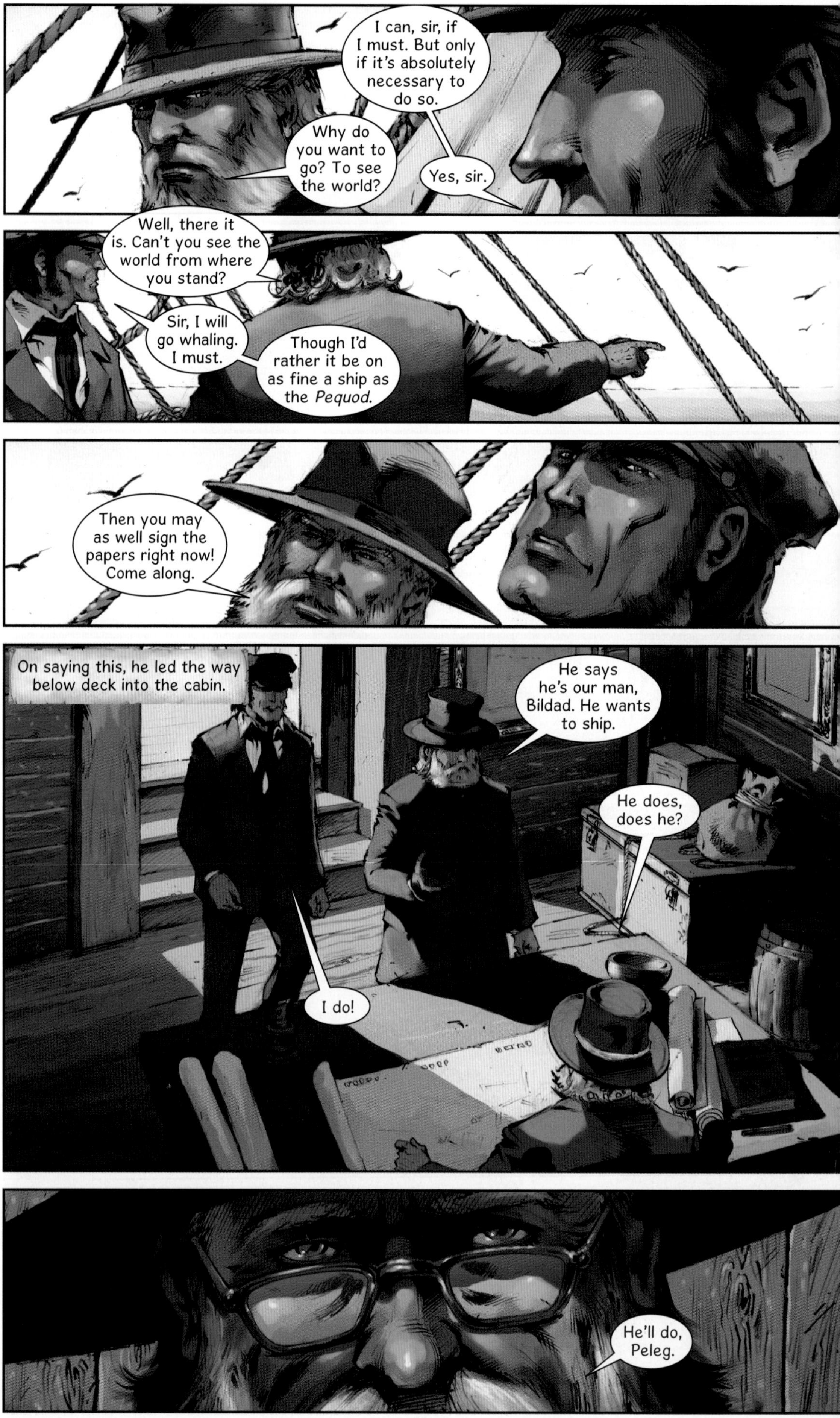
I can, sir, if I must. But only if it's absolutely necessary to do so.
Why do you want to go? To see the world?
Yes, sir.
Well, there it is. Can't you see the world from where you stand?
Sir, I will go whaling. I must.
Though I'd rather it be on as fine a ship as the *Pequod*.
Then you may as well sign the papers right now! Come along.
On saying this, he led the way below deck into the cabin.
He says he's our man, Bildad. He wants to ship.
He does, does he?
I do!
He'll do, Peleg.

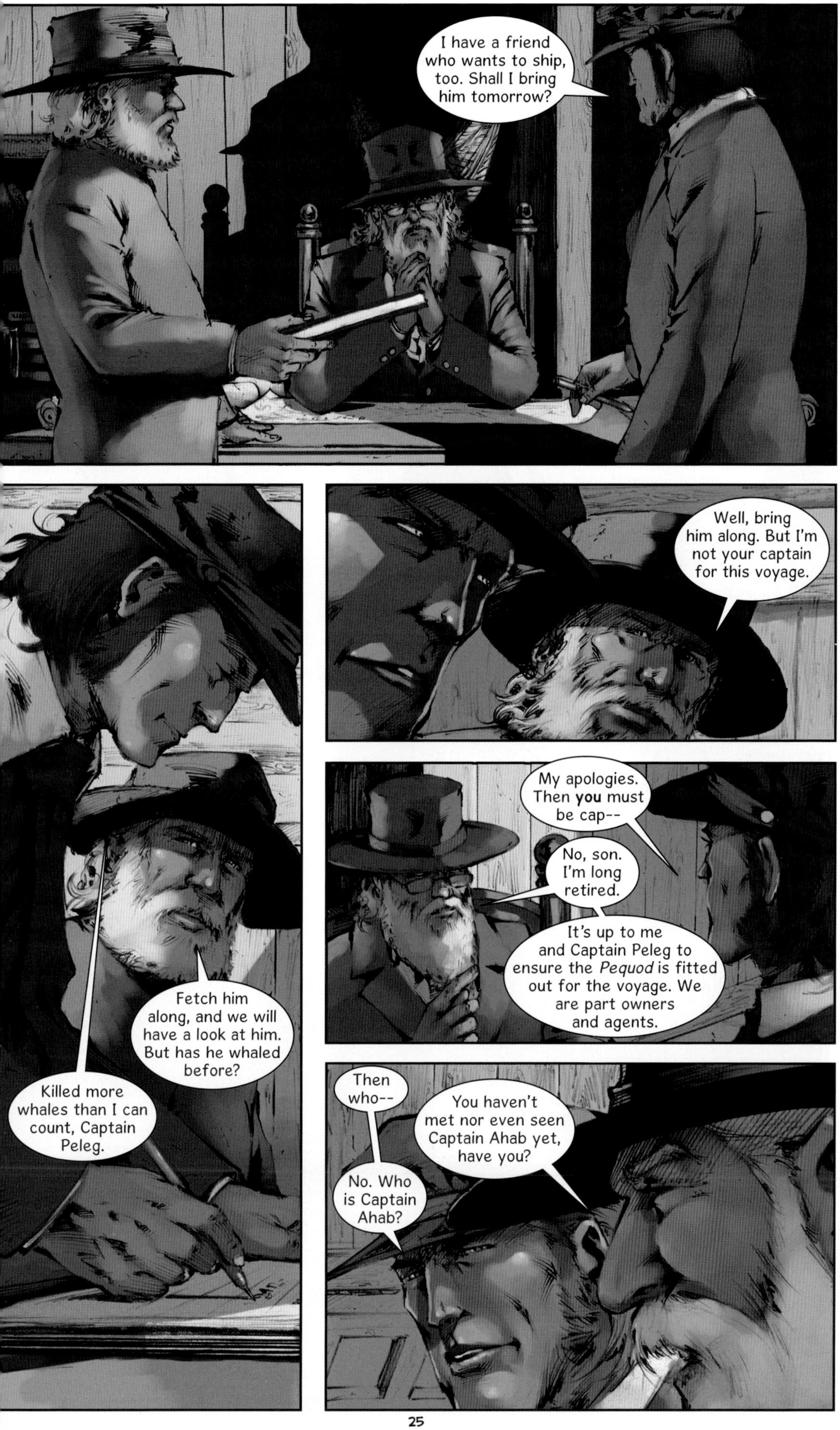
I have a friend who wants to ship, too. Shall I bring him tomorrow?
Fetch him along, and we will have a look at him. But has he whaled before?
Killed more whales than I can count, Captain Peleg.
Well, bring him along. But I'm not your captain for this voyage.
My apologies. Then **you** must be cap--
No, son. I'm long retired.
It's up to me and Captain Peleg to ensure the *Pequod* is fitted out for the voyage. We are part owners and agents.
Then who--
You haven't met nor even seen Captain Ahab yet, have you?
No. Who is Captain Ahab?

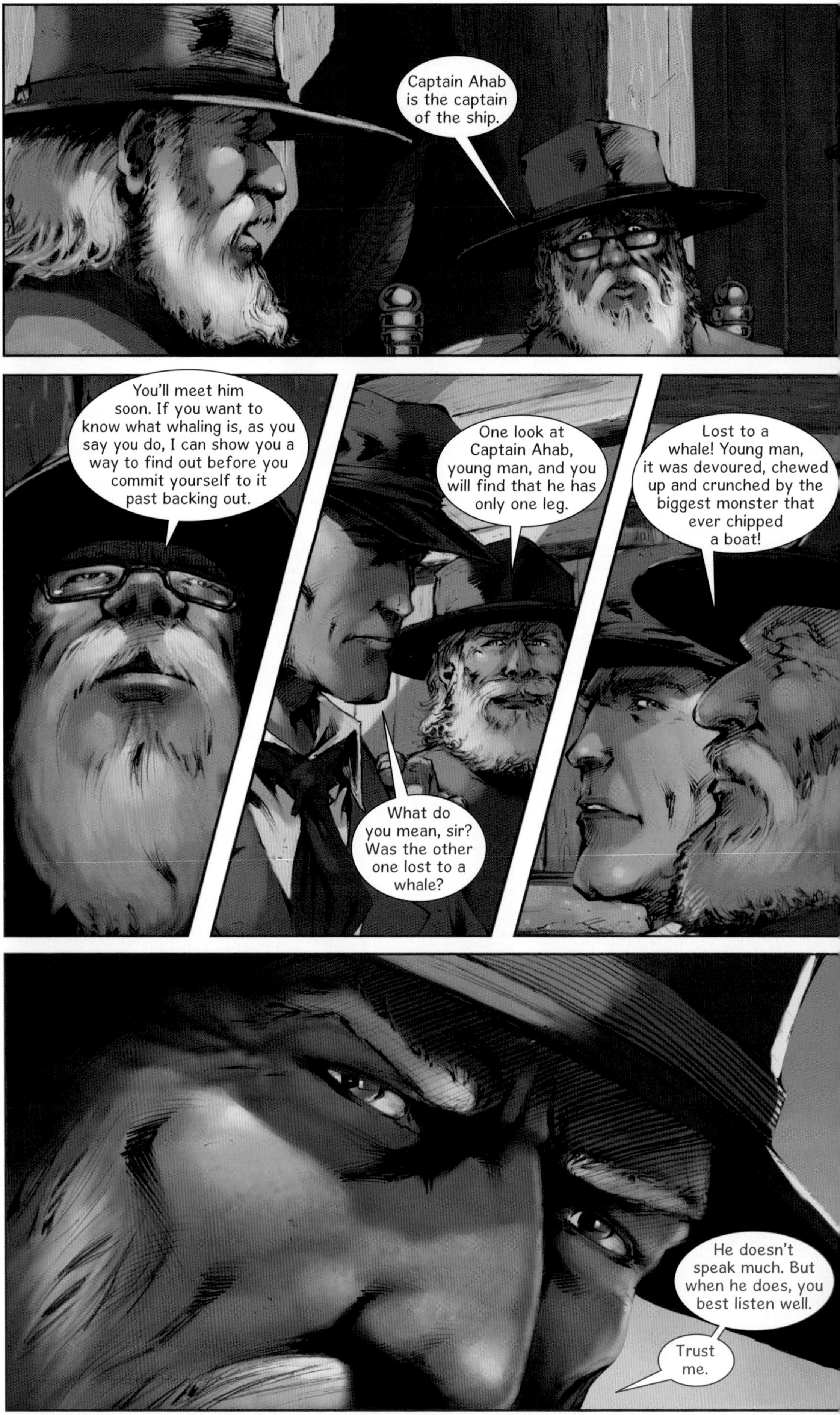
Captain Ahab is the captain of the ship.
You'll meet him soon. If you want to know what whaling is, as you say you do, I can show you a way to find out before you commit yourself to it past backing out.
One look at Captain Ahab, young man, and you will find that he has only one leg.
What do you mean, sir? Was the other one lost to a whale?
Lost to a whale! Young man, it was devoured, chewed up and crunched by the biggest monster that ever chipped a boat!
He doesn't speak much. But when he does, you best listen well.
Trust me.

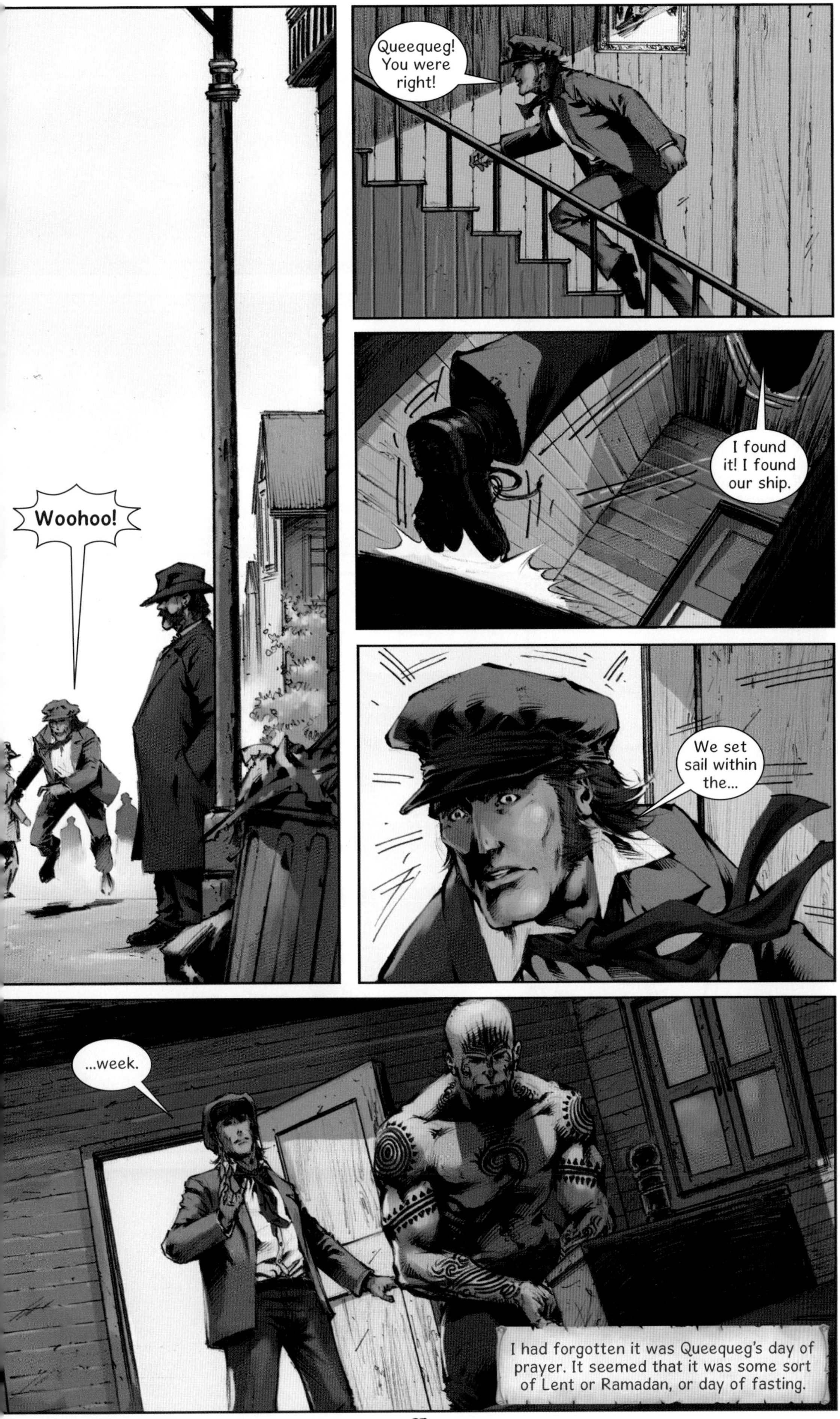
Queequeg! You were right!
I found it! I found our ship.
Woohoo!
We set sail within the...
...week.
I had forgotten it was Queequeg's day of prayer. It seemed that it was some sort of Lent or Ramadan, or day of fasting.

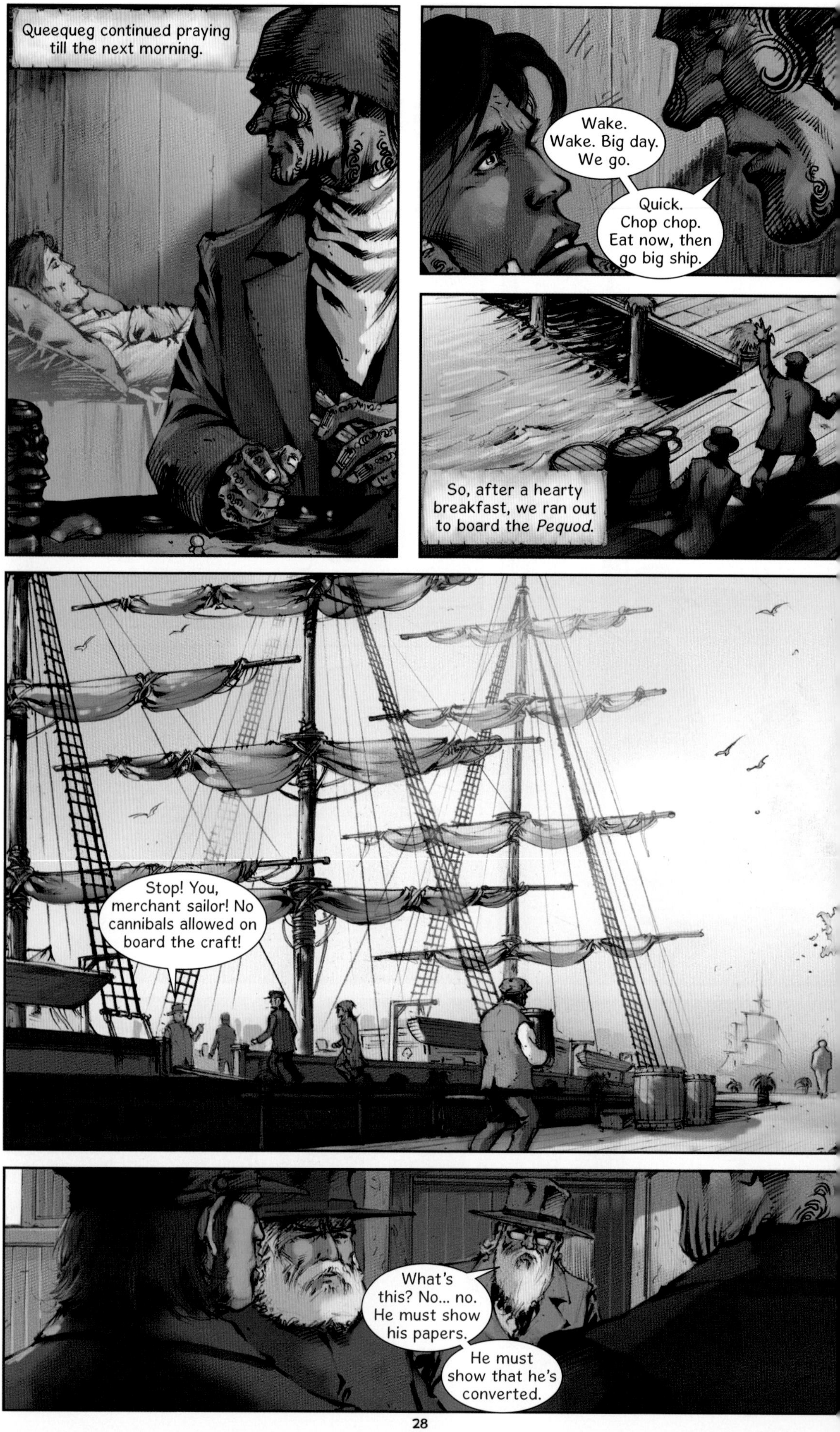

Queequeg continued praying till the next morning.
Wake. Wake. Big day. We go.
Quick. Chop chop. Eat now, then go big ship.
So, after a hearty breakfast, we ran out to board the *Pequod*.
Stop! You, merchant sailor! No cannibals allowed on board the craft!
What's this? No... no. He must show his papers.
He must show that he's converted.

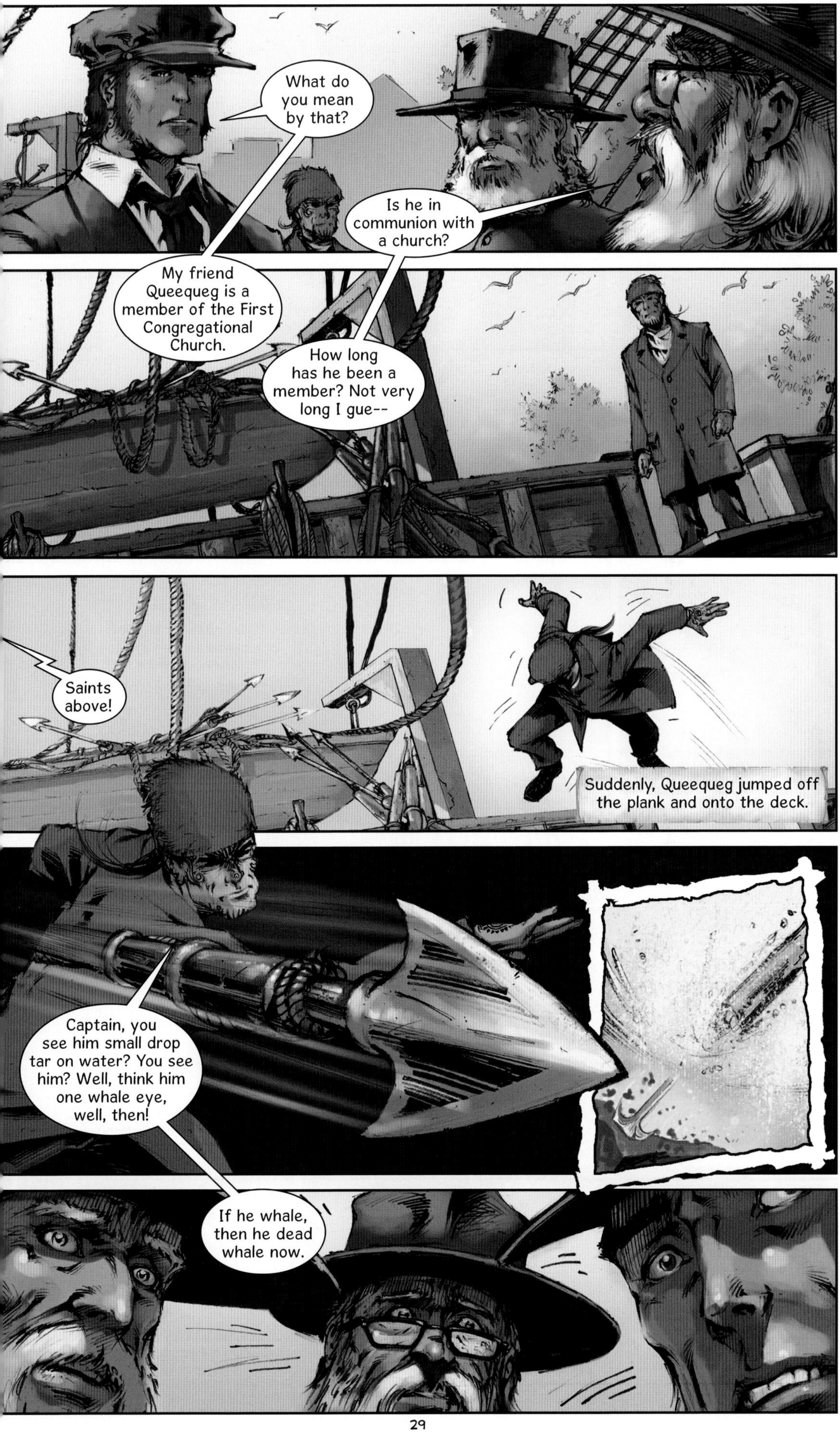
What do you mean by that?
Is he in communion with a church?
My friend Queequeg is a member of the First Congregational Church.
How long has he been a member? Not very long I gue--
Saints above!
Suddenly, Queequeg jumped off the plank and onto the deck.
Captain, you see him small drop tar on water? You see him? Well, think him one whale eye, well, then!
If he whale, then he dead whale now.

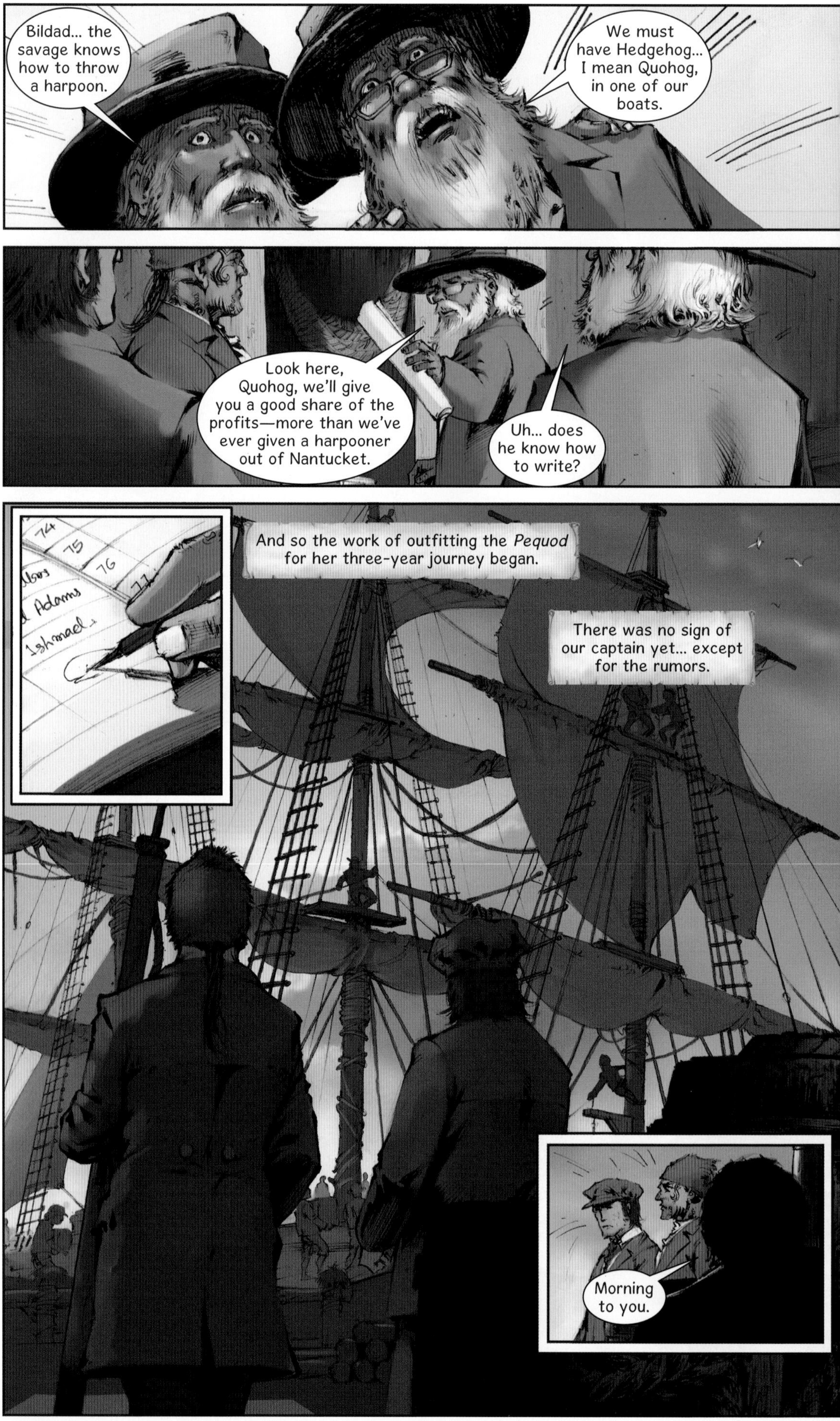

Bildad... the savage knows how to throw a harpoon.
We must have Hedgehog... I mean Quohog, in one of our boats.
Look here, Quohog, we'll give you a good share of the profits—more than we've ever given a harpooner out of Nantucket.
Uh... does he know how to write?
And so the work of outfitting the *Pequod* for her three-year journey began.
There was no sign of our captain yet... except for the rumors.
Morning to you.

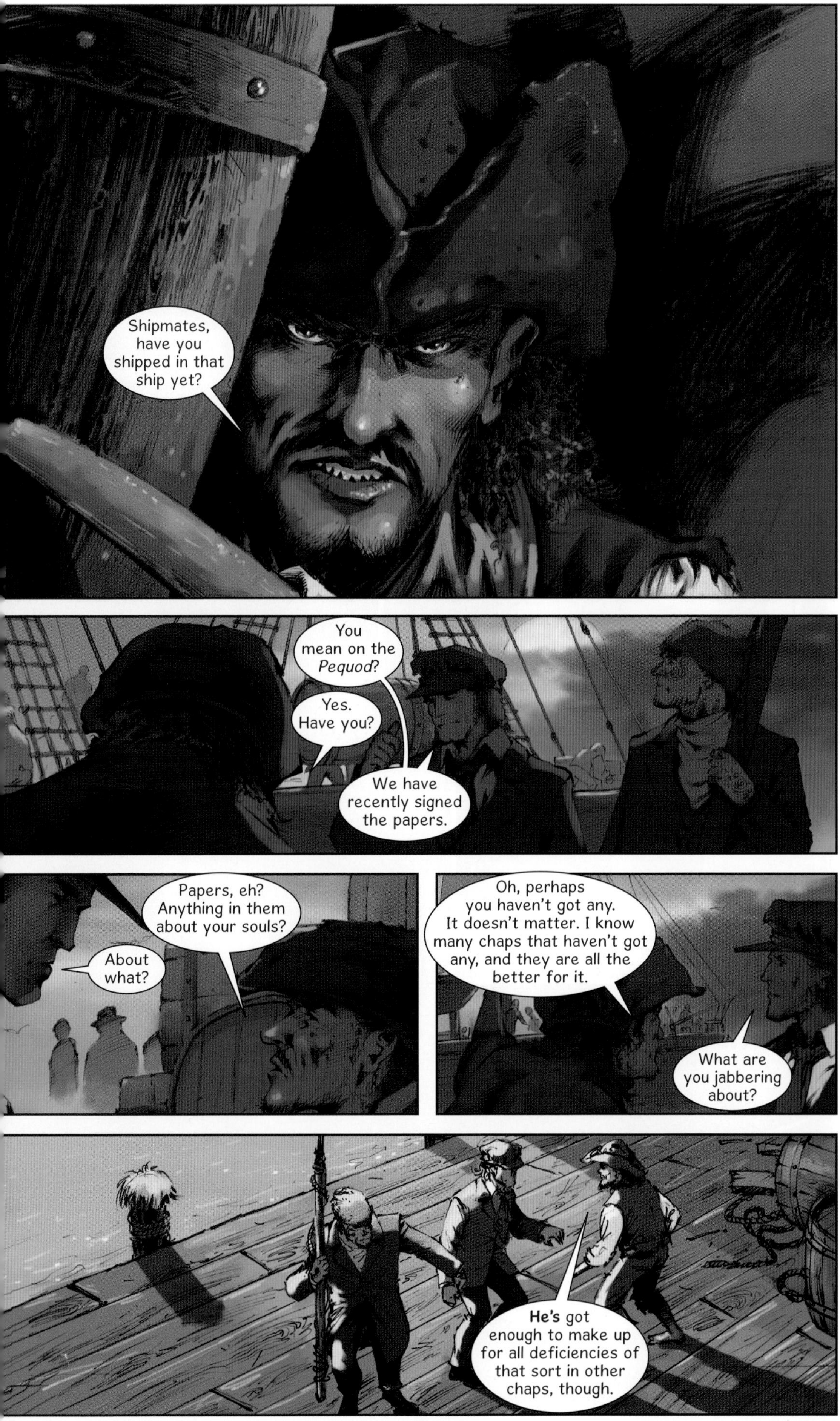
Shipmates, have you shipped in that ship yet?
You mean on the *Pequod*?
Yes. Have you?
We have recently signed the papers.
Papers, eh? Anything in them about your souls?
About what?
Oh, perhaps you haven't got any. It doesn't matter. I know many chaps that haven't got any, and they are all the better for it.
What are you jabbering about?
He's got enough to make up for all deficiencies of that sort in other chaps, though.

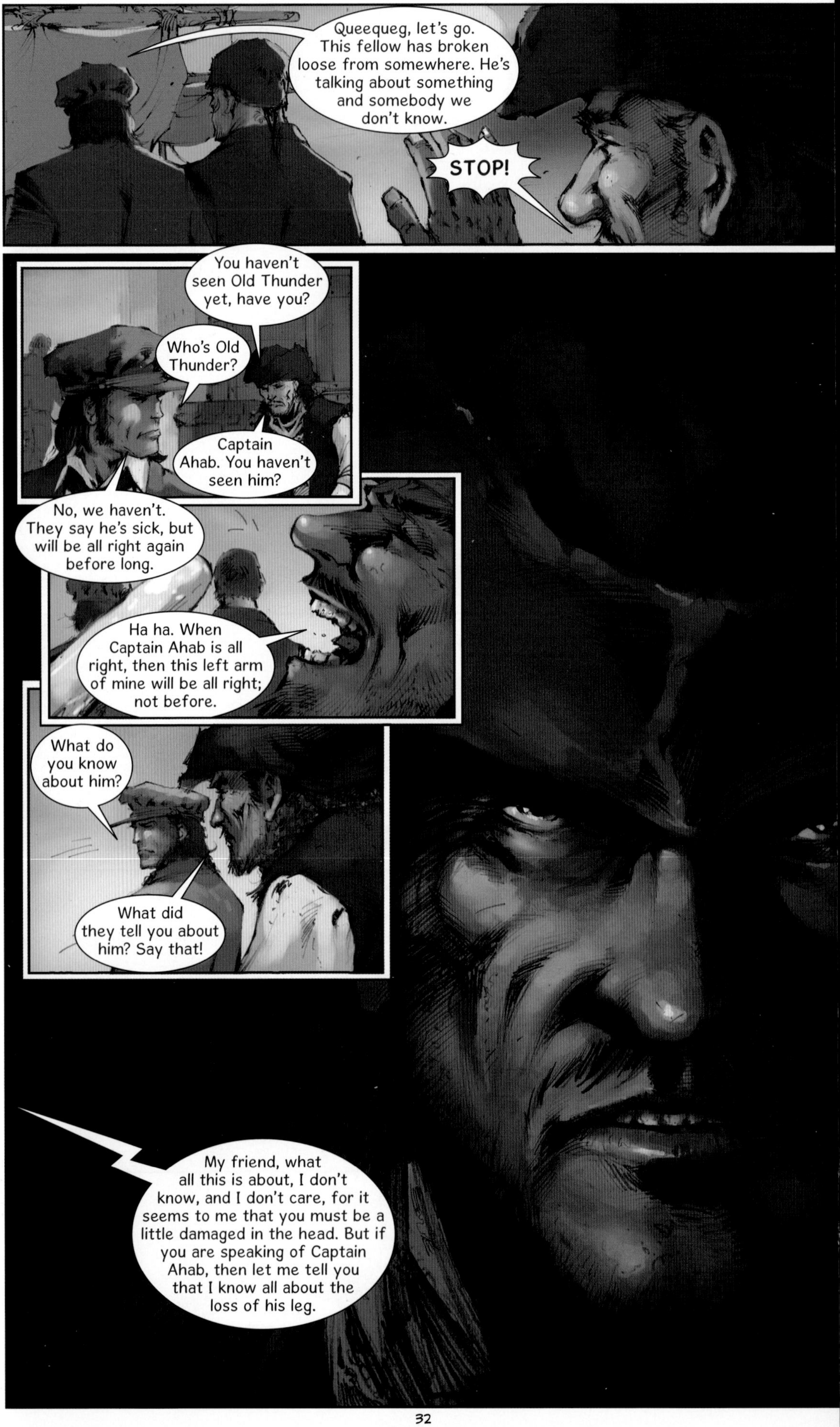
Queequeg, let's go. This fellow has broken loose from somewhere. He's talking about something and somebody we don't know.
STOP!
You haven't seen Old Thunder yet, have you?
Who's Old Thunder?
Captain Ahab. You haven't seen him?
No, we haven't. They say he's sick, but will be all right again before long.
Ha ha. When Captain Ahab is all right, then this left arm of mine will be all right; not before.
What do you know about him?
What did they tell you about him? Say that!
My friend, what all this is about, I don't know, and I don't care, for it seems to me that you must be a little damaged in the head. But if you are speaking of Captain Ahab, then let me tell you that I know all about the loss of his leg.

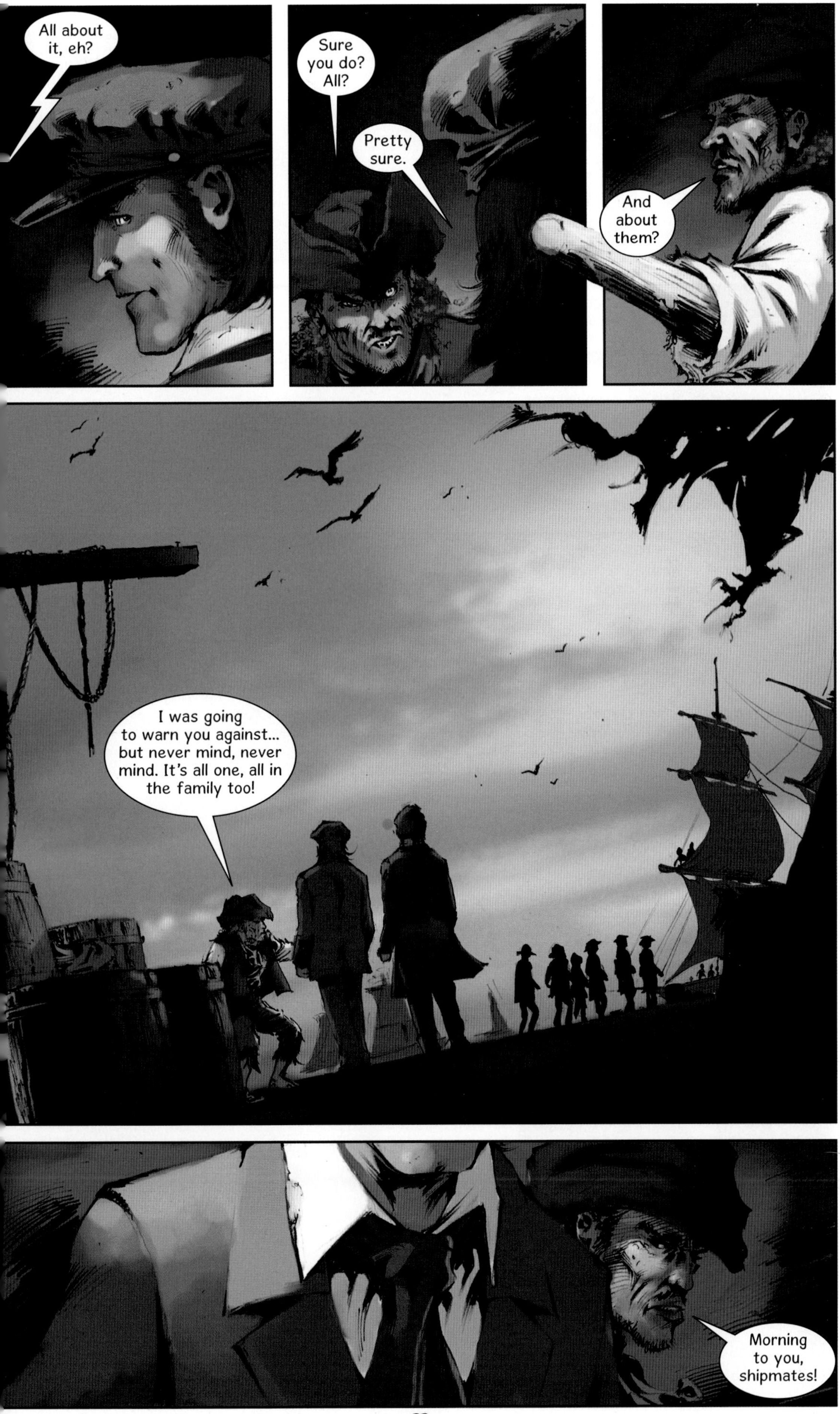
All about it, eh?
Sure you do? All?
Pretty sure.
And about them?
I was going to warn you against... but never mind, never mind. It's all one, all in the family too!
Morning to you, shipmates!

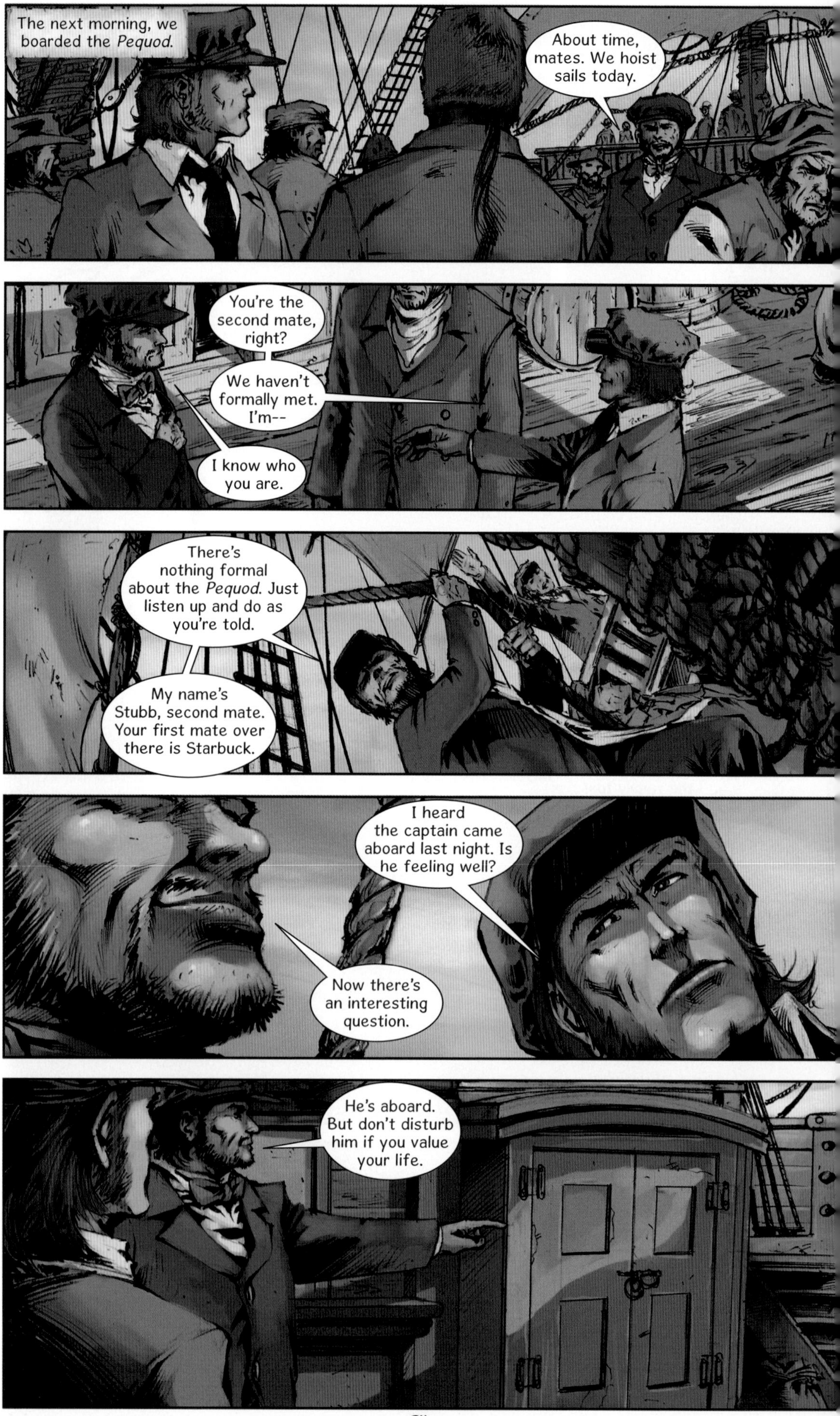
The next morning, we boarded the *Pequod*.
About time, mates. We hoist sails today.
You're the second mate, right?
We haven't formally met. I'm--
I know who you are.
There's nothing formal about the *Pequod*. Just listen up and do as you're told.
My name's Stubb, second mate. Your first mate over there is Starbuck.
I heard the captain came aboard last night. Is he feeling well?
Now there's an interesting question.
He's aboard. But don't disturb him if you value your life.

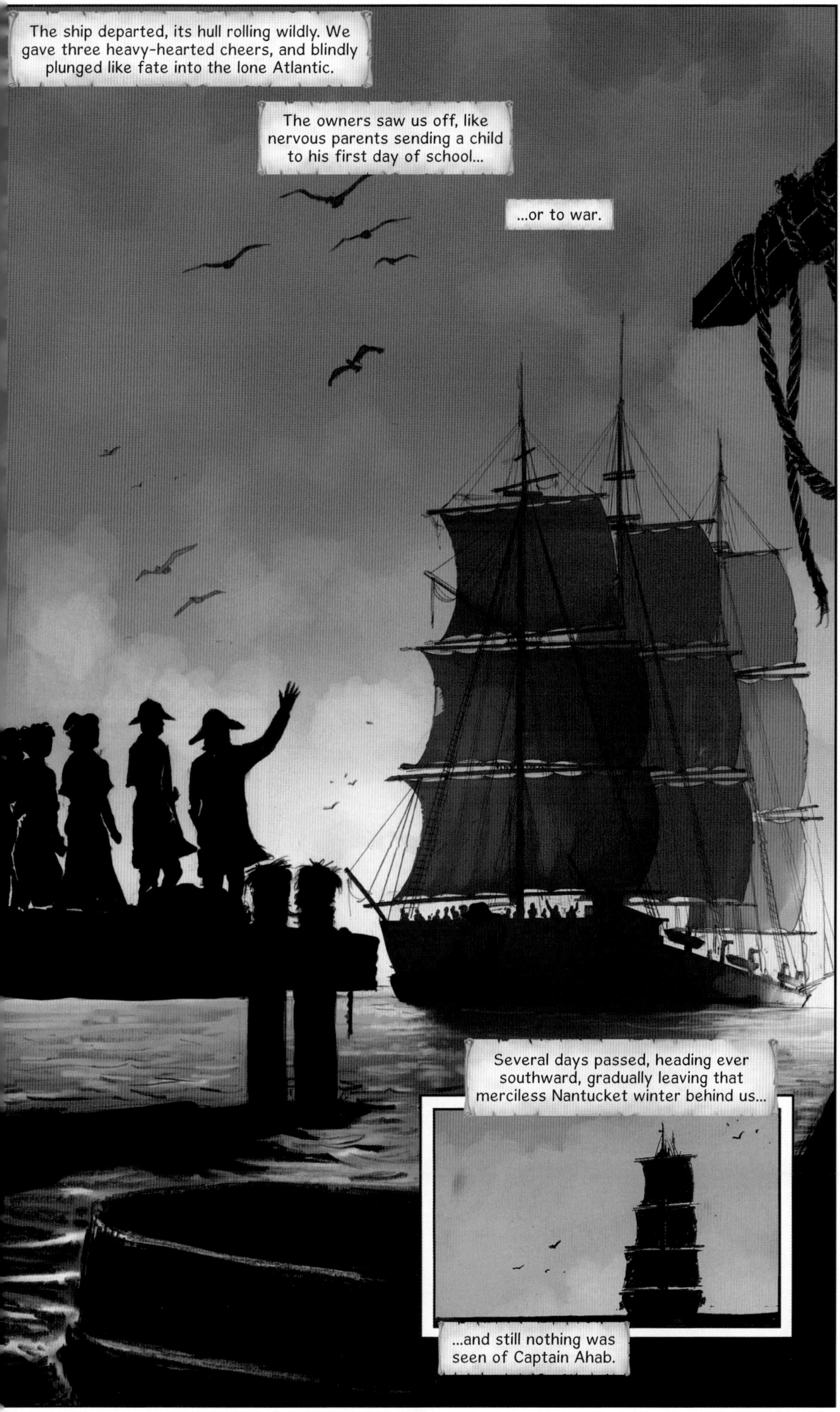
The ship departed, its hull rolling wildly. We gave three heavy-hearted cheers, and blindly plunged like fate into the lone Atlantic.
The owners saw us off, like nervous parents sending a child to his first day of school...
...or to war.
Several days passed, heading ever southward, gradually leaving that merciless Nantucket winter behind us...
...and still nothing was seen of Captain Ahab.

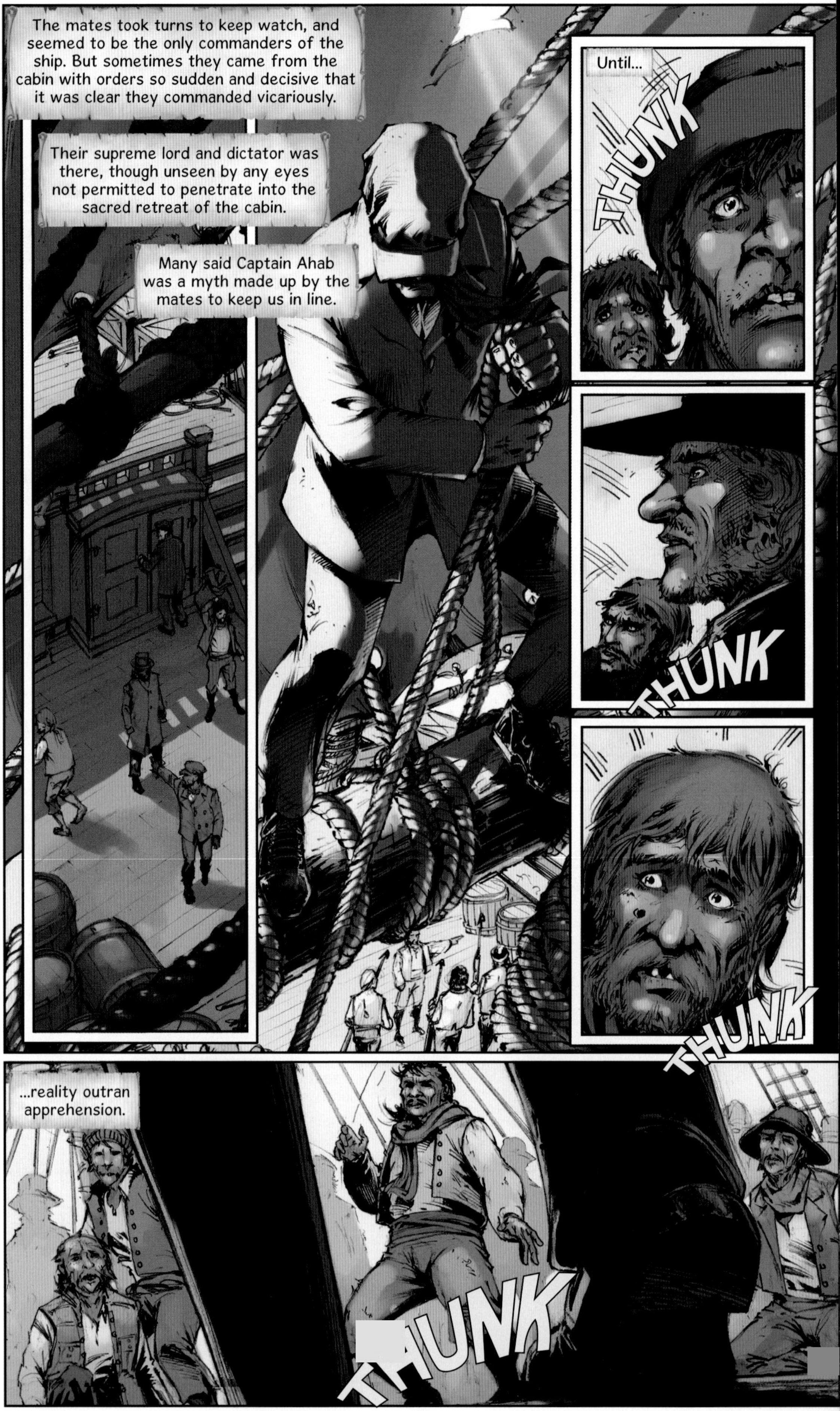
The mates took turns to keep watch, and seemed to be the only commanders of the ship. But sometimes they came from the cabin with orders so sudden and decisive that it was clear they commanded vicariously.
Their supreme lord and dictator was there, though unseen by any eyes not permitted to penetrate into the sacred retreat of the cabin.
Many said Captain Ahab was a myth made up by the mates to keep us in line.
Until...
THUNK
THUNK
THUNK
...reality outran apprehension.
THUNK

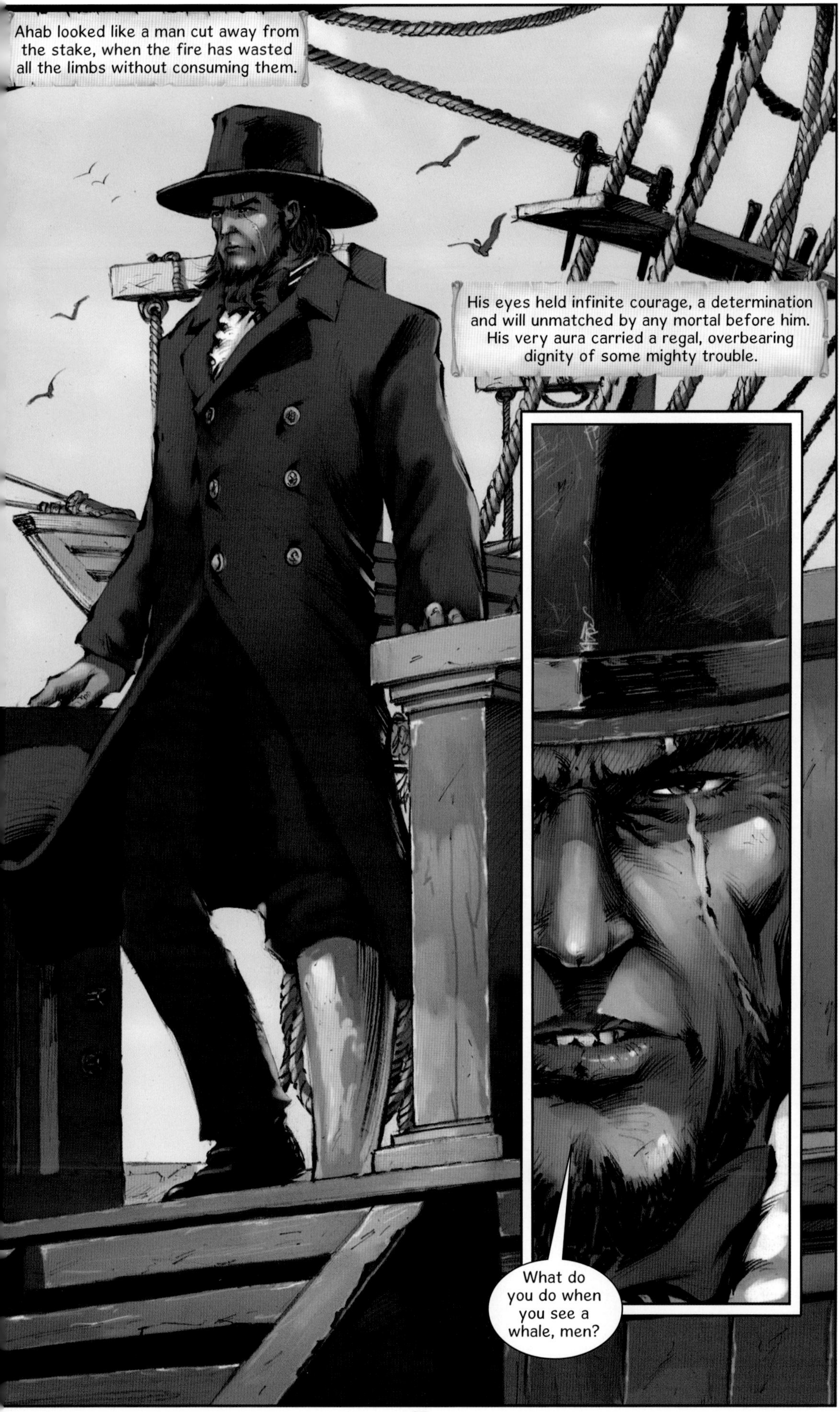
Ahab looked like a man cut away from the stake, when the fire has wasted all the limbs without consuming them.
His eyes held infinite courage, a determination and will unmatched by any mortal before him. His very aura carried a regal, overbearing dignity of some mighty trouble.
What do you do when you see a whale, men?

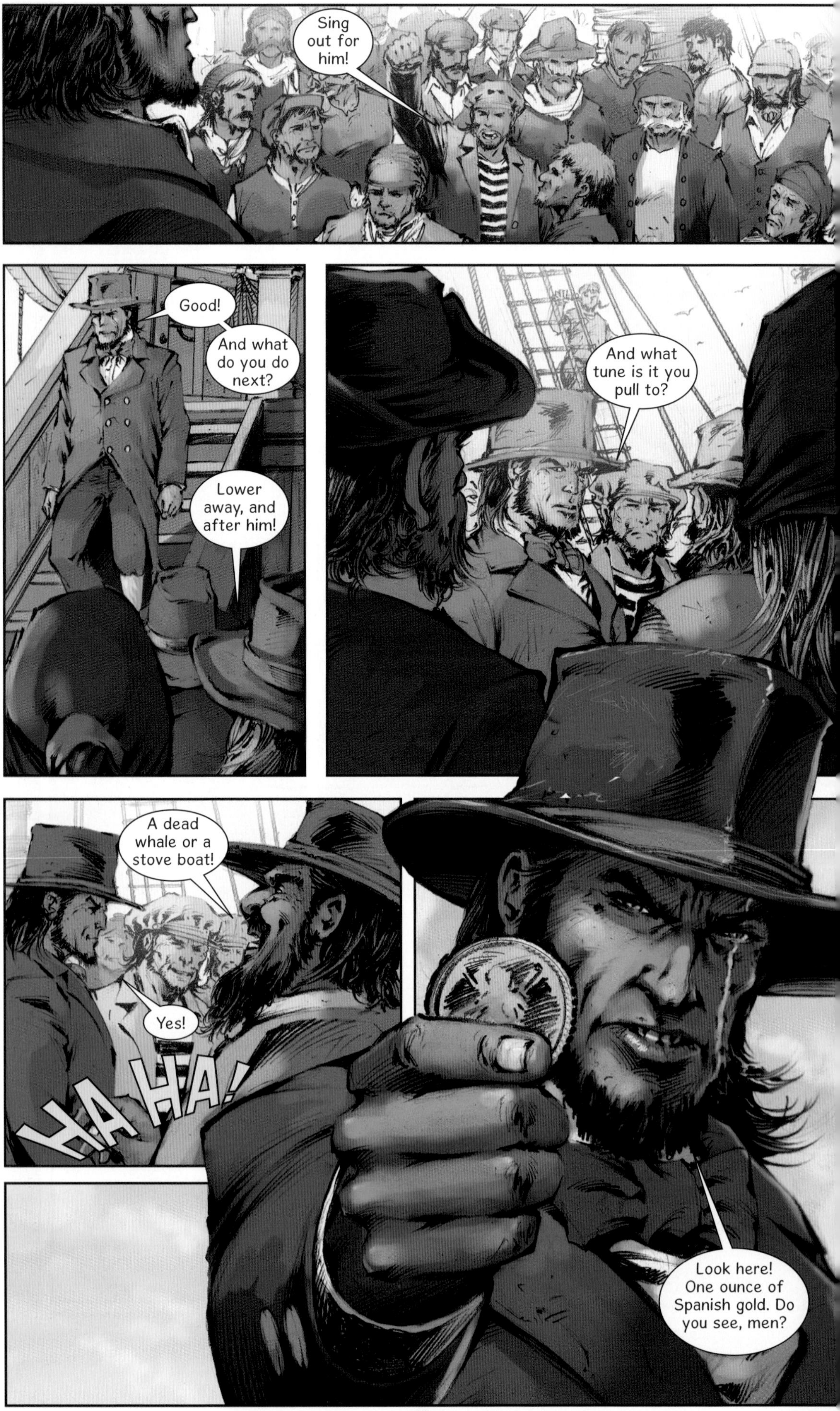
Sing out for him!
Good!
And what do you do next?
Lower away, and after him!
And what tune is it you pull to?
A dead whale or a stove boat!
Yes!
HA HA!
Look here! One ounce of Spanish gold. Do you see, men?

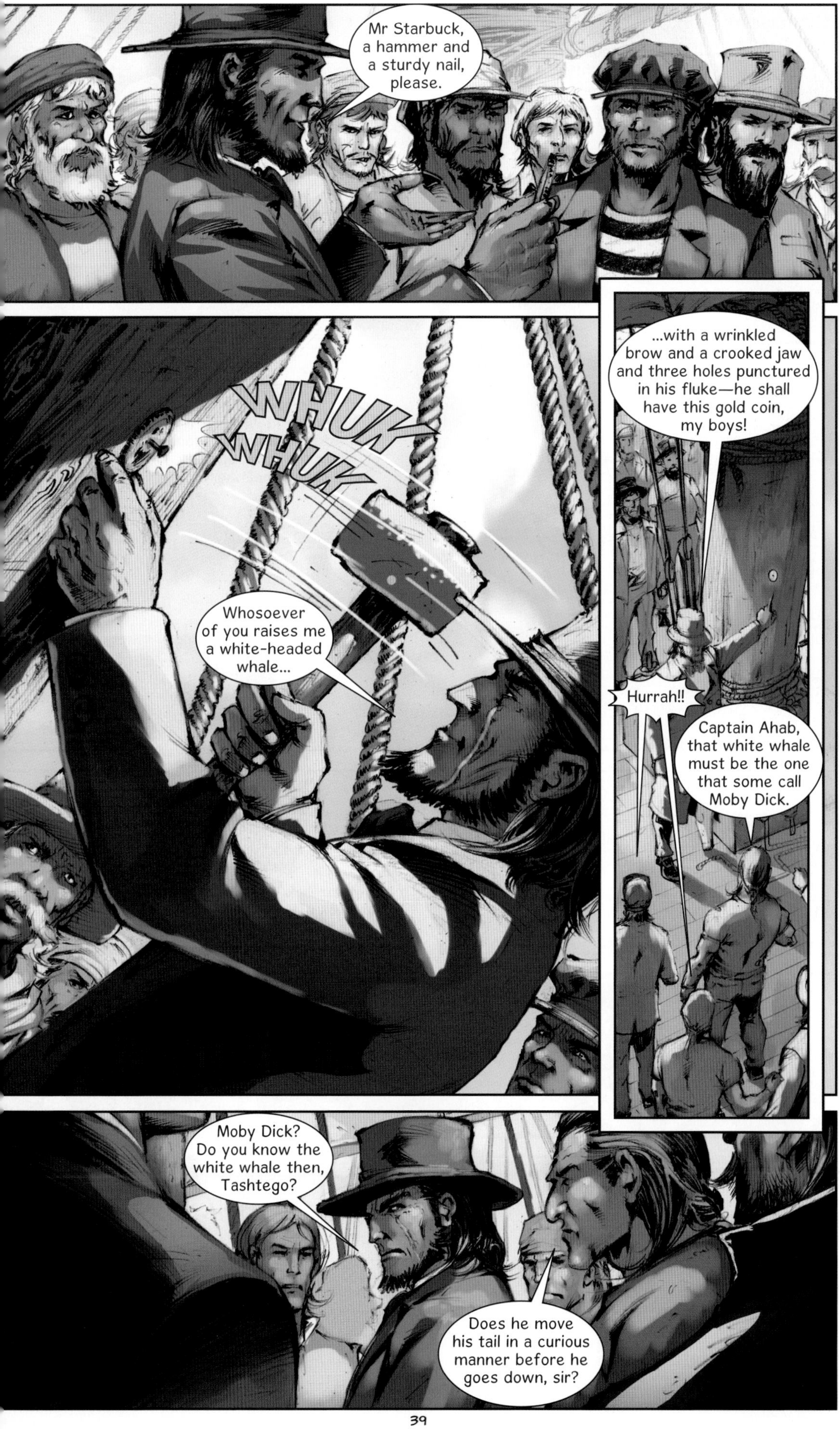
Mr Starbuck, a hammer and a sturdy nail, please.
WHUK WHUK
Whosoever of you raises me a white-headed whale...
...with a wrinkled brow and a crooked jaw and three holes punctured in his fluke—he shall have this gold coin, my boys!
Hurrah!!
Captain Ahab, that white whale must be the one that some call Moby Dick.
Moby Dick? Do you know the white whale then, Tashtego?
Does he move his tail in a curious manner before he goes down, sir?

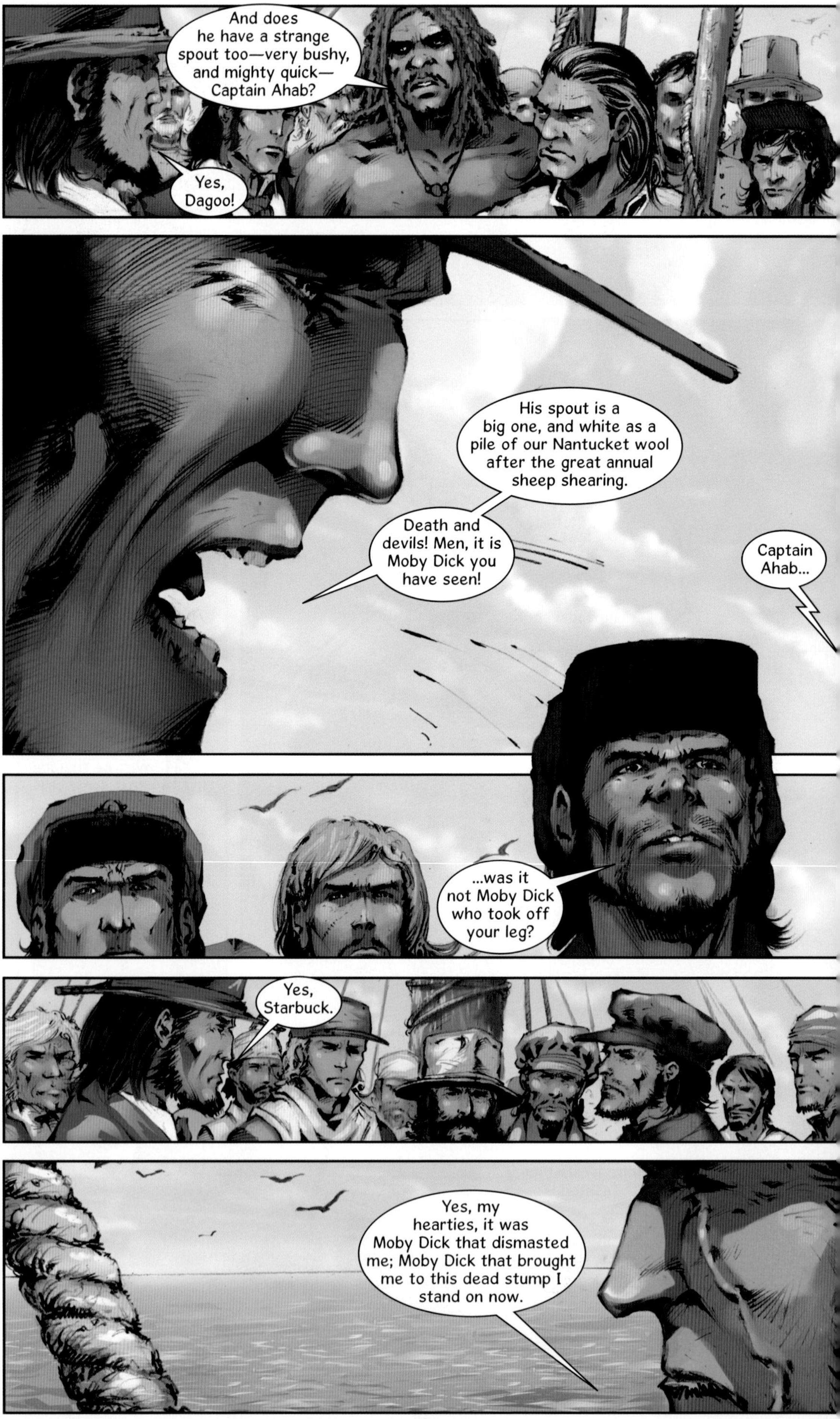
And does he have a strange spout too—very bushy, and mighty quick—Captain Ahab?
Yes, Dagoo!
His spout is a big one, and white as a pile of our Nantucket wool after the great annual sheep shearing.
Death and devils! Men, it is Moby Dick you have seen!
Captain Ahab...
...was it not Moby Dick who took off your leg?
Yes, Starbuck.
Yes, my hearties, it was Moby Dick that dismasted me; Moby Dick that brought me to this dead stump I stand on now.

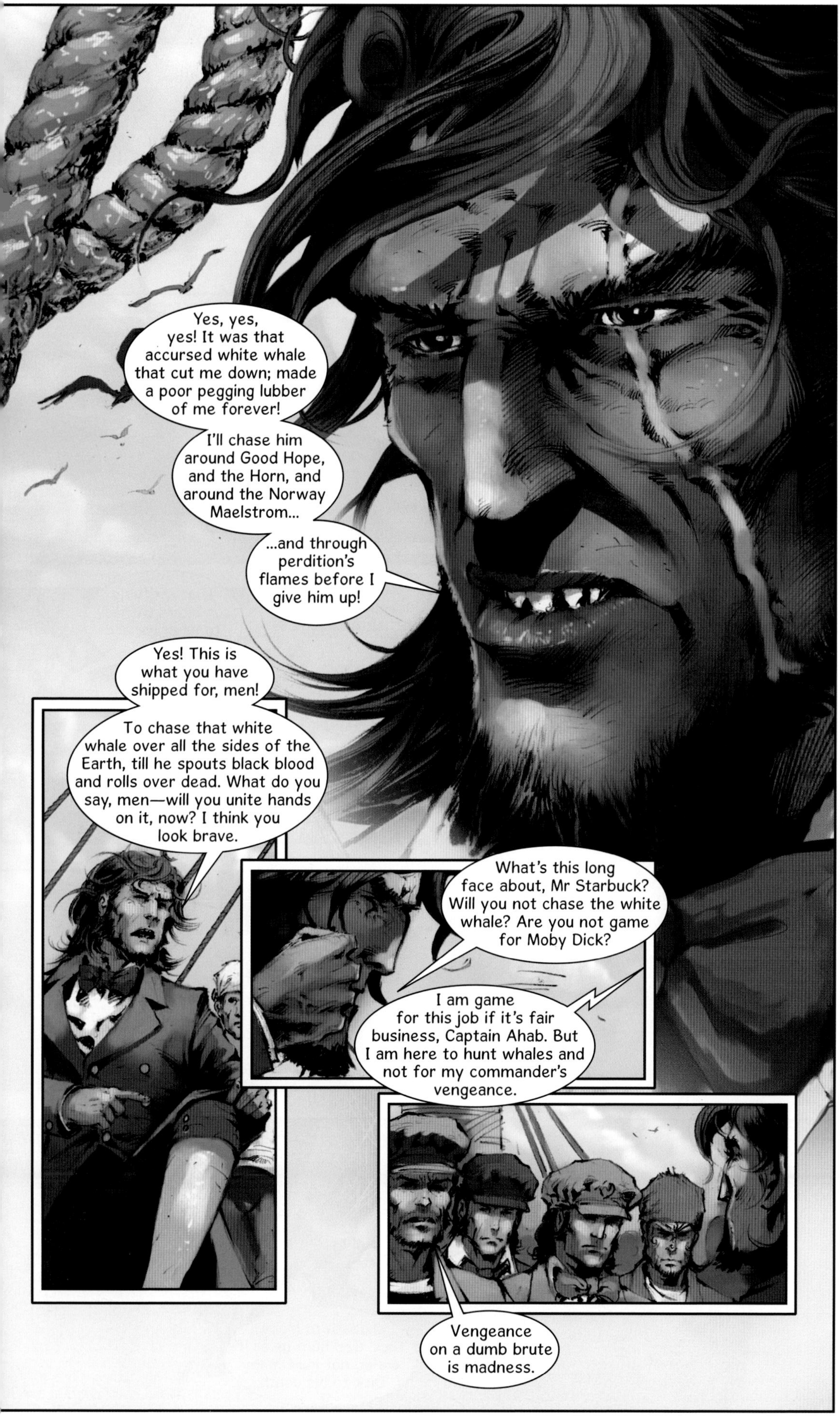
Yes, yes, yes! It was that accursed white whale that cut me down; made a poor pegging lubber of me forever!
I'll chase him around Good Hope, and the Horn, and around the Norway Maelstrom...
...and through perdition's flames before I give him up!
Yes! This is what you have shipped for, men!
To chase that white whale over all the sides of the Earth, till he spouts black blood and rolls over dead. What do you say, men—will you unite hands on it, now? I think you look brave.
What's this long face about, Mr Starbuck? Will you not chase the white whale? Are you not game for Moby Dick?
I am game for this job if it's fair business, Captain Ahab. But I am here to hunt whales and not for my commander's vengeance.
Vengeance on a dumb brute is madness.

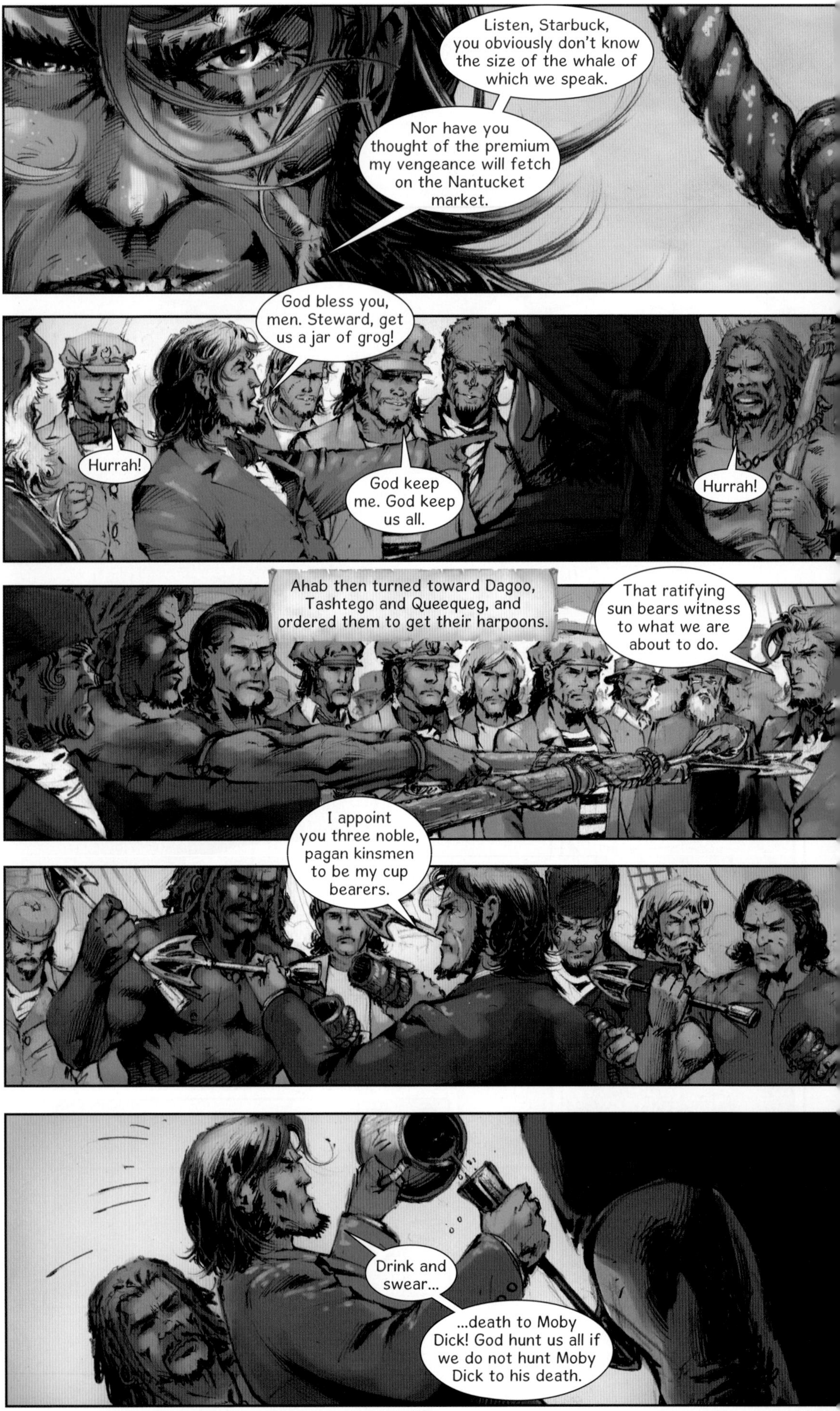

Listen, Starbuck, you obviously don't know the size of the whale of which we speak.
Nor have you thought of the premium my vengeance will fetch on the Nantucket market.
God bless you, men. Steward, get us a jar of grog!
Hurrah!
God keep me. God keep us all.
Hurrah!
Ahab then turned toward Dagoo, Tashtego and Queequeg, and ordered them to get their harpoons.
That ratifying sun bears witness to what we are about to do.
I appoint you three noble, pagan kinsmen to be my cup bearers.
Drink and swear...
...death to Moby Dick! God hunt us all if we do not hunt Moby Dick to his death.

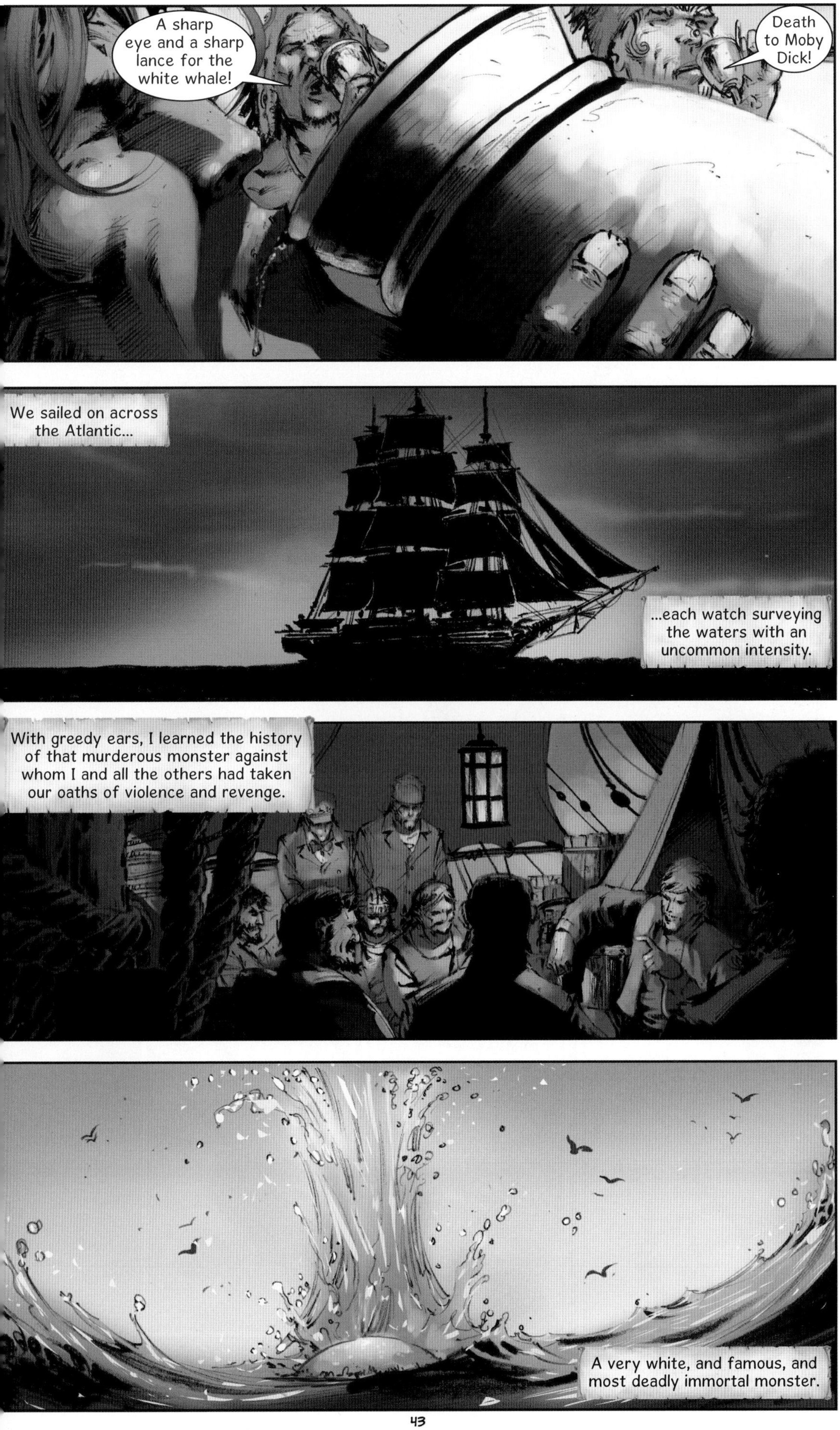
A sharp eye and a sharp lance for the white whale!
Death to Moby Dick!
We sailed on across the Atlantic...
...each watch surveying the waters with an uncommon intensity.
With greedy ears, I learned the history of that murderous monster against whom I and all the others had taken our oaths of violence and revenge.
A very white, and famous, and most deadly immortal monster.

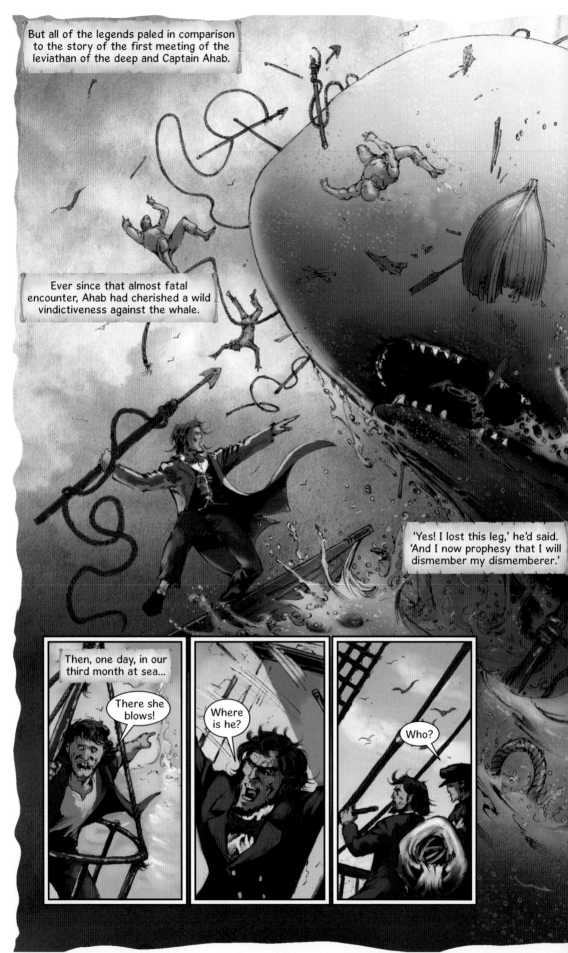

But all of the legends paled in comparison to the story of the first meeting of the leviathan of the deep and Captain Ahab.

Ever since that almost fatal encounter, Ahab had cherished a wild vindictiveness against the whale.

'Yes! I lost this leg,' he'd said. 'And I now prophesy that I will dismember my dismemberer.'

Then, one day, in our third month at sea...

There she blows!

Where is he?

Who?

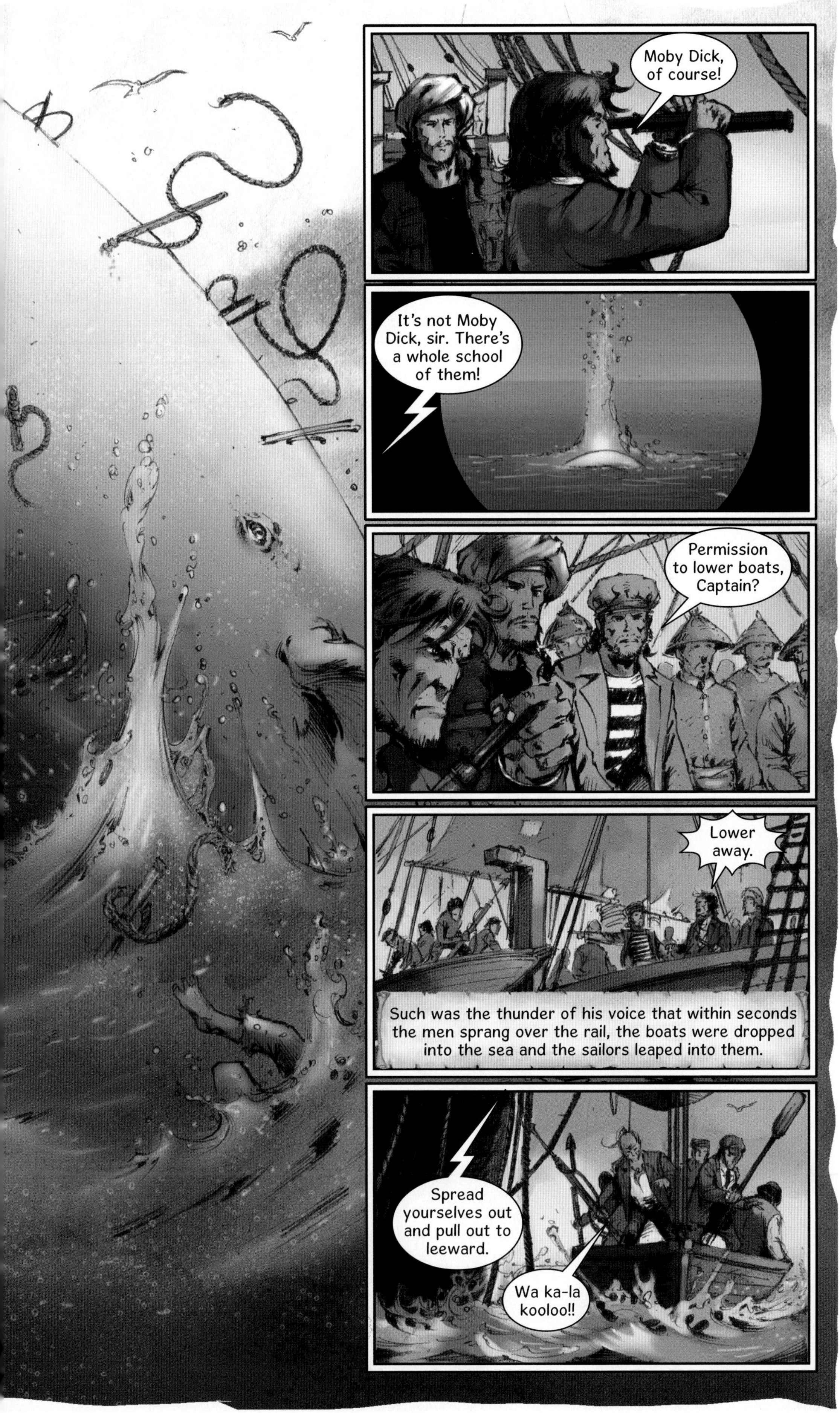

Moby Dick, of course!
It's not Moby Dick, sir. There's a whole school of them!
Permission to lower boats, Captain?
Lower away.
Such was the thunder of his voice that within seconds the men sprang over the rail, the boats were dropped into the sea and the sailors leaped into them.
Spread yourselves out and pull out to leeward.
Wa ka-la kooloo!!

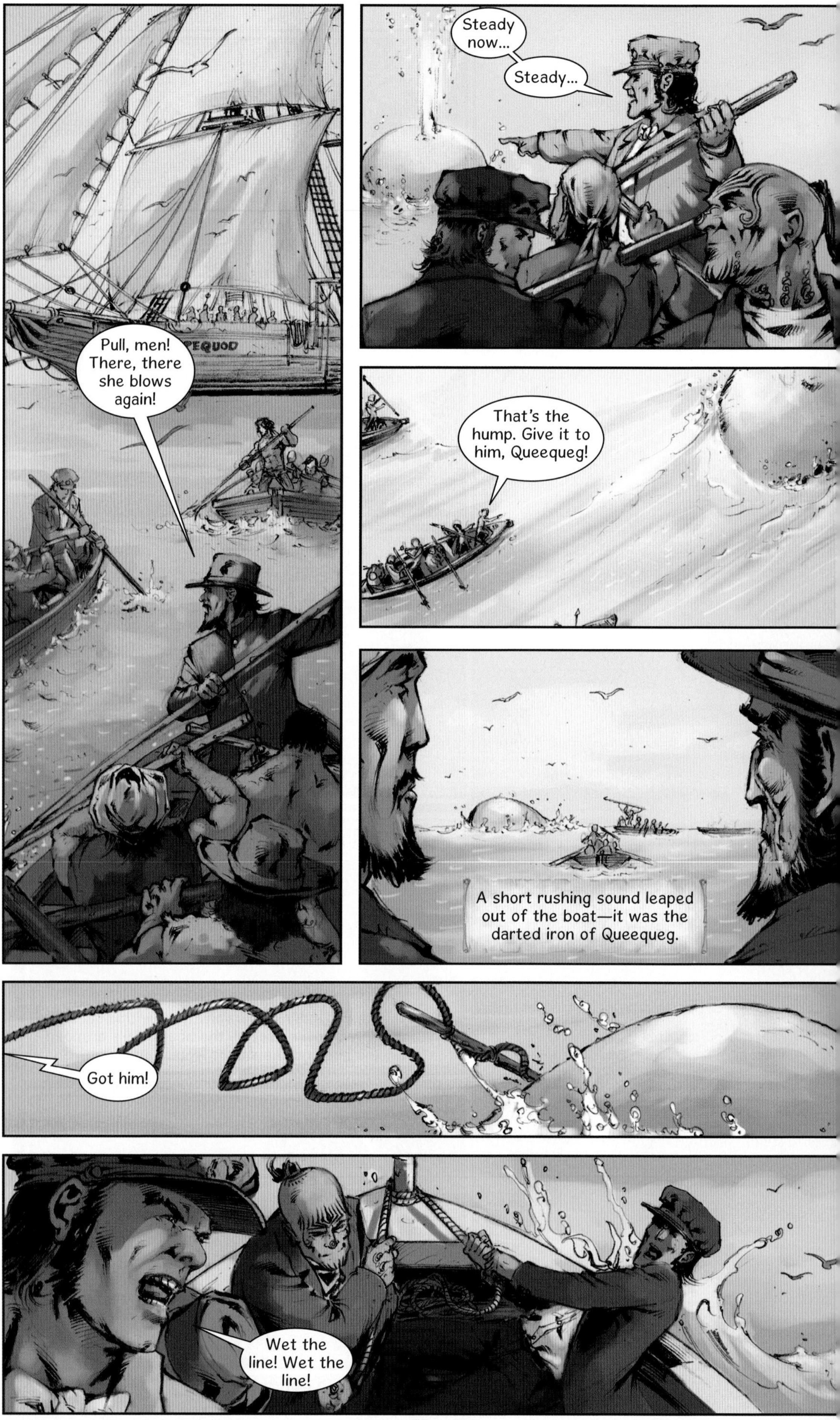
PEQUOD
Pull, men! There, there she blows again!
Steady now...
Steady...
That's the hump. Give it to him, Queequeg!
A short rushing sound leaped out of the boat—it was the darted iron of Queequeg.
Got him!
Wet the line! Wet the line!

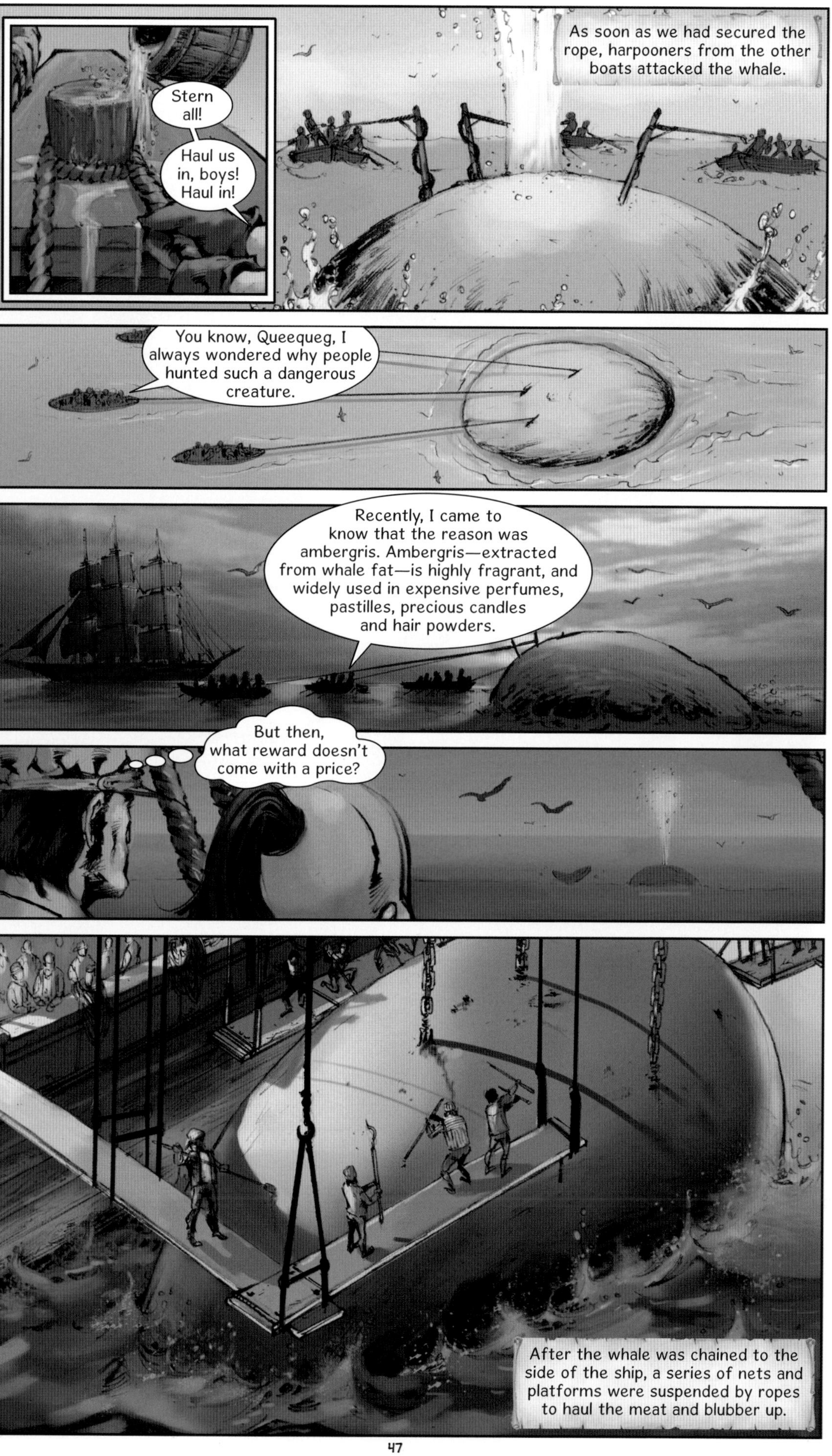
Stern all!
Haul us in, boys! Haul in!
As soon as we had secured the rope, harpooners from the other boats attacked the whale.
You know, Queequeg, I always wondered why people hunted such a dangerous creature.
Recently, I came to know that the reason was ambergris. Ambergris—extracted from whale fat—is highly fragrant, and widely used in expensive perfumes, pastilles, precious candles and hair powders.
But then, what reward doesn't come with a price?
After the whale was chained to the side of the ship, a series of nets and platforms were suspended by ropes to haul the meat and blubber up.

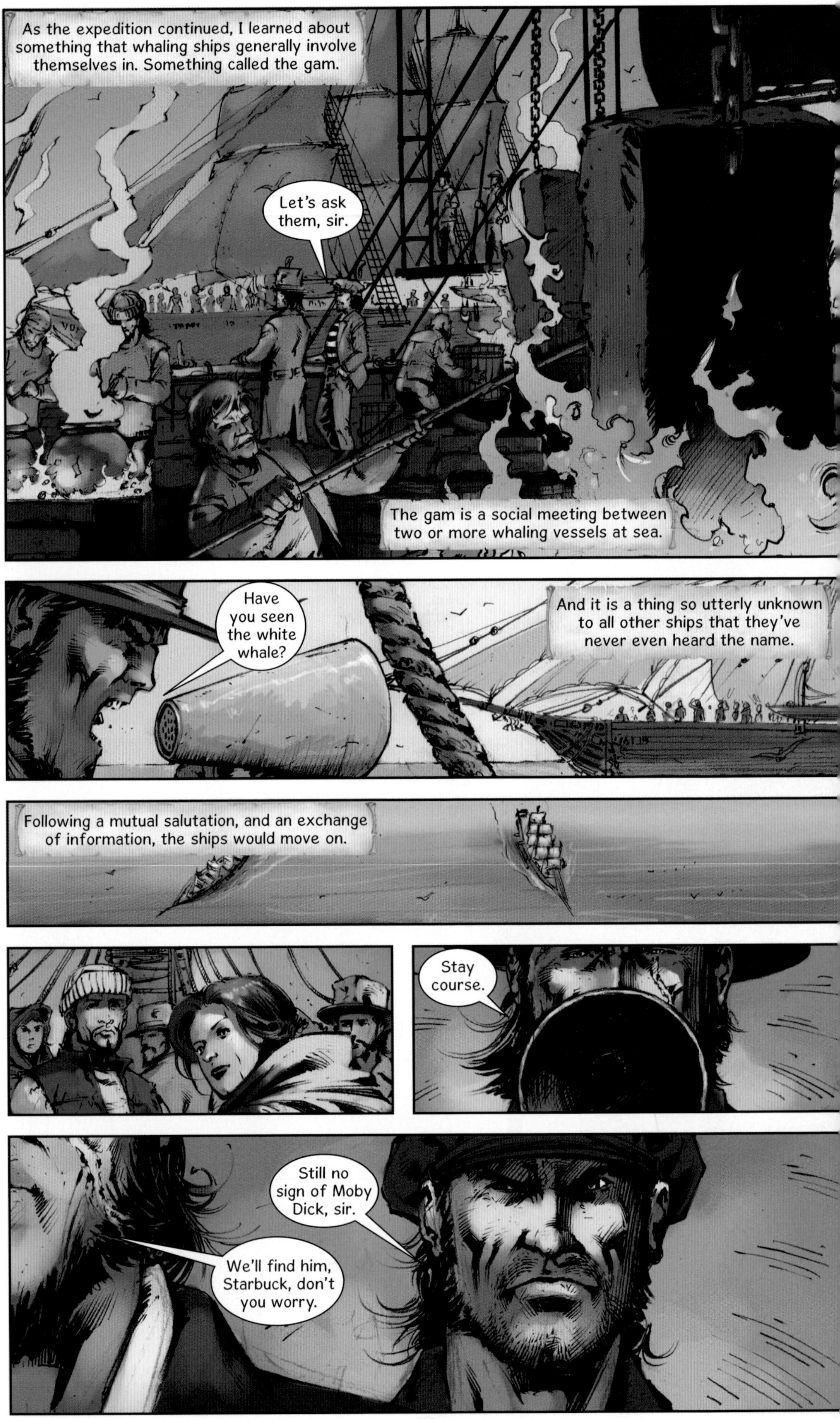
As the expedition continued, I learned about something that whaling ships generally involve themselves in. Something called the gam.
Let's ask them, sir.
The gam is a social meeting between two or more whaling vessels at sea.
Have you seen the white whale?
And it is a thing so utterly unknown to all other ships that they've never even heard the name.
Following a mutual salutation, and an exchange of information, the ships would move on.
Stay course.
Still no sign of Moby Dick, sir.
We'll find him, Starbuck, don't you worry.

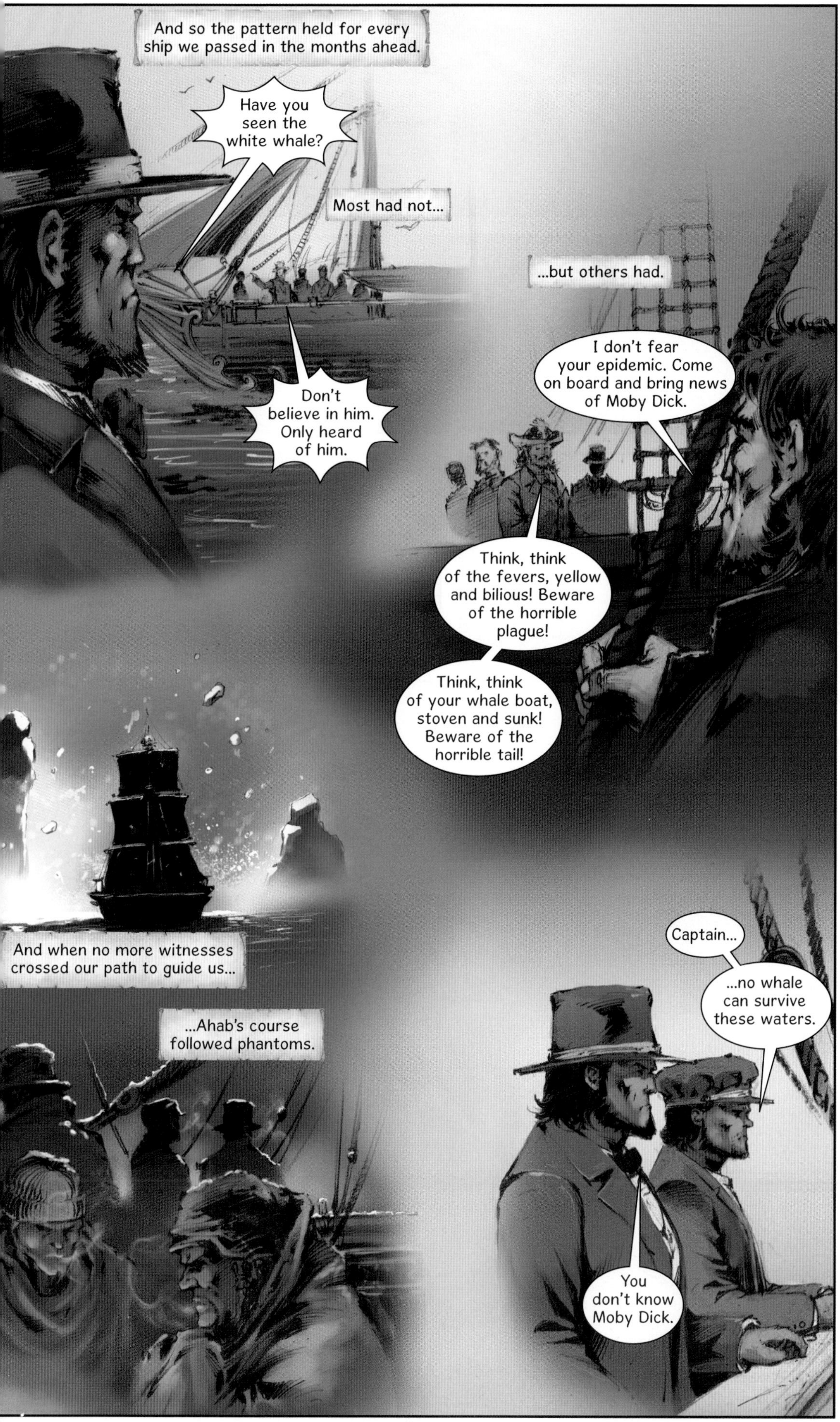

And so the pattern held for every ship we passed in the months ahead.
Have you seen the white whale?
Most had not...
Don't believe in him. Only heard of him.
...but others had.
I don't fear your epidemic. Come on board and bring news of Moby Dick.
Think, think of the fevers, yellow and bilious! Beware of the horrible plague!
Think, think of your whale boat, stoven and sunk! Beware of the horrible tail!
And when no more witnesses crossed our path to guide us...
...Ahab's course followed phantoms.
Captain...
...no whale can survive these waters.
You don't know Moby Dick.

Then, one day, after turning north beyond Cape Horn...

There... there again! There she breaches!

It's him! A great white hump ahead to starboard!

Moby Dick. I knew we'd find you.

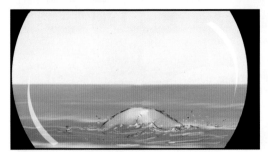

Lower the boats!

I have you now, Moby Dick!

Face me, Moby Dick!

And then...

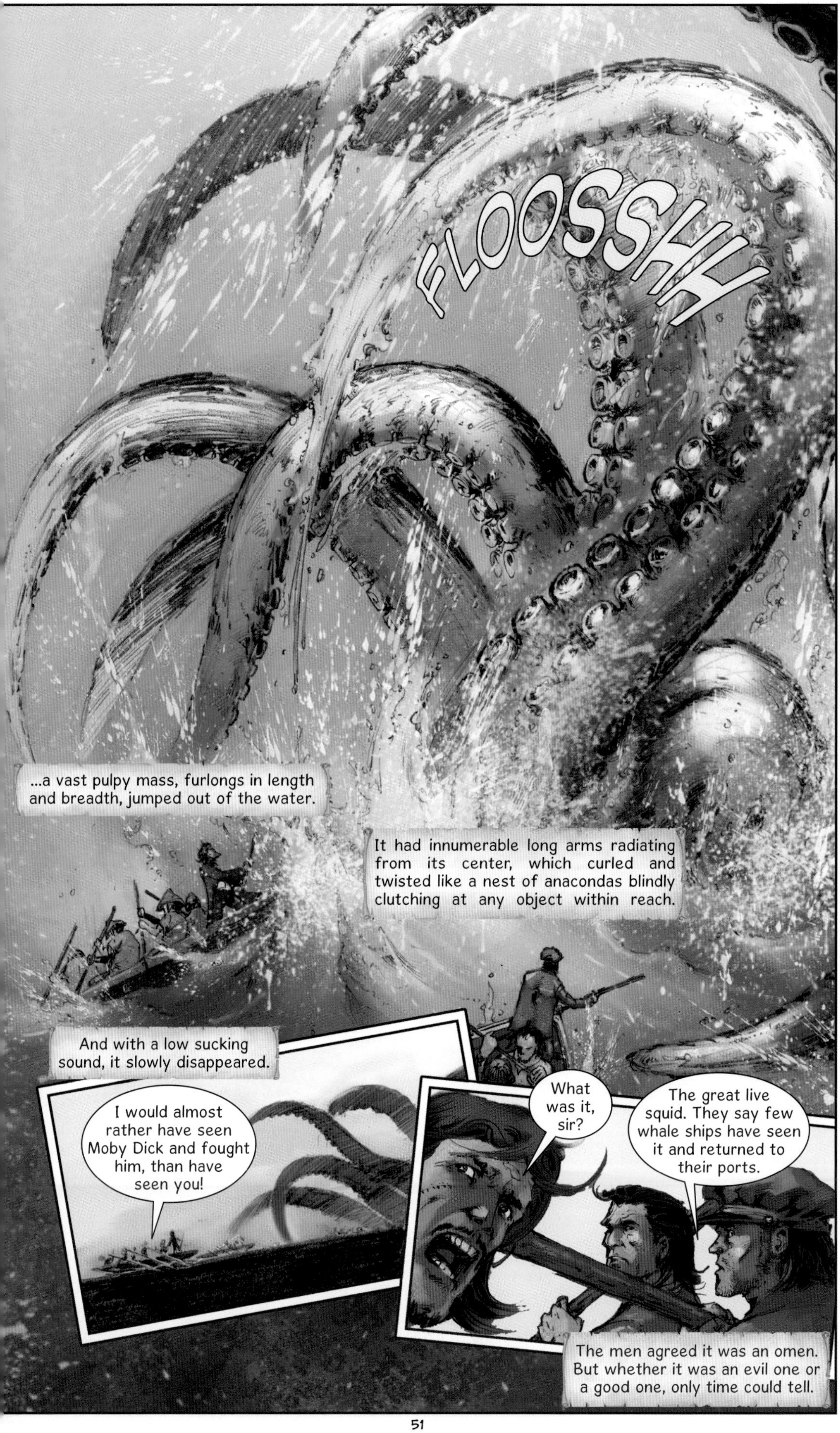

FLOOSSHH
...a vast pulpy mass, furlongs in length and breadth, jumped out of the water.
It had innumerable long arms radiating from its center, which curled and twisted like a nest of anacondas blindly clutching at any object within reach.
And with a low sucking sound, it slowly disappeared.
I would almost rather have seen Moby Dick and fought him, than have seen you!
What was it, sir?
The great live squid. They say few whale ships have seen it and returned to their ports.
The men agreed it was an omen. But whether it was an evil one or a good one, only time could tell.

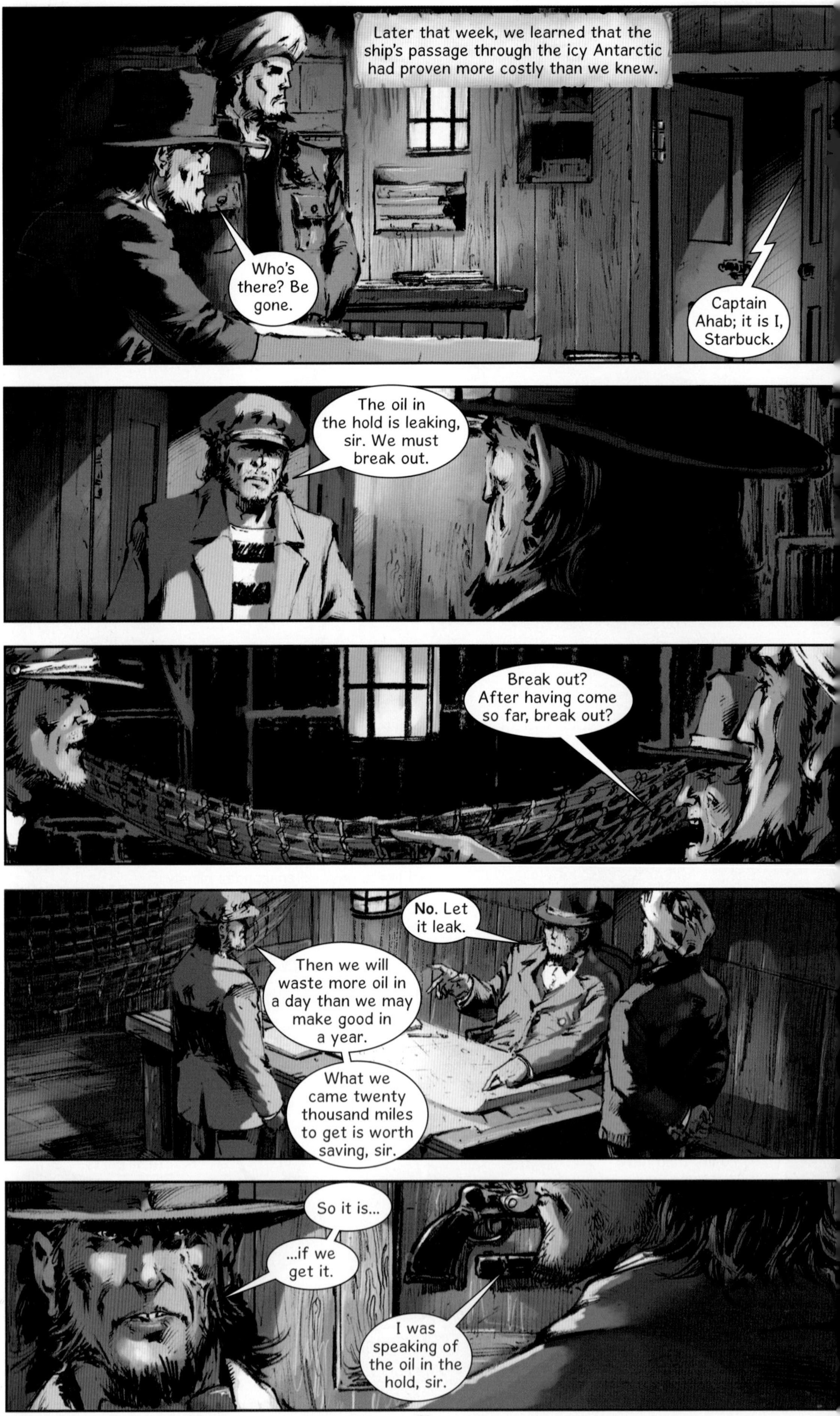
Later that week, we learned that the ship's passage through the icy Antarctic had proven more costly than we knew.
Who's there? Be gone.
Captain Ahab; it is I, Starbuck.
The oil in the hold is leaking, sir. We must break out.
Break out? After having come so far, break out?
No. Let it leak.
Then we will waste more oil in a day than we may make good in a year.
What we came twenty thousand miles to get is worth saving, sir.
So it is...
...if we get it.
I was speaking of the oil in the hold, sir.

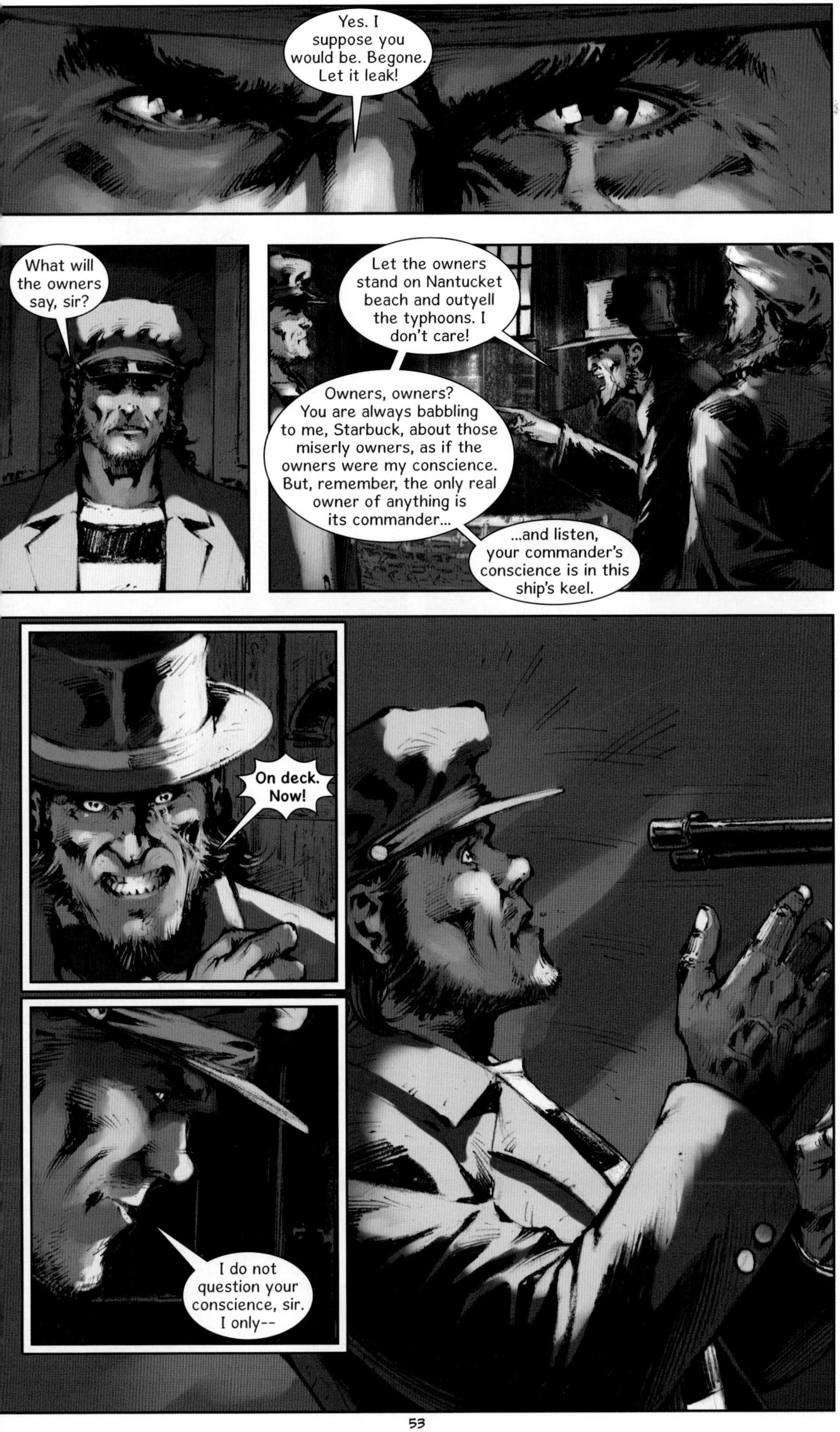

Yes. I suppose you would be. Begone. Let it leak!
What will the owners say, sir?
Let the owners stand on Nantucket beach and outyell the typhoons. I don't care!
Owners, owners? You are always babbling to me, Starbuck, about those miserly owners, as if the owners were my conscience. But, remember, the only real owner of anything is its commander...
...and listen, your commander's conscience is in this ship's keel.
On deck. Now!
I do not question your conscience, sir. I only--

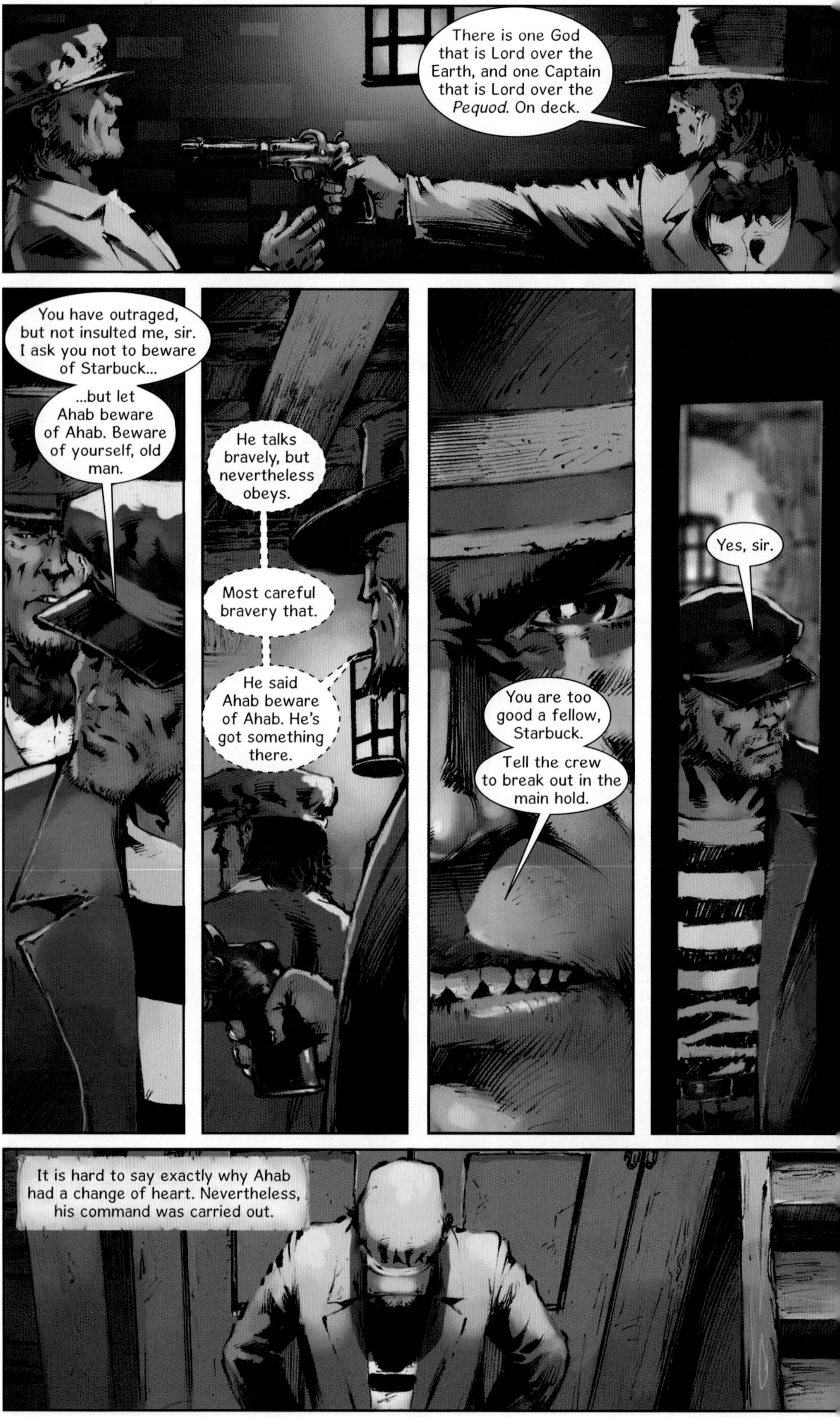
There is one God that is Lord over the Earth, and one Captain that is Lord over the *Pequod*. On deck.
You have outraged, but not insulted me, sir. I ask you not to beware of Starbuck...
...but let Ahab beware of Ahab. Beware of yourself, old man.
He talks bravely, but nevertheless obeys.
Most careful bravery that.
He said Ahab beware of Ahab. He's got something there.
You are too good a fellow, Starbuck.
Tell the crew to break out in the main hold.
Yes, sir.
It is hard to say exactly why Ahab had a change of heart. Nevertheless, his command was carried out.

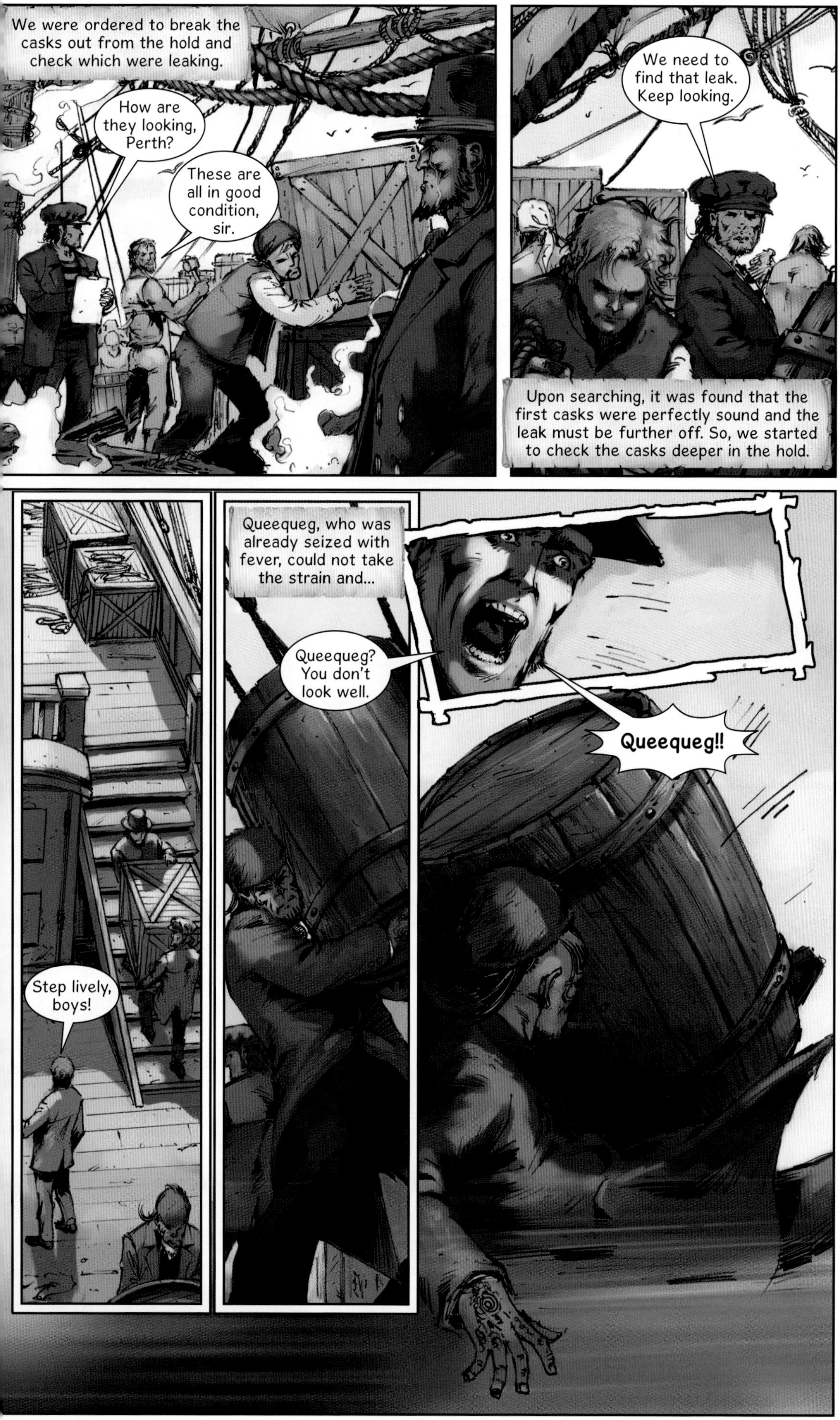
We were ordered to break the casks out from the hold and check which were leaking.
How are they looking, Perth?
These are all in good condition, sir.
We need to find that leak. Keep looking.
Upon searching, it was found that the first casks were perfectly sound and the leak must be further off. So, we started to check the casks deeper in the hold.
Step lively, boys!
Queequeg, who was already seized with fever, could not take the strain and...
Queequeg? You don't look well.
Queequeg!!

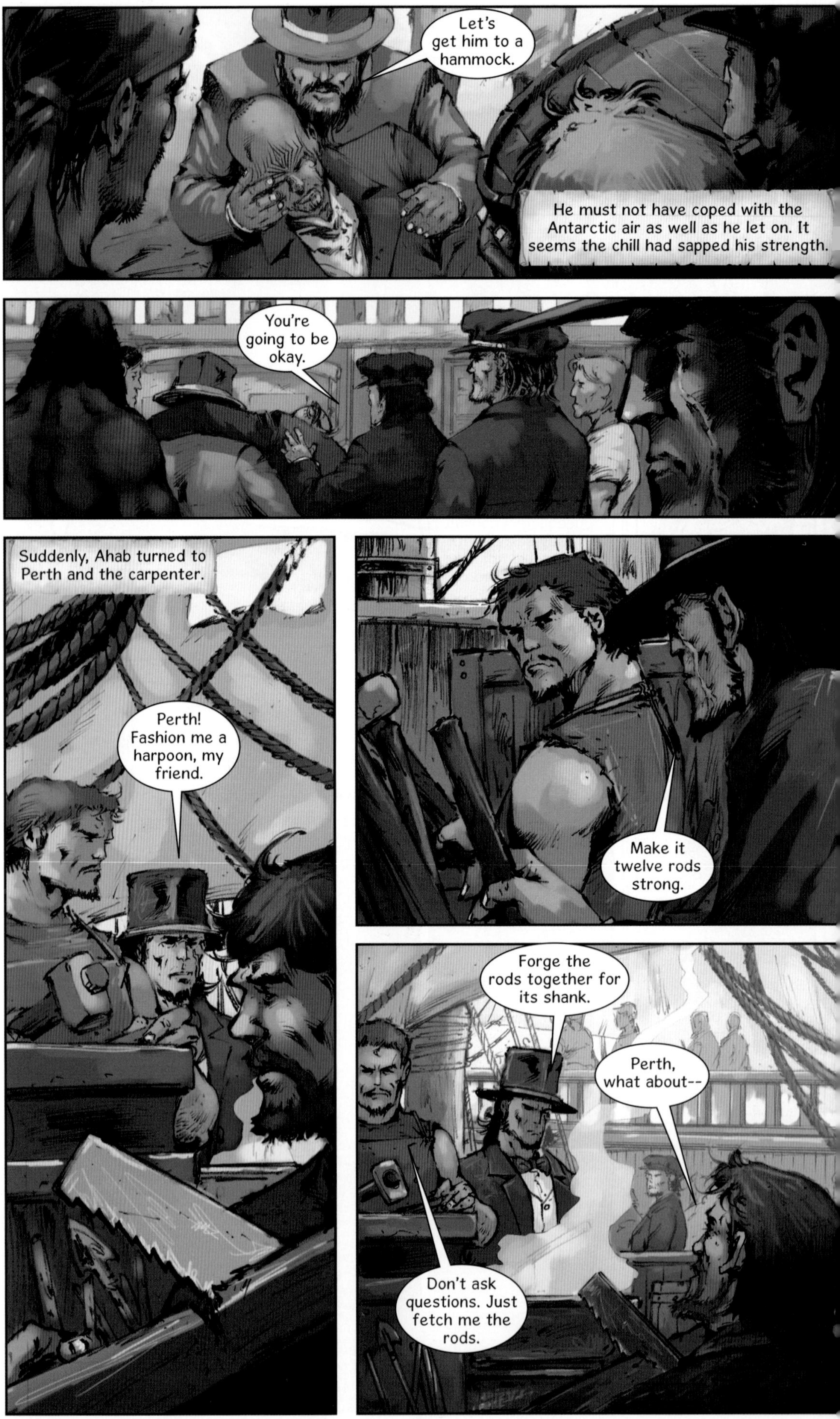
Let's get him to a hammock.
He must not have coped with the Antarctic air as well as he let on. It seems the chill had sapped his strength.
You're going to be okay.
Suddenly, Ahab turned to Perth and the carpenter.
Perth! Fashion me a harpoon, my friend.
Make it twelve rods strong.
Forge the rods together for its shank.
Perth, what about--
Don't ask questions. Just fetch me the rods.

Below deck, Queequeg was not faring too well.

He's delirious.

ᚼᛝᛏᚼᚼᛩᚠ ᚱᛏᚼᛝᛏᚤᚾ ᛏᛩᛏᚾᛝᛏᛙᛁ

Ishmael, please...

Ishmael, make me a--

No, my friend. Don't ask me to do that.

Back on the deck...

Here. I will neither shave nor eat until the white whale is dead.

I want that harpoon. And I want Moby Dick dead!

Queequeg wants a coffin. While in Nantucket, he saw some small canoes made of dark wood. He came to know that all whalemen who died in Nantucket were laid in those canoes. The idea really pleased him.

He hates the thought of being buried in his hammock, to be food for the sharks, according to the usual sea custom.

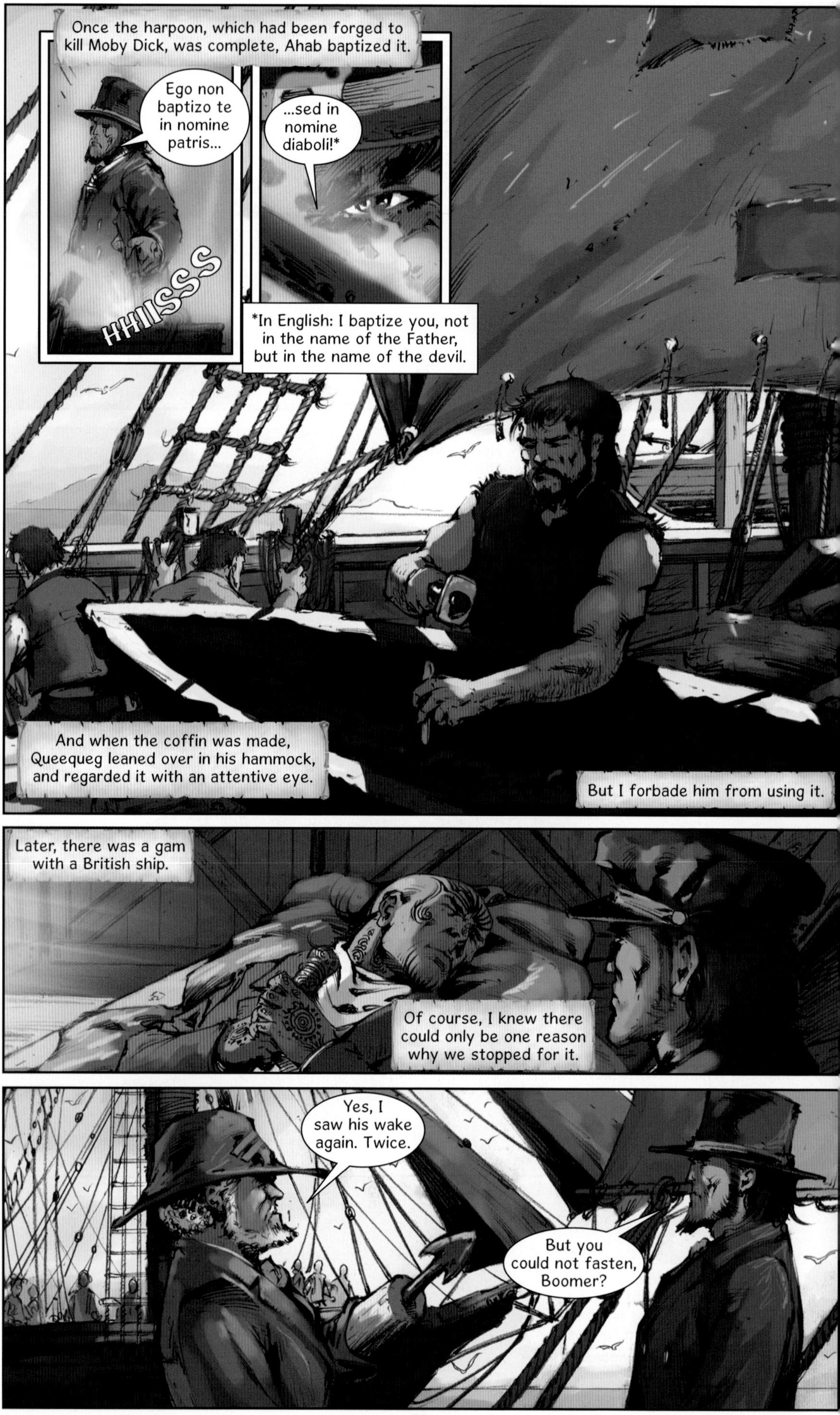
Once the harpoon, which had been forged to kill Moby Dick, was complete, Ahab baptized it.
Ego non baptizo te in nomine patris...
HHIISSS
...sed in nomine diaboli!*
*In English: I baptize you, not in the name of the Father, but in the name of the devil.
And when the coffin was made, Queequeg leaned over in his hammock, and regarded it with an attentive eye.
But I forbade him from using it.
Later, there was a gam with a British ship.
Of course, I knew there could only be one reason why we stopped for it.
Yes, I saw his wake again. Twice.
But you could not fasten, Boomer?

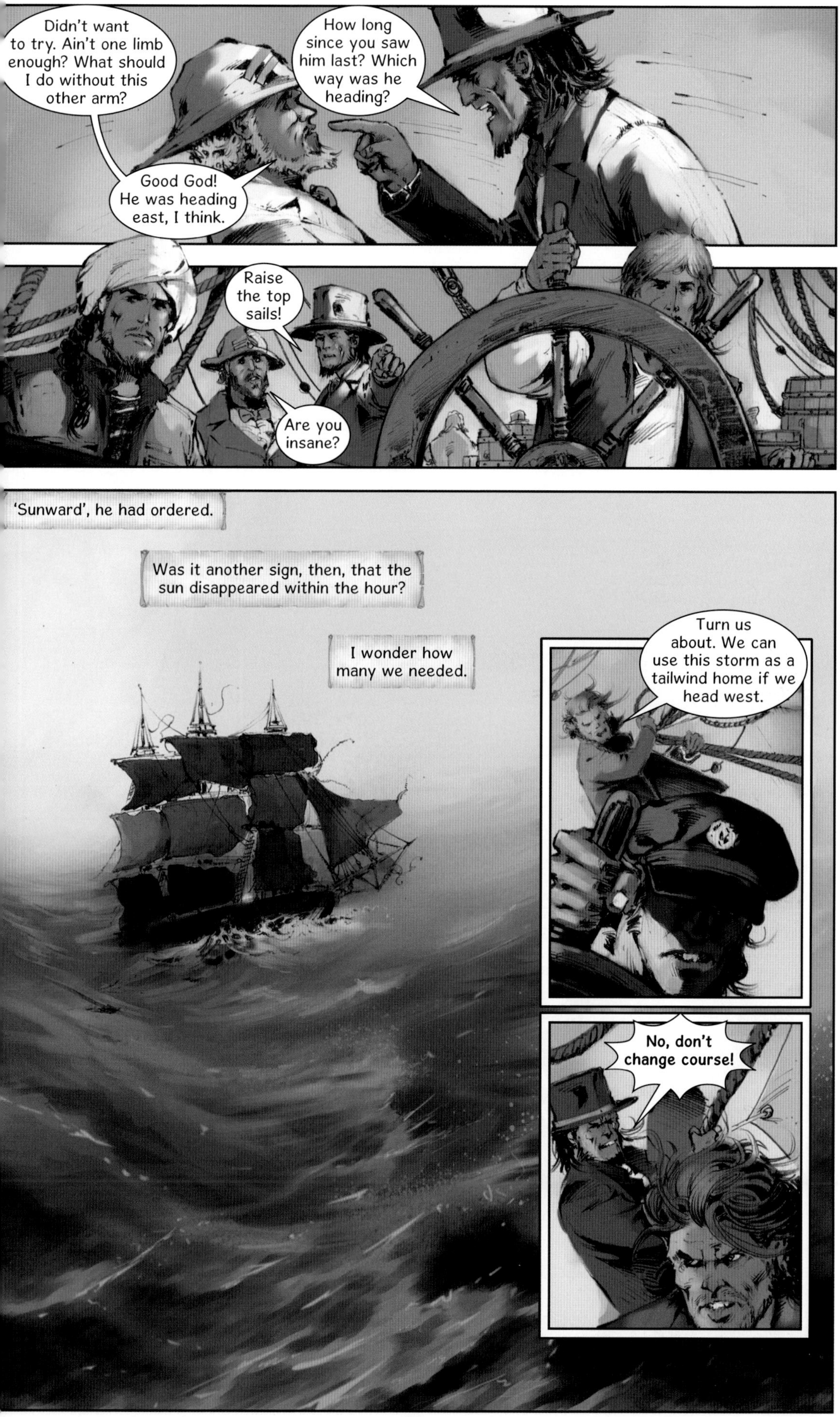

Didn't want to try. Ain't one limb enough? What should I do without this other arm?
How long since you saw him last? Which way was he heading?
Good God! He was heading east, I think.
Raise the top sails!
Are you insane?
'Sunward', he had ordered.
Was it another sign, then, that the sun disappeared within the hour?
I wonder how many we needed.
Turn us about. We can use this storm as a tailwind home if we head west.
No, don't change course!

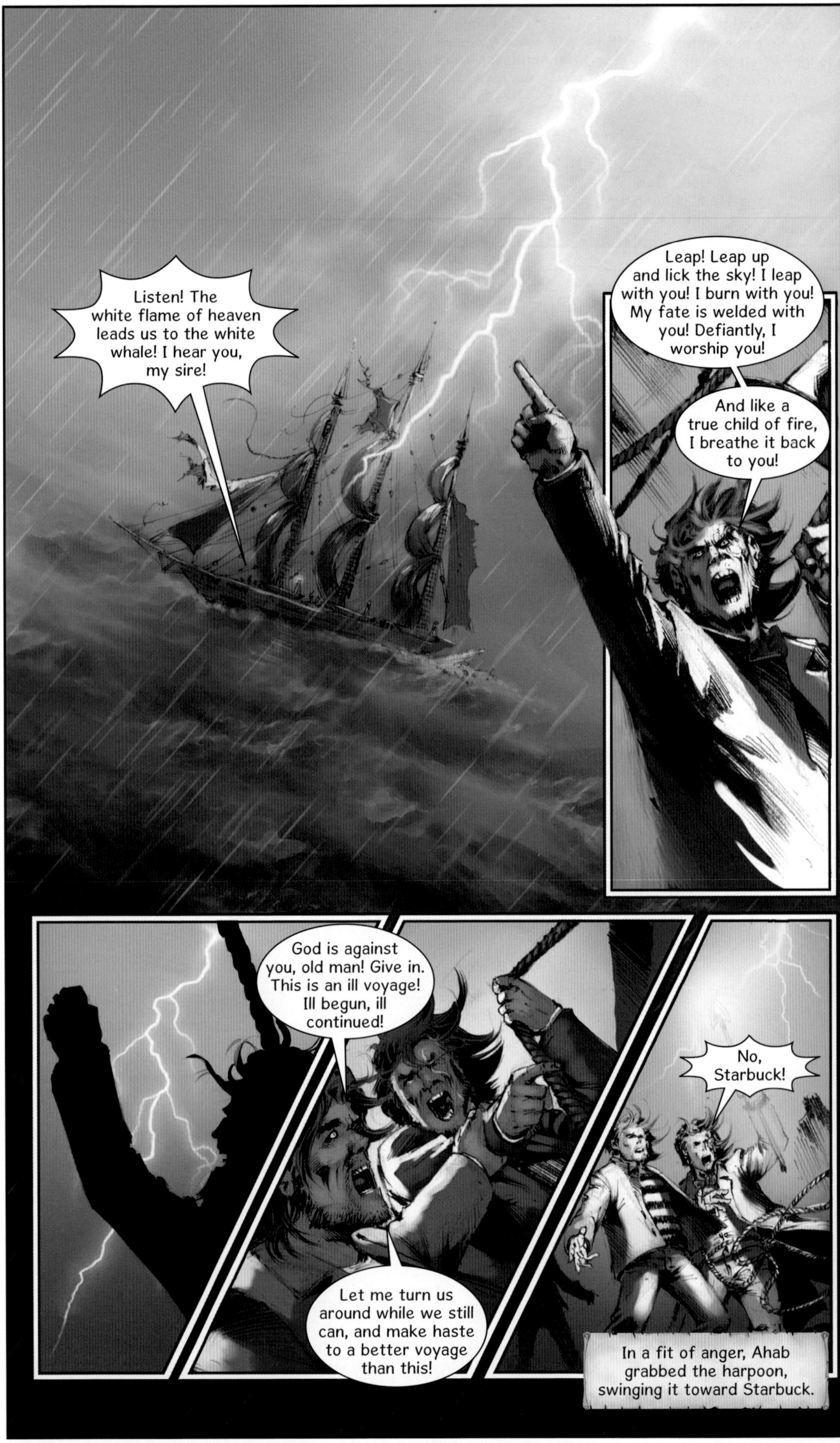
Listen! The white flame of heaven leads us to the white whale! I hear you, my sire!
Leap! Leap up and lick the sky! I leap with you! I burn with you! My fate is welded with you! Defiantly, I worship you!
And like a true child of fire, I breathe it back to you!
God is against you, old man! Give in. This is an ill voyage! Ill begun, ill continued!
Let me turn us around while we still can, and make haste to a better voyage than this!
No, Starbuck!
In a fit of anger, Ahab grabbed the harpoon, swinging it toward Starbuck.

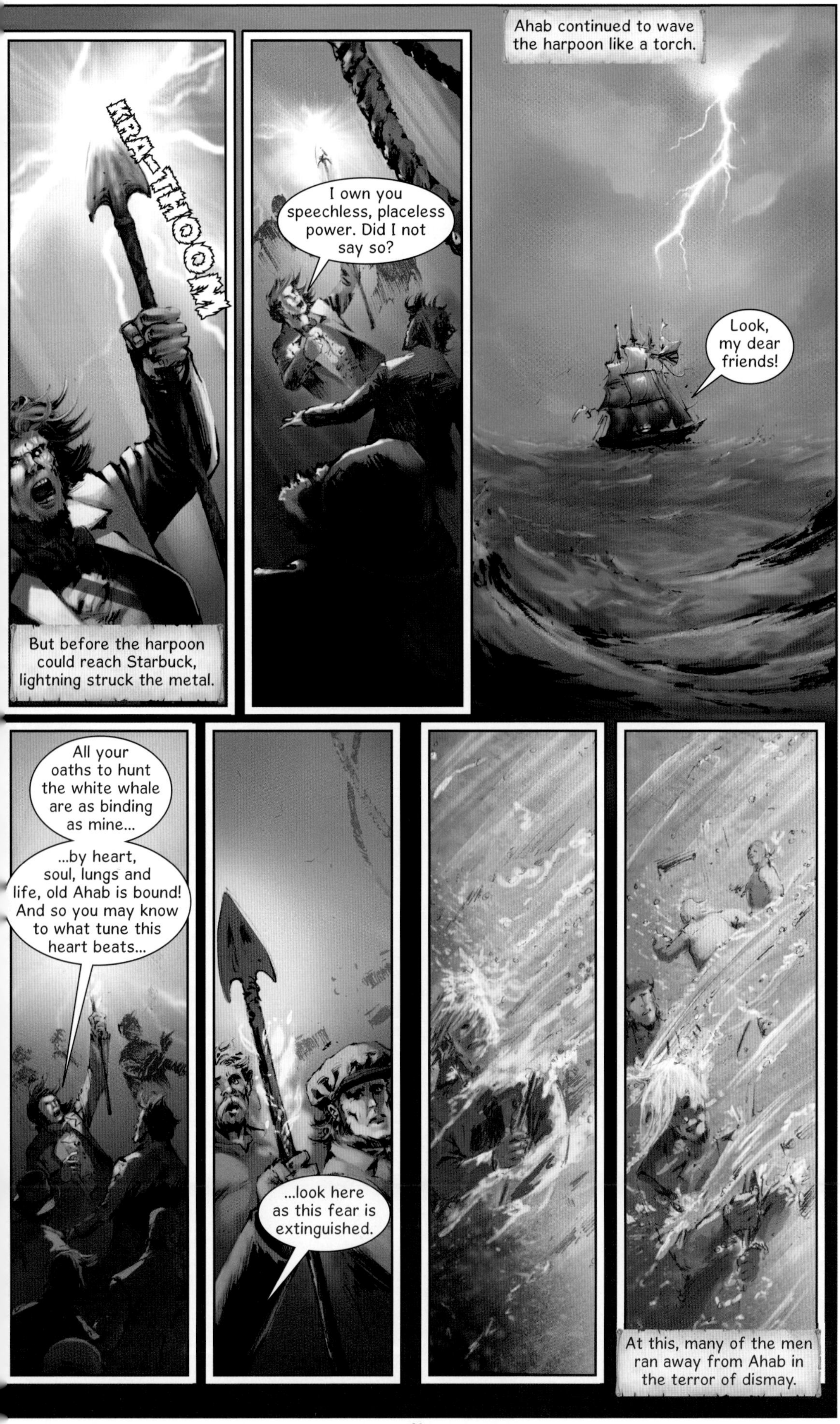
KRA-THOOM
But before the harpoon could reach Starbuck, lightning struck the metal.
I own you speechless, placeless power. Did I not say so?
Ahab continued to wave the harpoon like a torch.
Look, my dear friends!
All your oaths to hunt the white whale are as binding as mine...
...by heart, soul, lungs and life, old Ahab is bound! And so you may know to what tune this heart beats...
...look here as this fear is extinguished.
At this, many of the men ran away from Ahab in the terror of dismay.

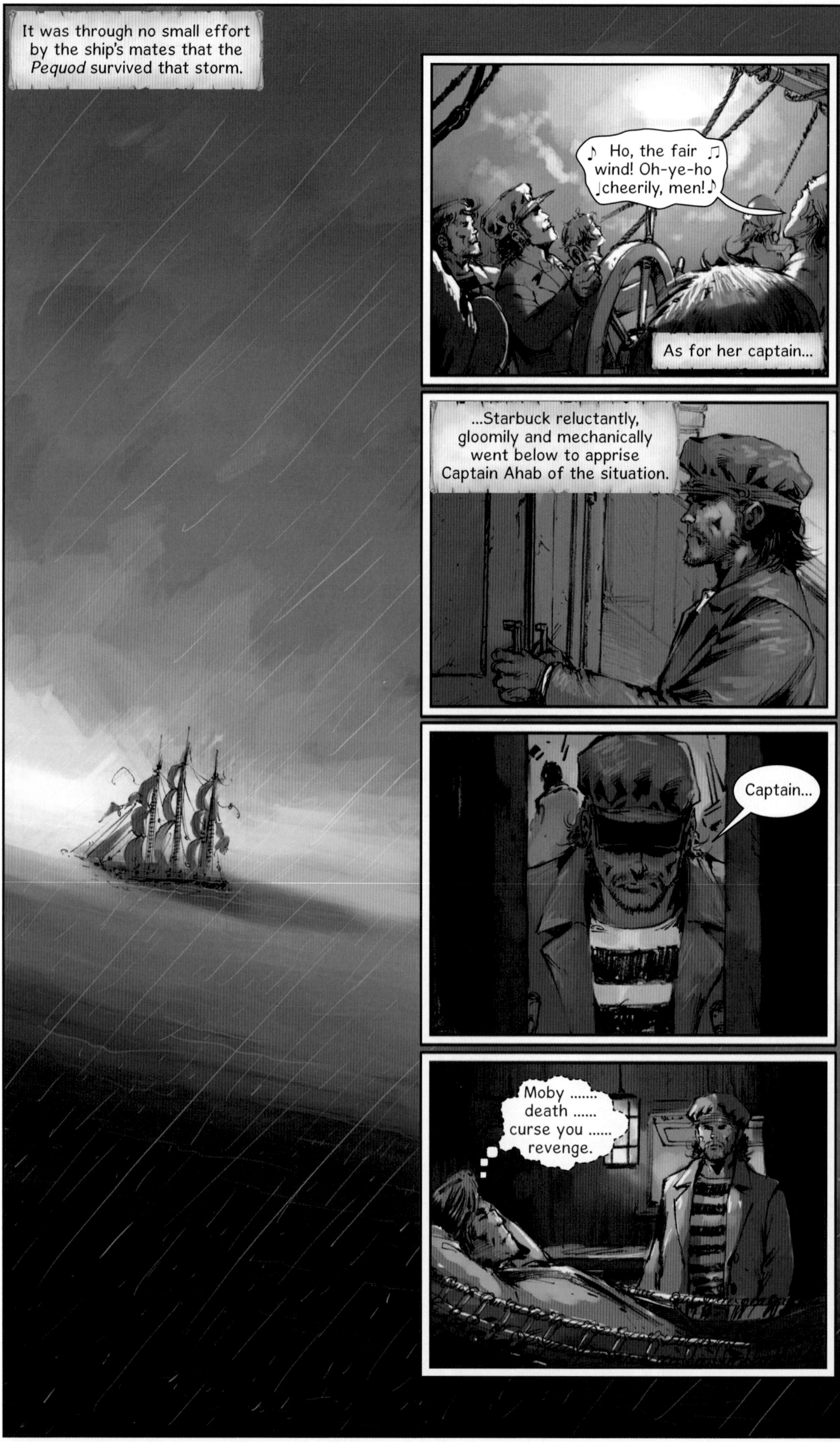
It was through no small effort by the ship's mates that the *Pequod* survived that storm.
♪ Ho, the fair ♫ wind! Oh-ye-ho ♩cheerily, men!♪
As for her captain...
...Starbuck reluctantly, gloomily and mechanically went below to apprise Captain Ahab of the situation.
Captain...
Moby ...... death ...... curse you ...... revenge.

Strange! I have handled so many deadly lances, so why am I shaking now?

I have come to report a fair wind to him. But how fair? Fair for death and doom—that's fair for Moby Dick. A fair wind is only fair for that accursed whale!

The very gun he pointed at me—the very one. He would have killed me with it. And he would gladly kill all his crew.

Stern all... oh Moby Dick, I clutch your heart at last.

Is heaven a murderer when its lightning strikes a would-be murderer in his bed? And would I be a murderer if...

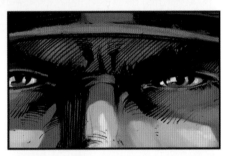

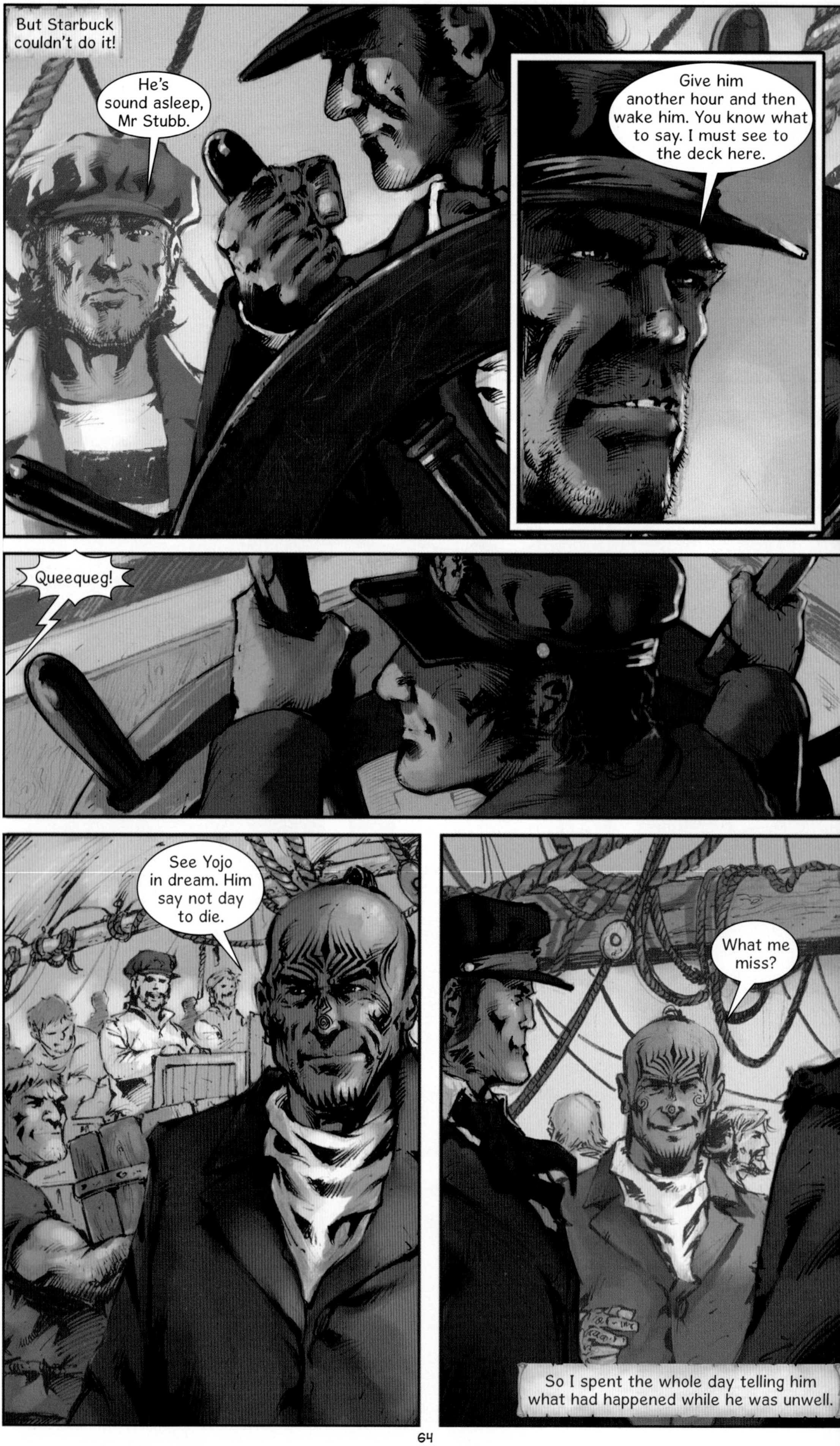

But Starbuck couldn't do it!
He's sound asleep, Mr Stubb.
Give him another hour and then wake him. You know what to say. I must see to the deck here.
Queequeg!
See Yojo in dream. Him say not day to die.
What me miss?
So I spent the whole day telling him what had happened while he was unwell.

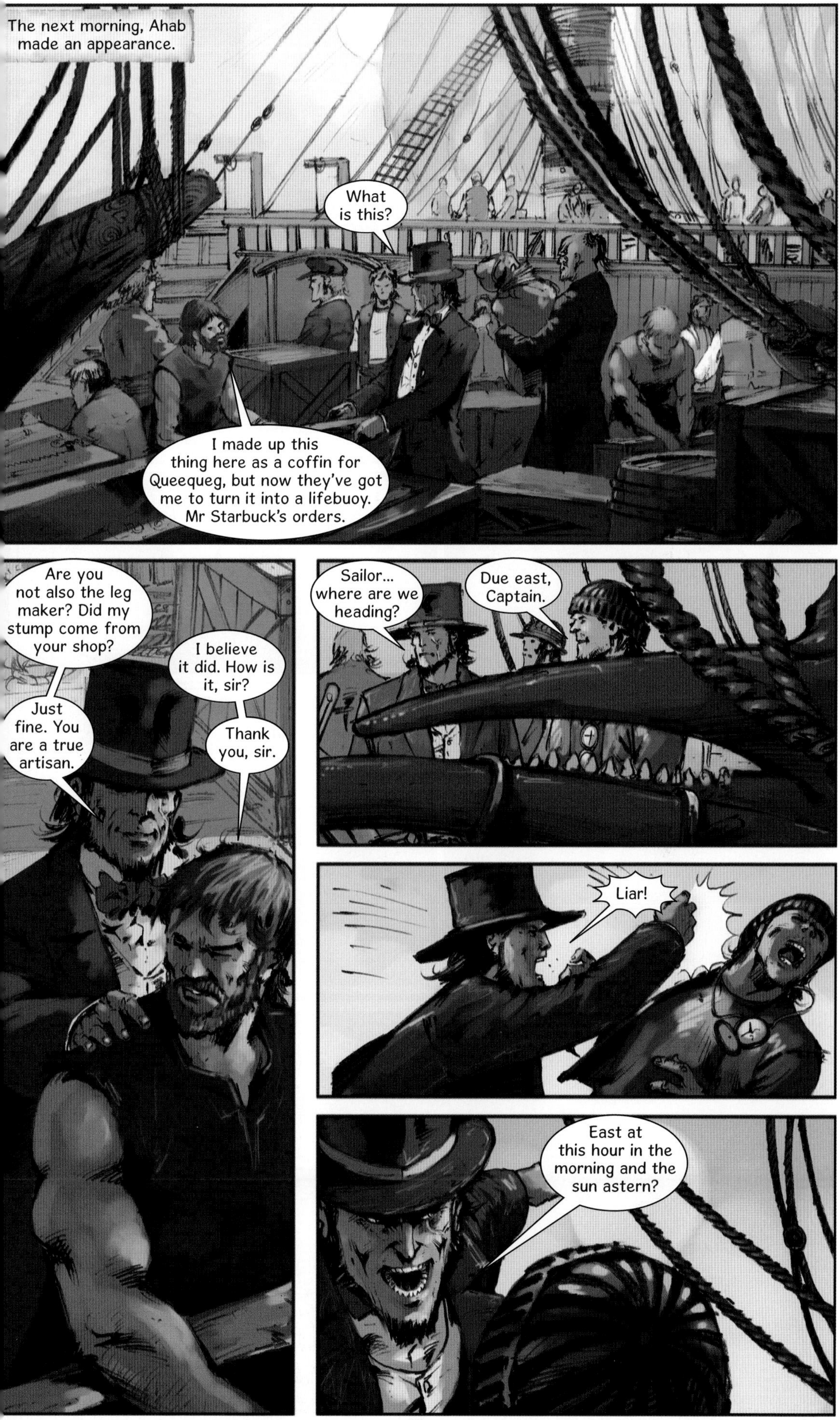
The next morning, Ahab made an appearance.
What is this?
I made up this thing here as a coffin for Queequeg, but now they've got me to turn it into a lifebuoy. Mr Starbuck's orders.
Are you not also the leg maker? Did my stump come from your shop?
I believe it did. How is it, sir?
Just fine. You are a true artisan.
Thank you, sir.
Sailor... where are we heading?
Due east, Captain.
Liar!
East at this hour in the morning and the sun astern?

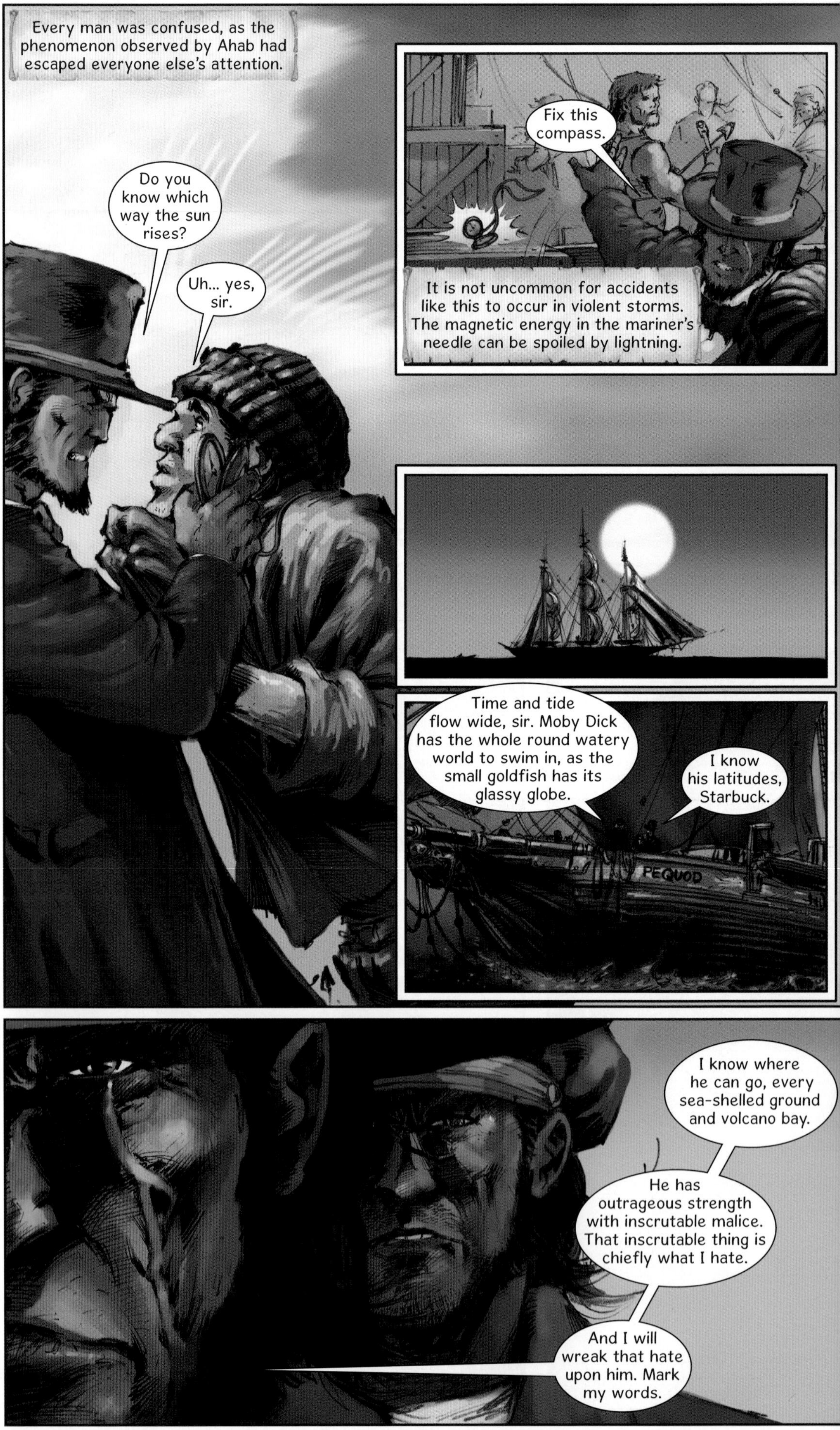
Every man was confused, as the phenomenon observed by Ahab had escaped everyone else's attention.
Do you know which way the sun rises?
Uh... yes, sir.
Fix this compass.
It is not uncommon for accidents like this to occur in violent storms. The magnetic energy in the mariner's needle can be spoiled by lightning.
Time and tide flow wide, sir. Moby Dick has the whole round watery world to swim in, as the small goldfish has its glassy globe.
I know his latitudes, Starbuck.
PEQUOD
I know where he can go, every sea-shelled ground and volcano bay.
He has outrageous strength with inscrutable malice. That inscrutable thing is chiefly what I hate.
And I will wreak that hate upon him. Mark my words.

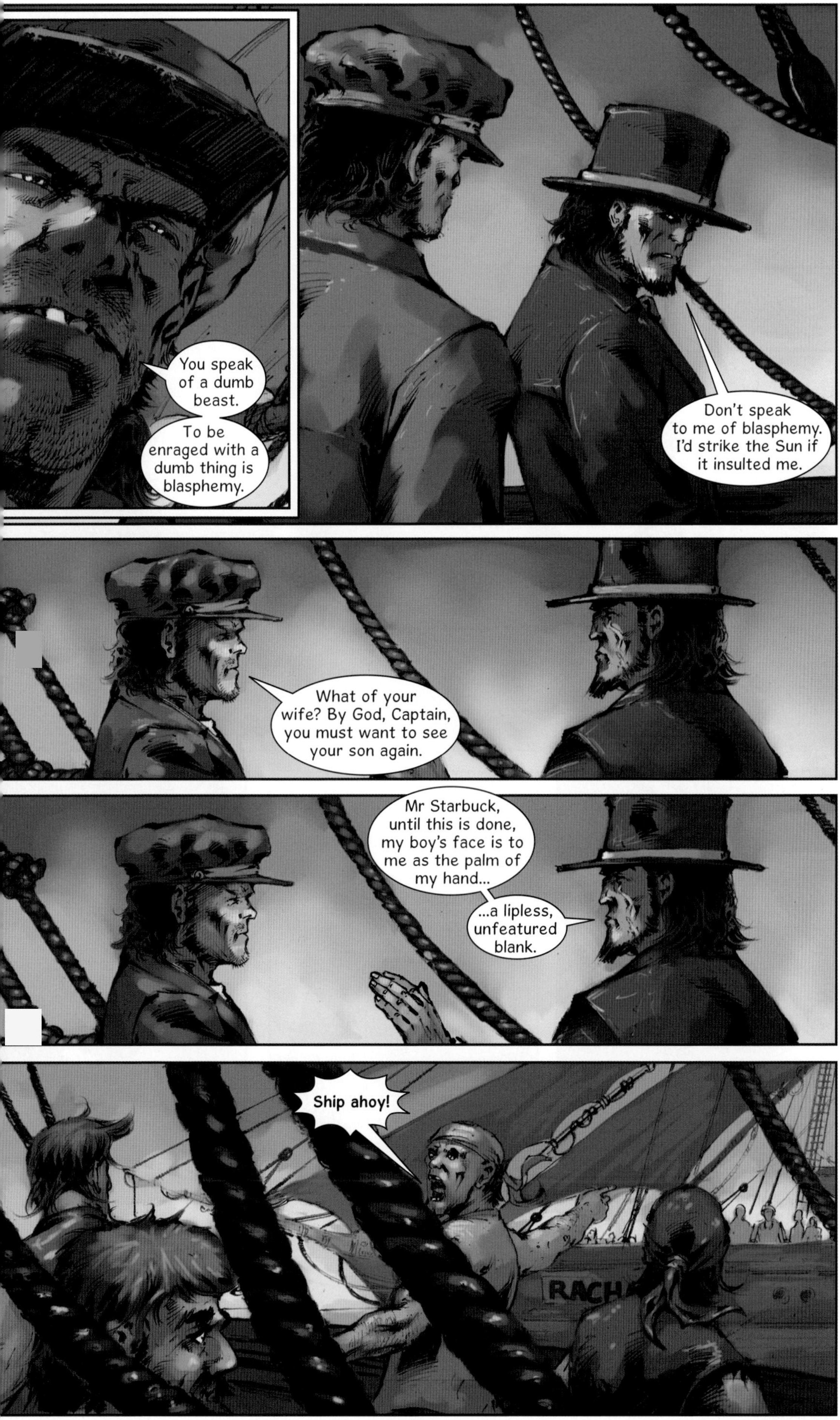
You speak of a dumb beast.
To be enraged with a dumb thing is blasphemy.
Don't speak to me of blasphemy. I'd strike the Sun if it insulted me.
What of your wife? By God, Captain, you must want to see your son again.
Mr Starbuck, until this is done, my boy's face is to me as the palm of my hand...
...a lipless, unfeatured blank.
Ship ahoy!
RACH

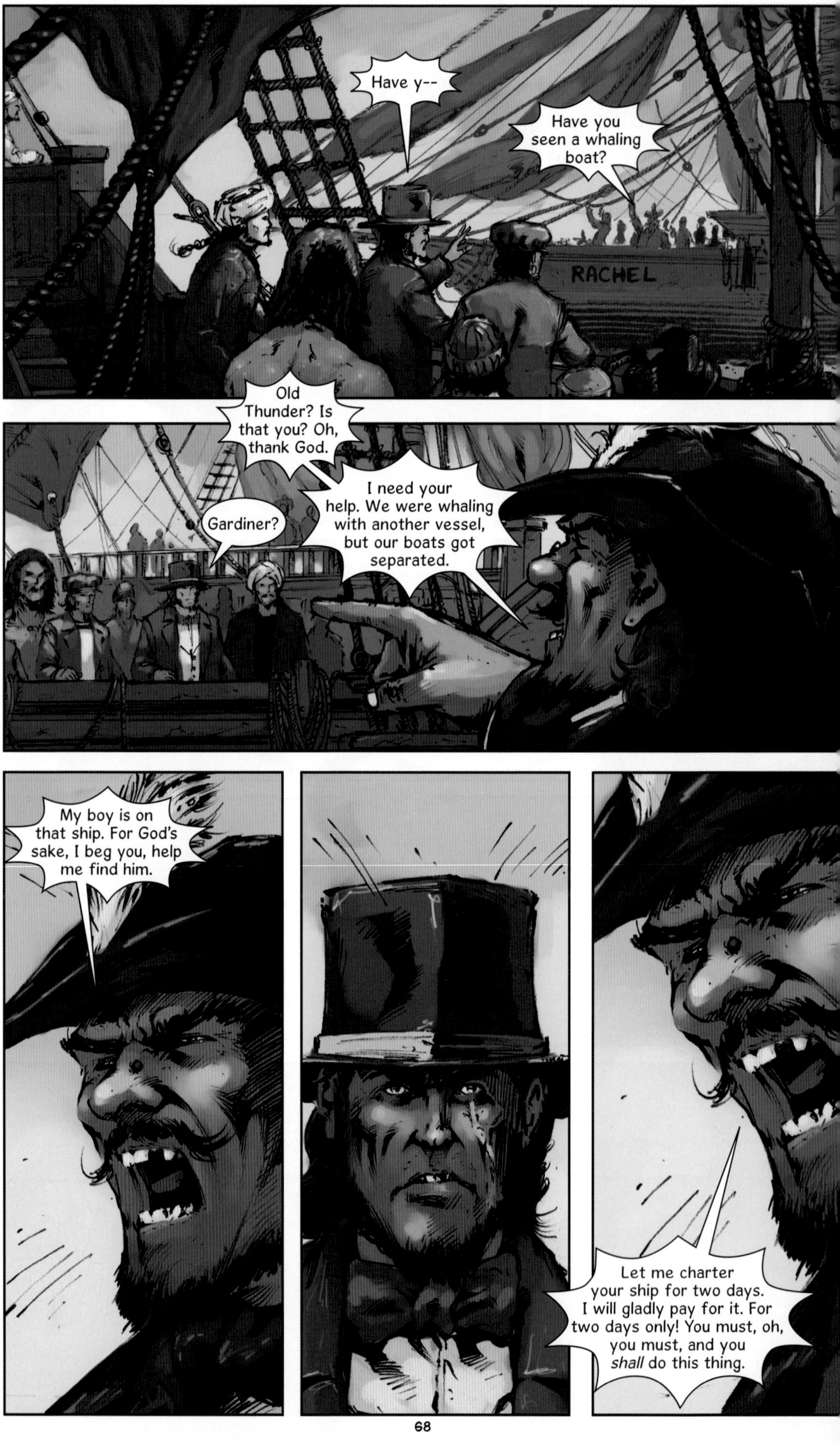
Have y--
Have you seen a whaling boat?
RACHEL
Old Thunder? Is that you? Oh, thank God.
Gardiner?
I need your help. We were whaling with another vessel, but our boats got separated.
My boy is on that ship. For God's sake, I beg you, help me find him.
Let me charter your ship for two days. I will gladly pay for it. For two days only! You must, oh, you must, and you *shall* do this thing.

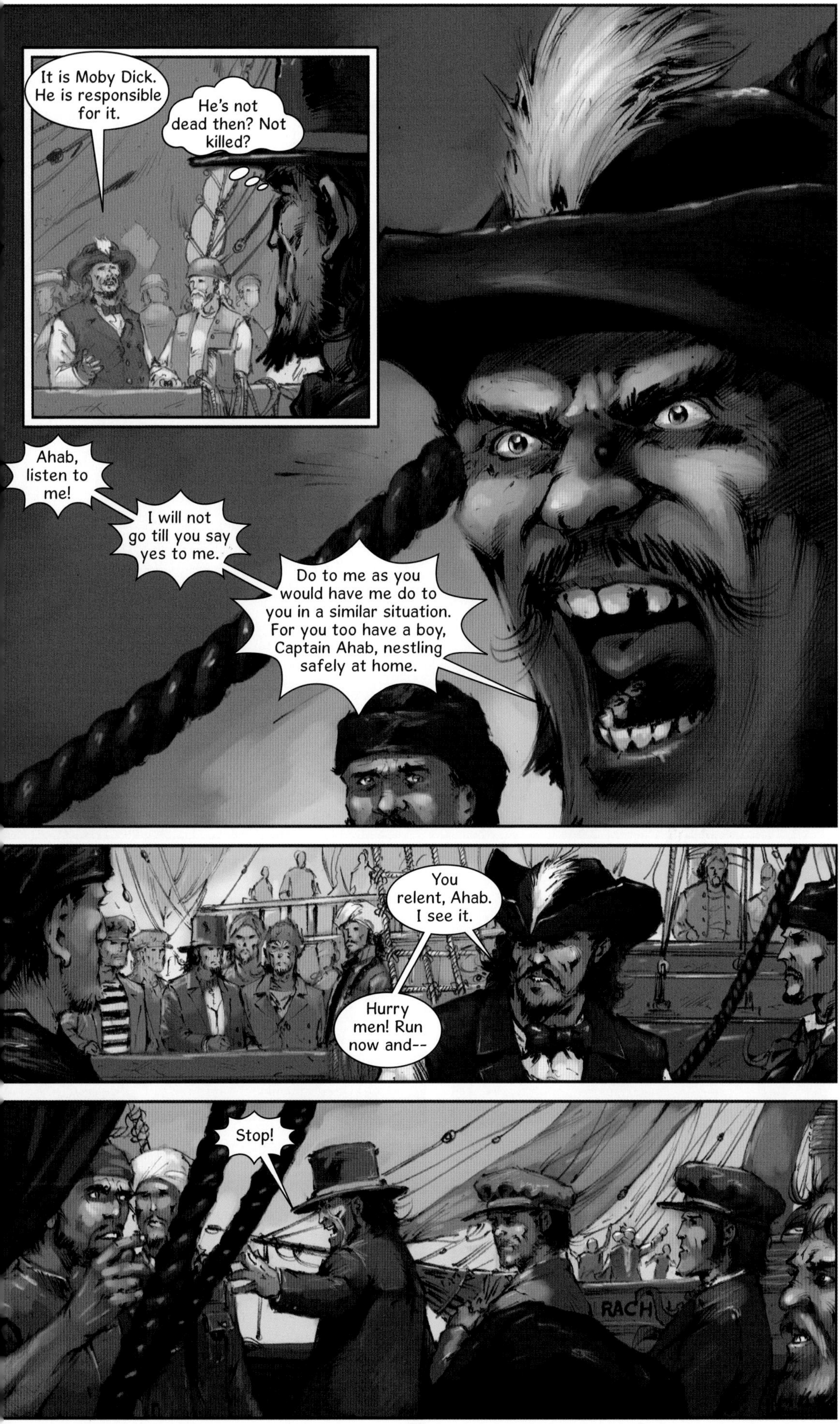
It is Moby Dick. He is responsible for it.
He's not dead then? Not killed?
Ahab, listen to me!
I will not go till you say yes to me.
Do to me as you would have me do to you in a similar situation. For you too have a boy, Captain Ahab, nestling safely at home.
You relent, Ahab. I see it.
Hurry men! Run now and--
Stop!
RACH

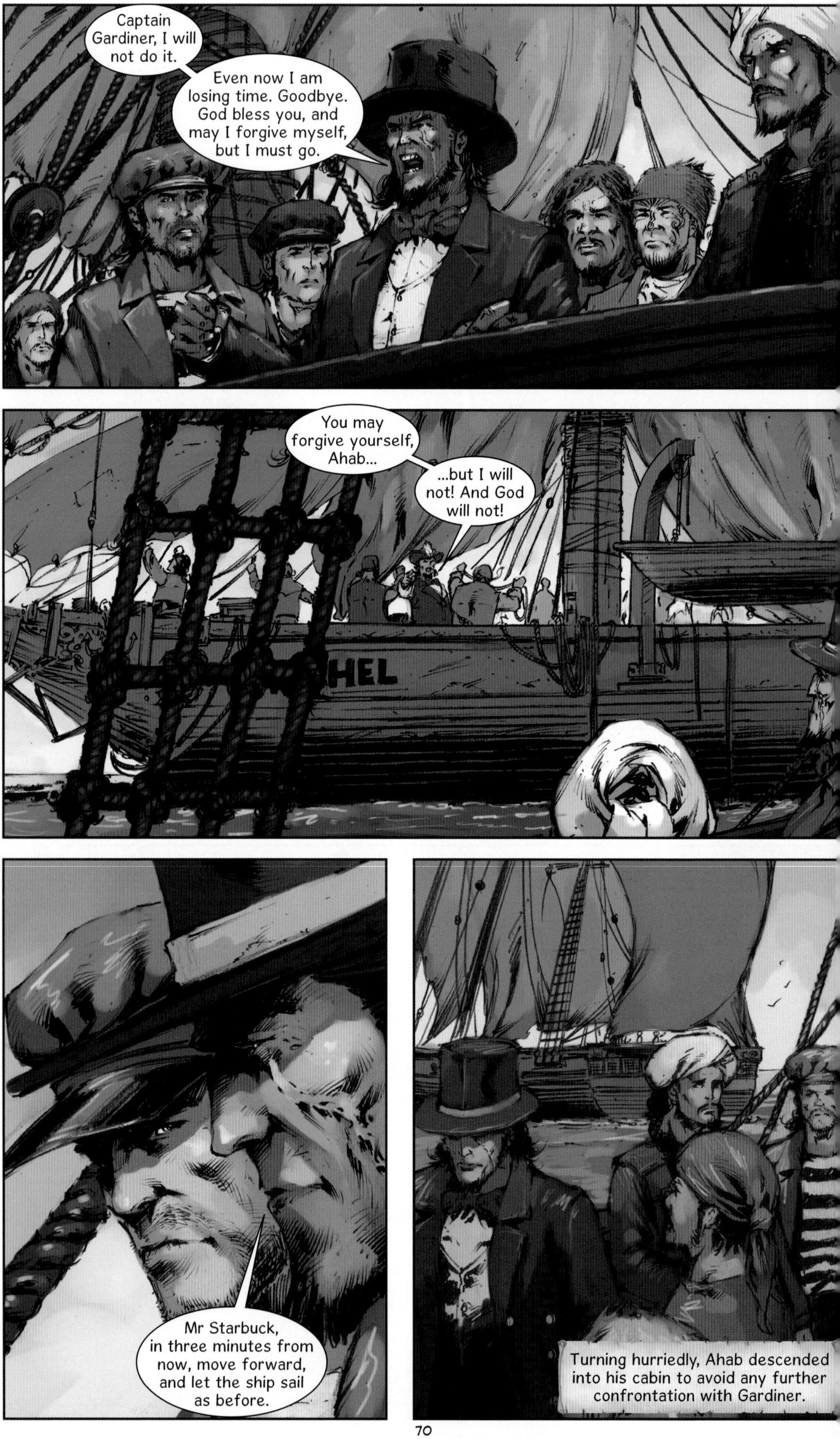
Captain Gardiner, I will not do it.
Even now I am losing time. Goodbye. God bless you, and may I forgive myself, but I must go.
You may forgive yourself, Ahab...
...but I will not! And God will not!
HEL
Mr Starbuck, in three minutes from now, move forward, and let the ship sail as before.
Turning hurriedly, Ahab descended into his cabin to avoid any further confrontation with Gardiner.

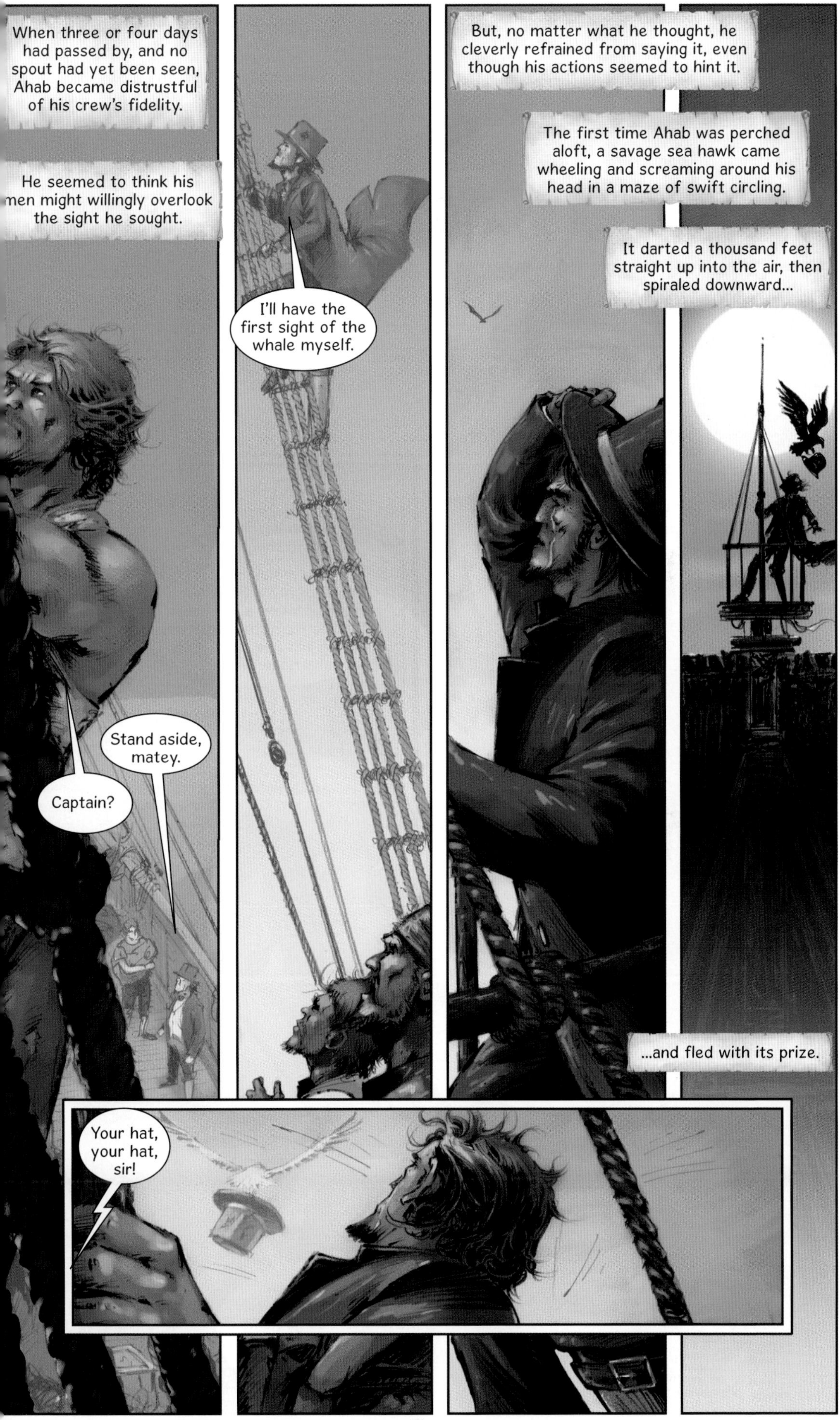
When three or four days had passed by, and no spout had yet been seen, Ahab became distrustful of his crew's fidelity.
He seemed to think his men might willingly overlook the sight he sought.
Captain?
Stand aside, matey.
I'll have the first sight of the whale myself.
But, no matter what he thought, he cleverly refrained from saying it, even though his actions seemed to hint it.
The first time Ahab was perched aloft, a savage sea hawk came wheeling and screaming around his head in a maze of swift circling.
It darted a thousand feet straight up into the air, then spiraled downward...
...and fled with its prize.
Your hat, your hat, sir!

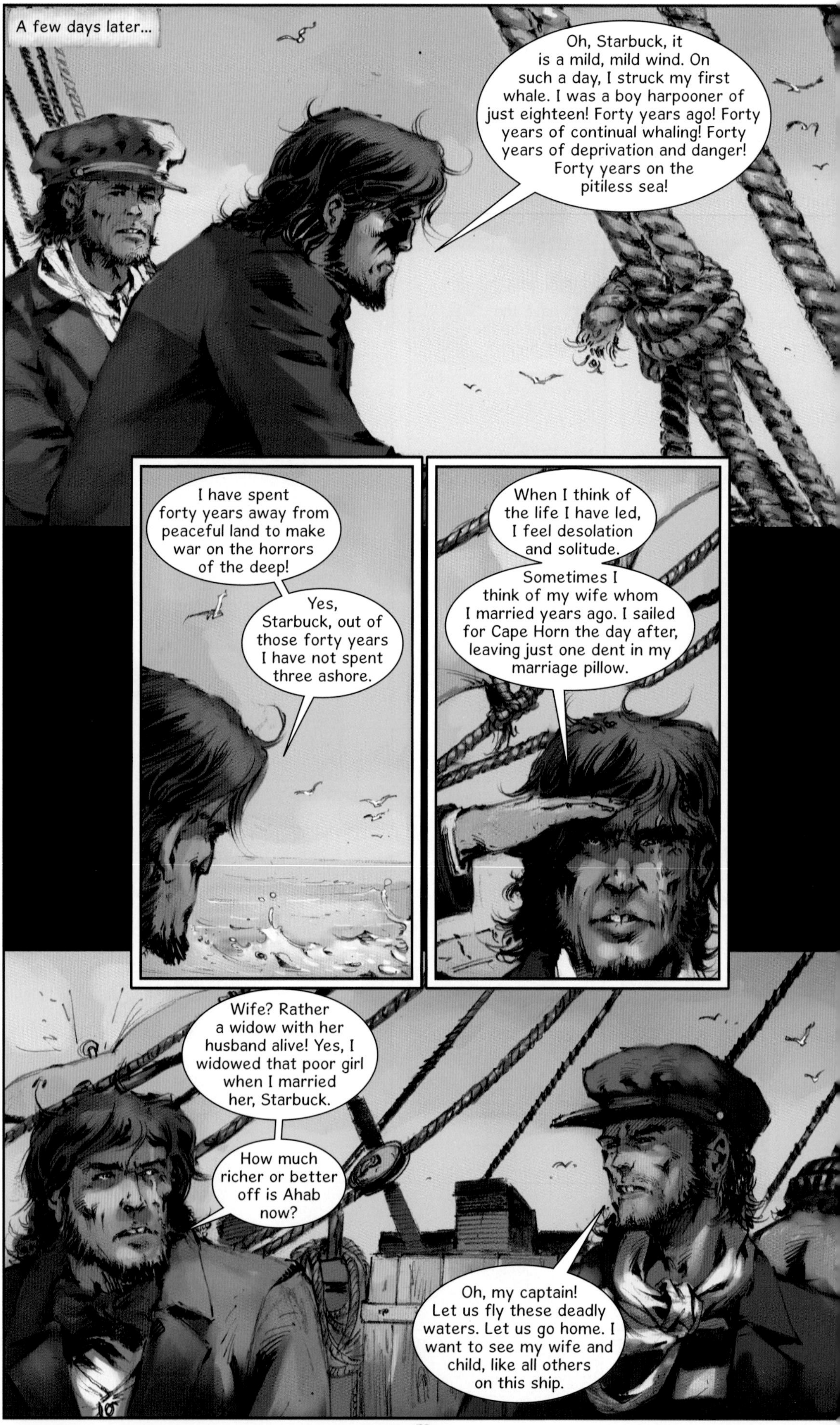
A few days later...
Oh, Starbuck, it is a mild, mild wind. On such a day, I struck my first whale. I was a boy harpooner of just eighteen! Forty years ago! Forty years of continual whaling! Forty years of deprivation and danger! Forty years on the pitiless sea!
I have spent forty years away from peaceful land to make war on the horrors of the deep!
Yes, Starbuck, out of those forty years I have not spent three ashore.
When I think of the life I have led, I feel desolation and solitude.
Sometimes I think of my wife whom I married years ago. I sailed for Cape Horn the day after, leaving just one dent in my marriage pillow.
Wife? Rather a widow with her husband alive! Yes, I widowed that poor girl when I married her, Starbuck.
How much richer or better off is Ahab now?
Oh, my captain! Let us fly these deadly waters. Let us go home. I want to see my wife and child, like all others on this ship.

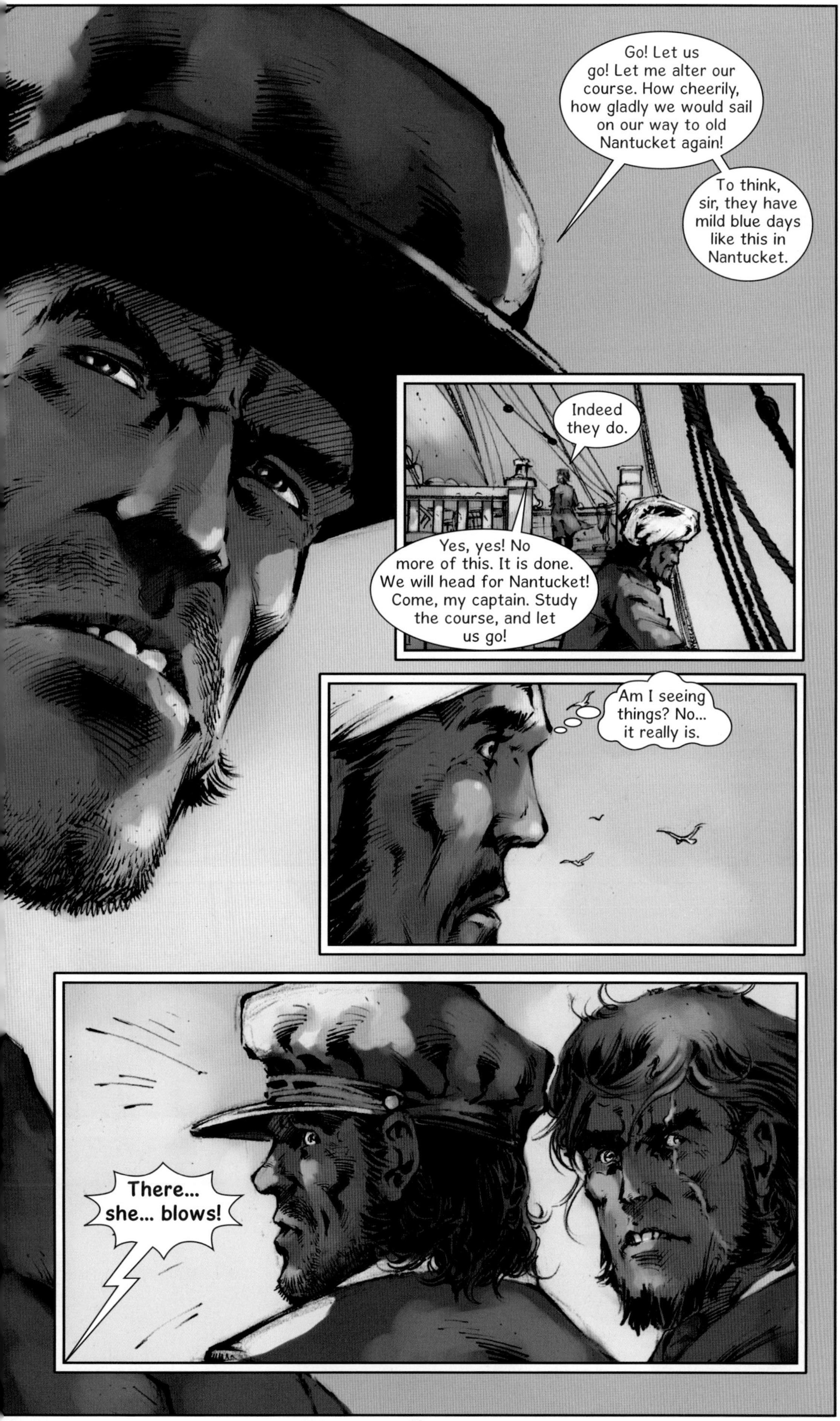
Go! Let us go! Let me alter our course. How cheerily, how gladly we would sail on our way to old Nantucket again!
To think, sir, they have mild blue days like this in Nantucket.
Indeed they do.
Yes, yes! No more of this. It is done. We will head for Nantucket! Come, my captain. Study the course, and let us go!
Am I seeing things? No... it really is.
There... she... blows!

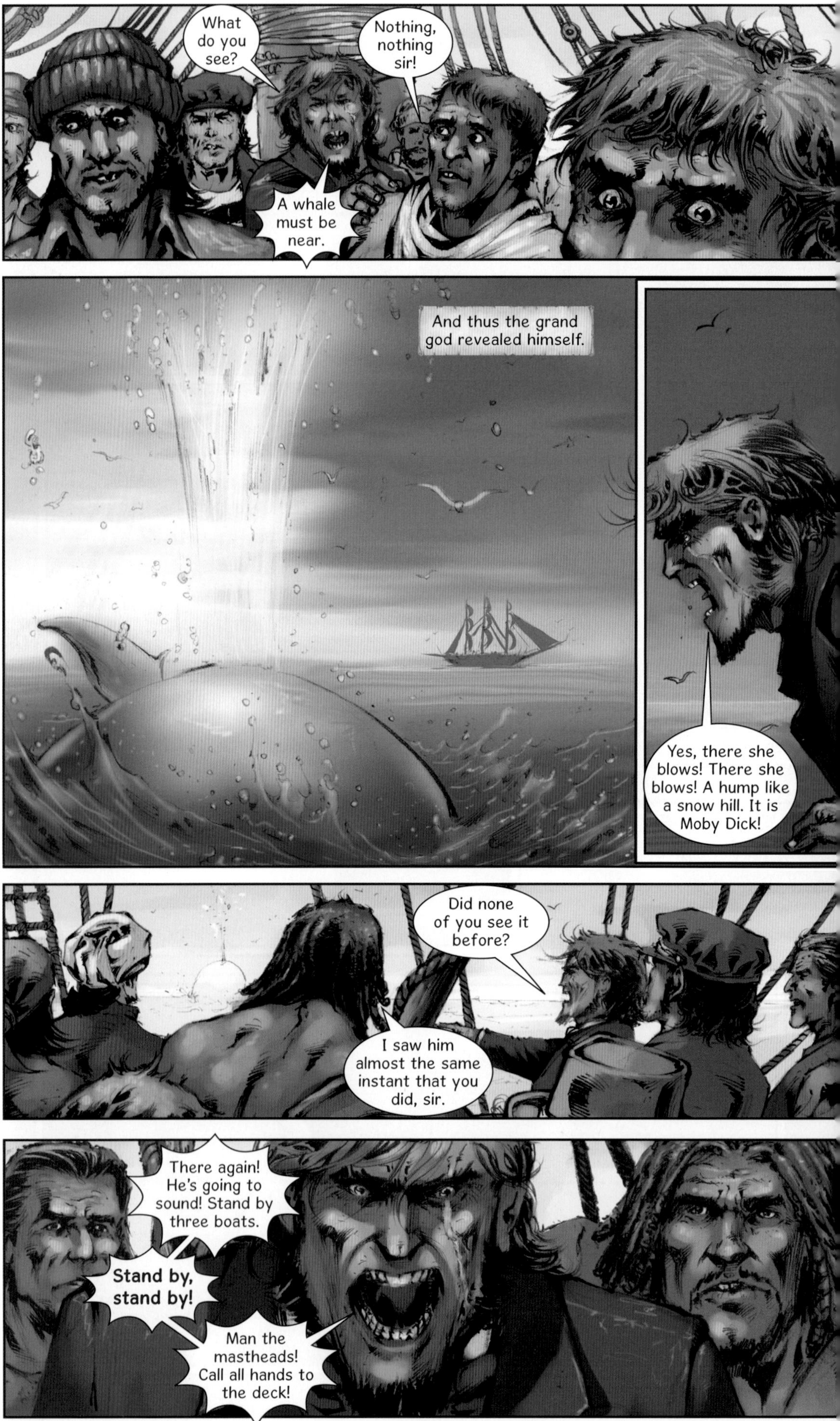
What do you see?
Nothing, nothing sir!
A whale must be near.
And thus the grand god revealed himself.
Yes, there she blows! There she blows! A hump like a snow hill. It is Moby Dick!
Did none of you see it before?
I saw him almost the same instant that you did, sir.
There again! He's going to sound! Stand by three boats.
Stand by, stand by!
Man the mastheads! Call all hands to the deck!

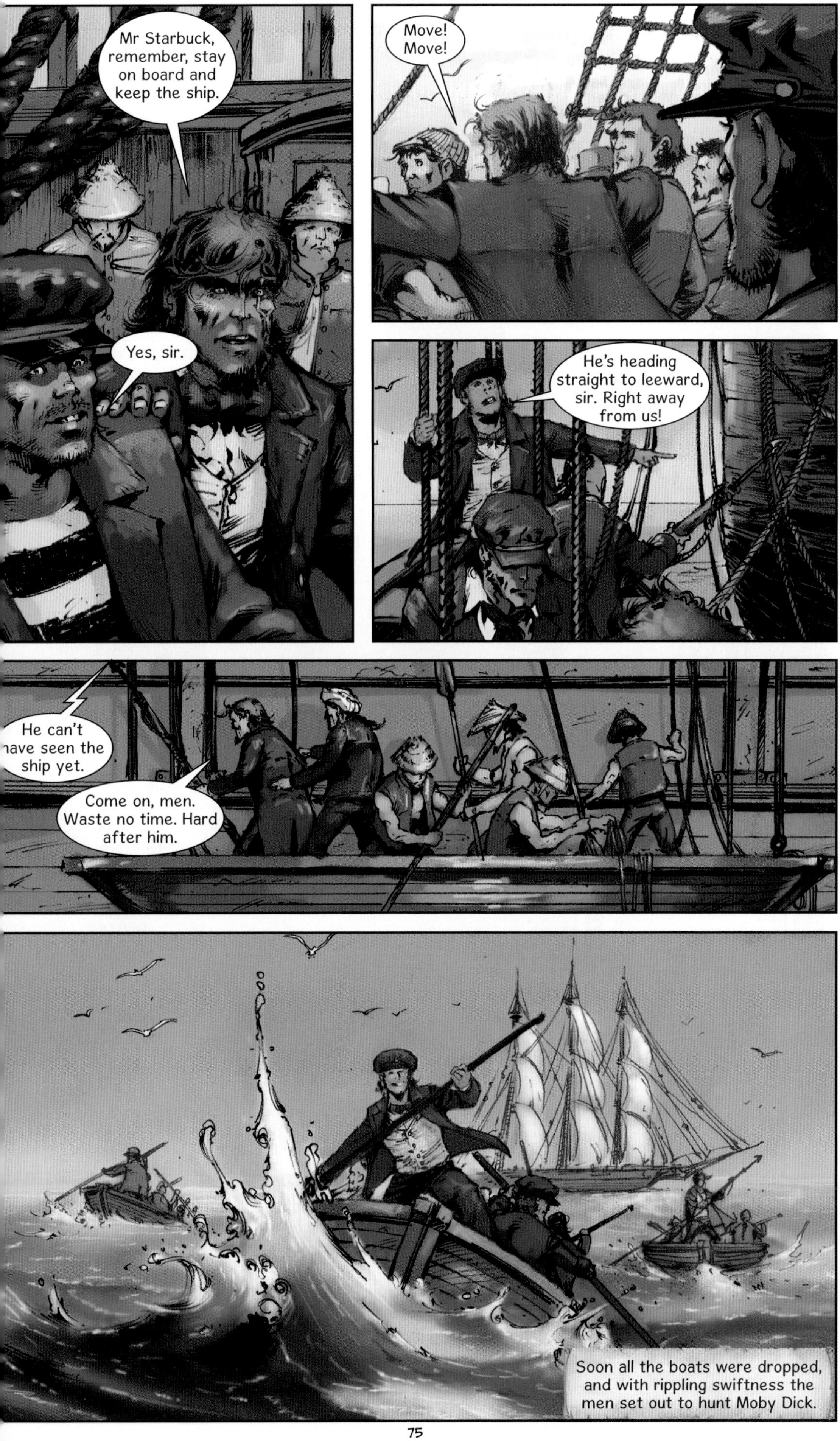
Mr Starbuck, remember, stay on board and keep the ship.
Yes, sir.
Move! Move!
He's heading straight to leeward, sir. Right away from us!
He can't have seen the ship yet.
Come on, men. Waste no time. Hard after him.
Soon all the boats were dropped, and with rippling swiftness the men set out to hunt Moby Dick.

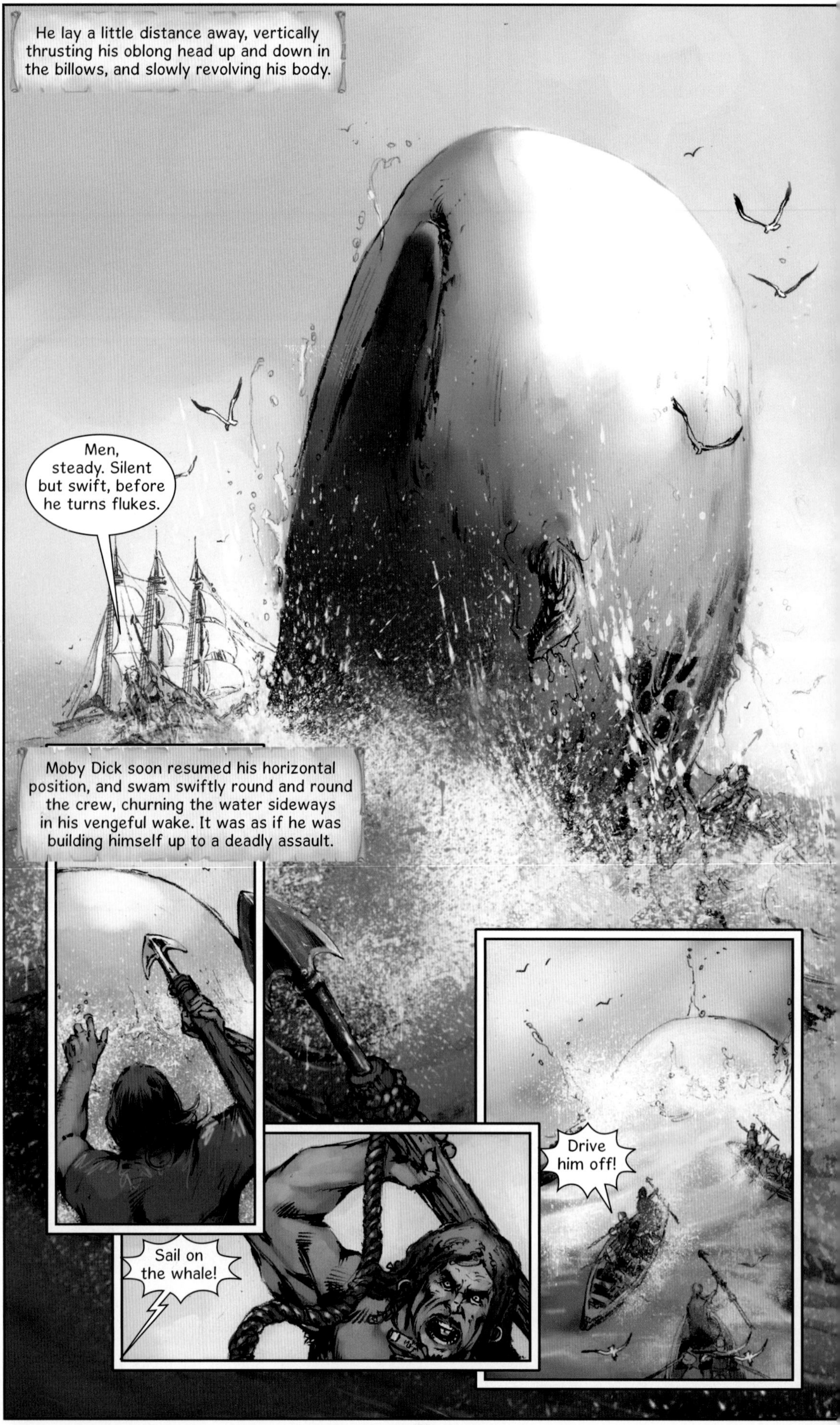
He lay a little distance away, vertically thrusting his oblong head up and down in the billows, and slowly revolving his body.
Men, steady. Silent but swift, before he turns flukes.
Moby Dick soon resumed his horizontal position, and swam swiftly round and round the crew, churning the water sideways in his vengeful wake. It was as if he was building himself up to a deadly assault.
Sail on the whale!
Drive him off!

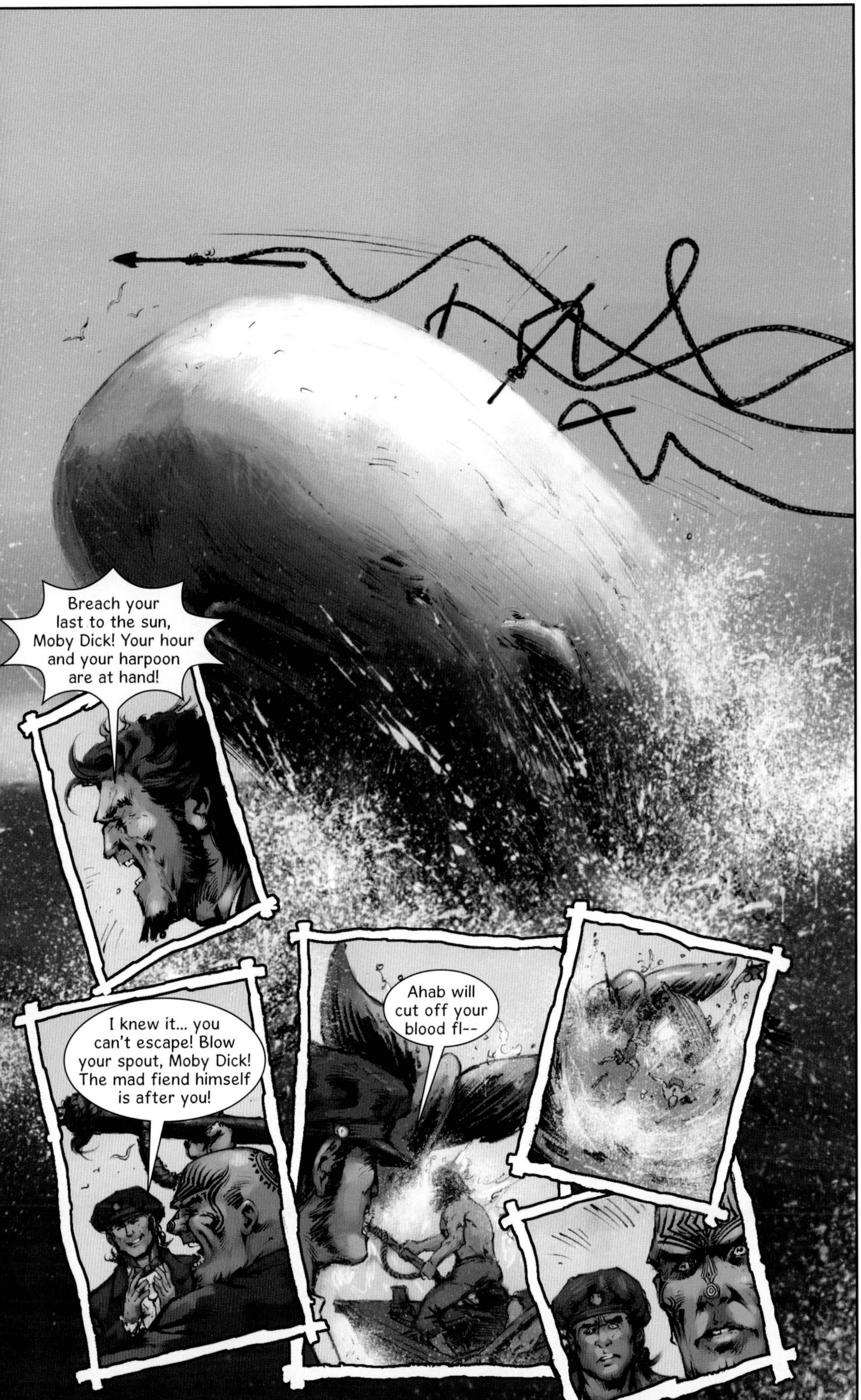
Breach your last to the sun, Moby Dick! Your hour and your harpoon are at hand!
I knew it... you can't escape! Blow your spout, Moby Dick! The mad fiend himself is after you!
Ahab will cut off your blood fl--

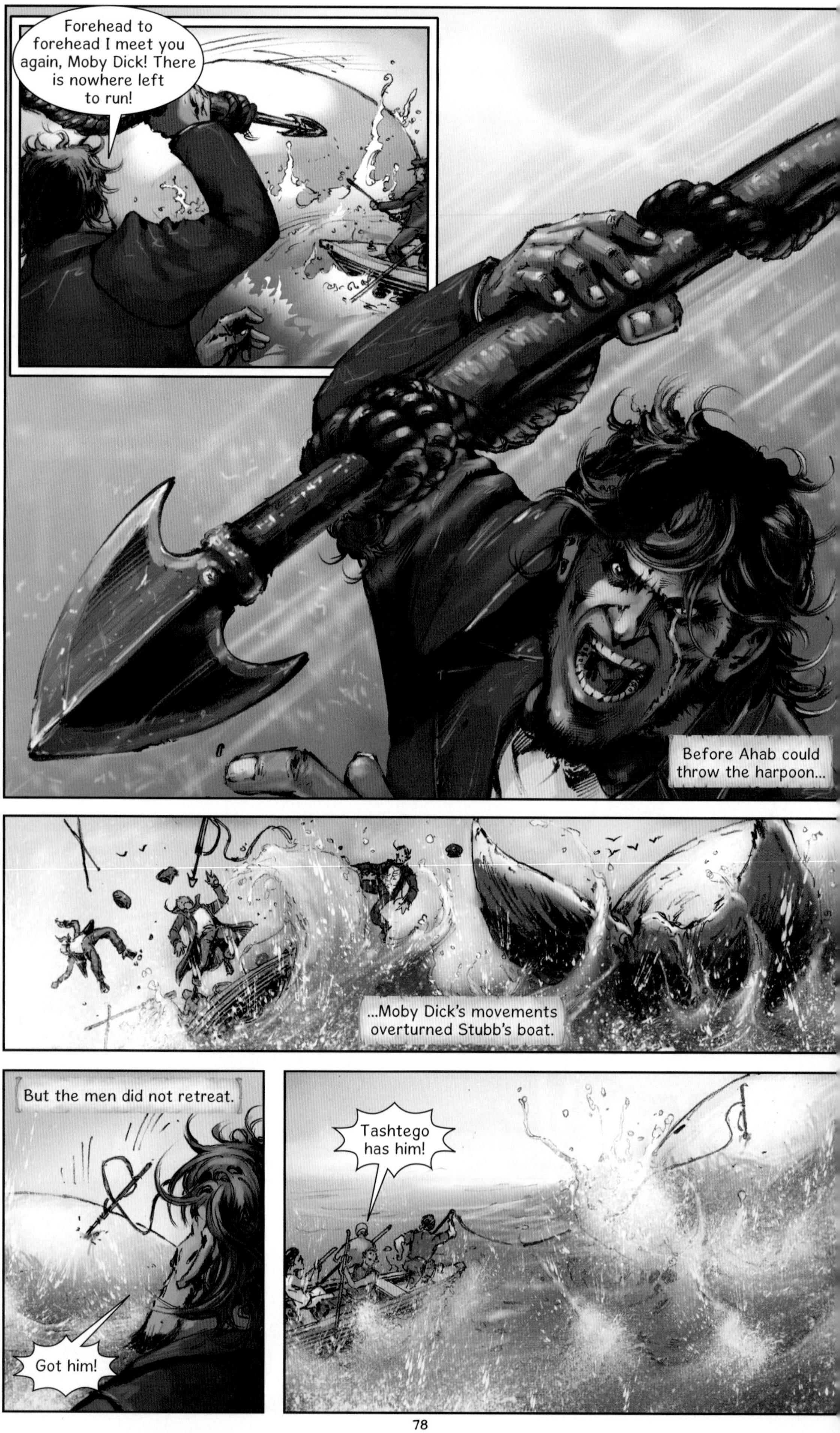

Forehead to forehead I meet you again, Moby Dick! There is nowhere left to run!
Before Ahab could throw the harpoon...
...Moby Dick's movements overturned Stubb's boat.
But the men did not retreat.
Got him!
Tashtego has him!

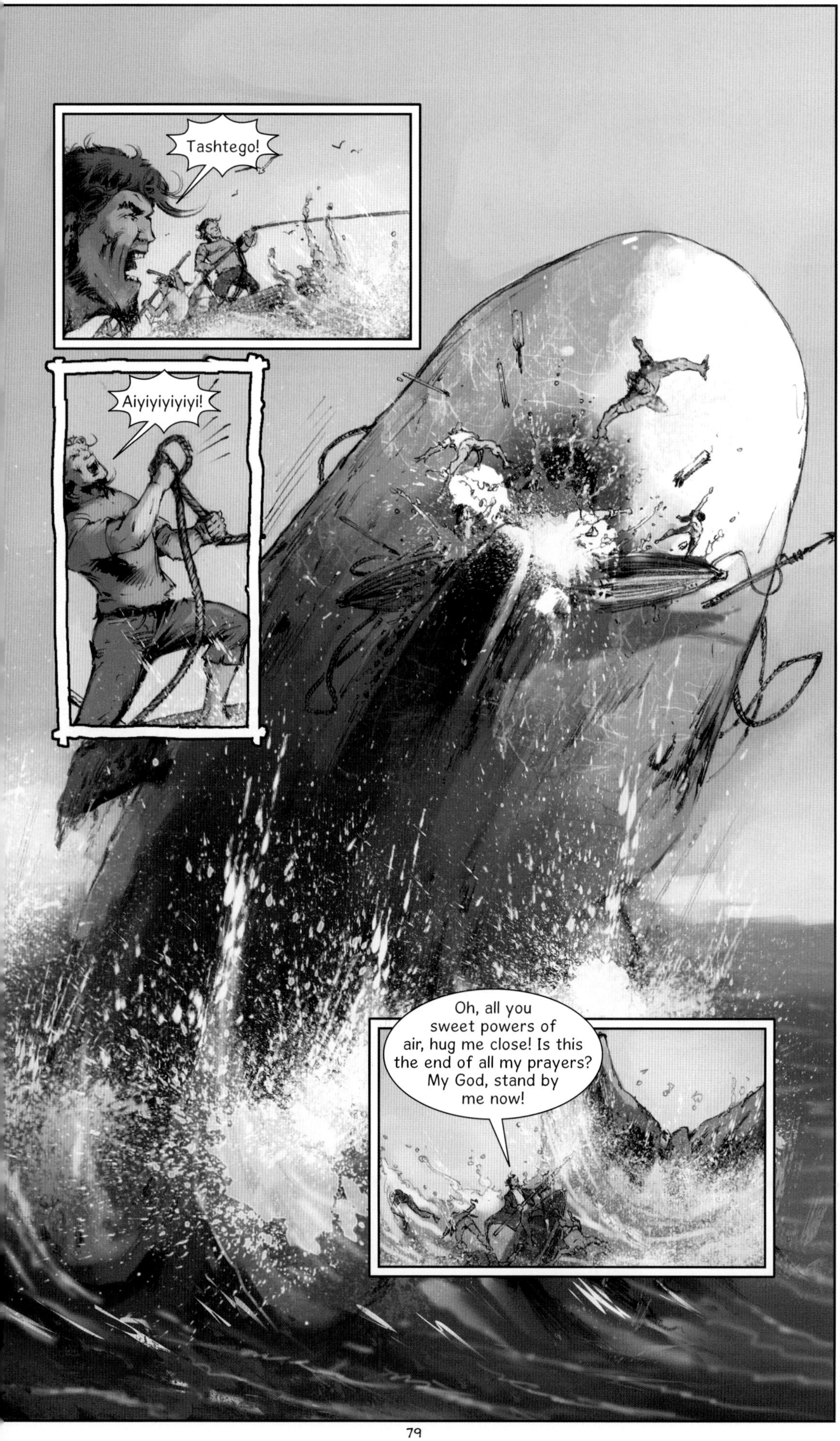
Tashtego!
Aiyiyiyiyiyi!
Oh, all you sweet powers of air, hug me close! Is this the end of all my prayers? My God, stand by me now!

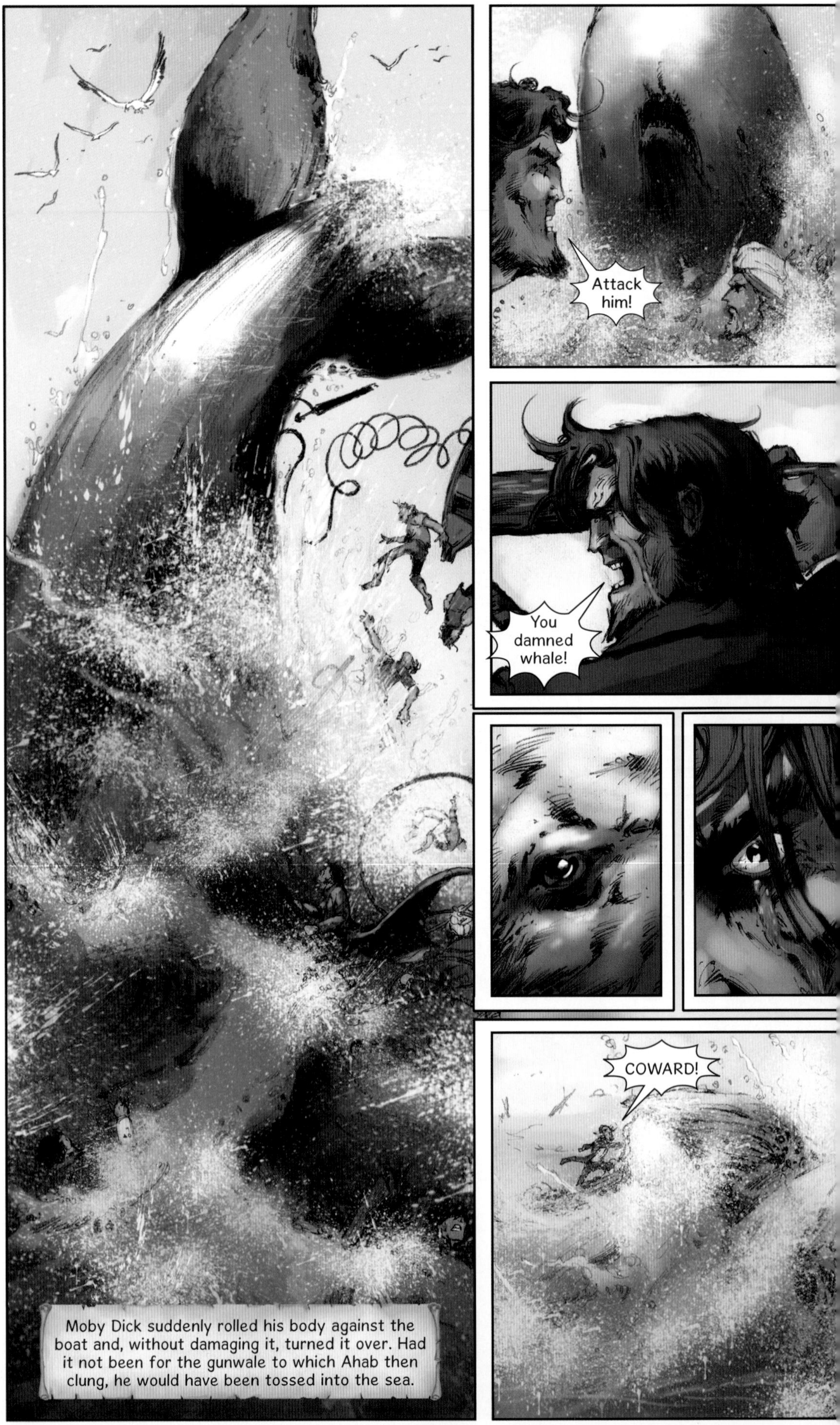
Attack him!
You damned whale!
COWARD!
Moby Dick suddenly rolled his body against the boat and, without damaging it, turned it over. Had it not been for the gunwale to which Ahab then clung, he would have been tossed into the sea.

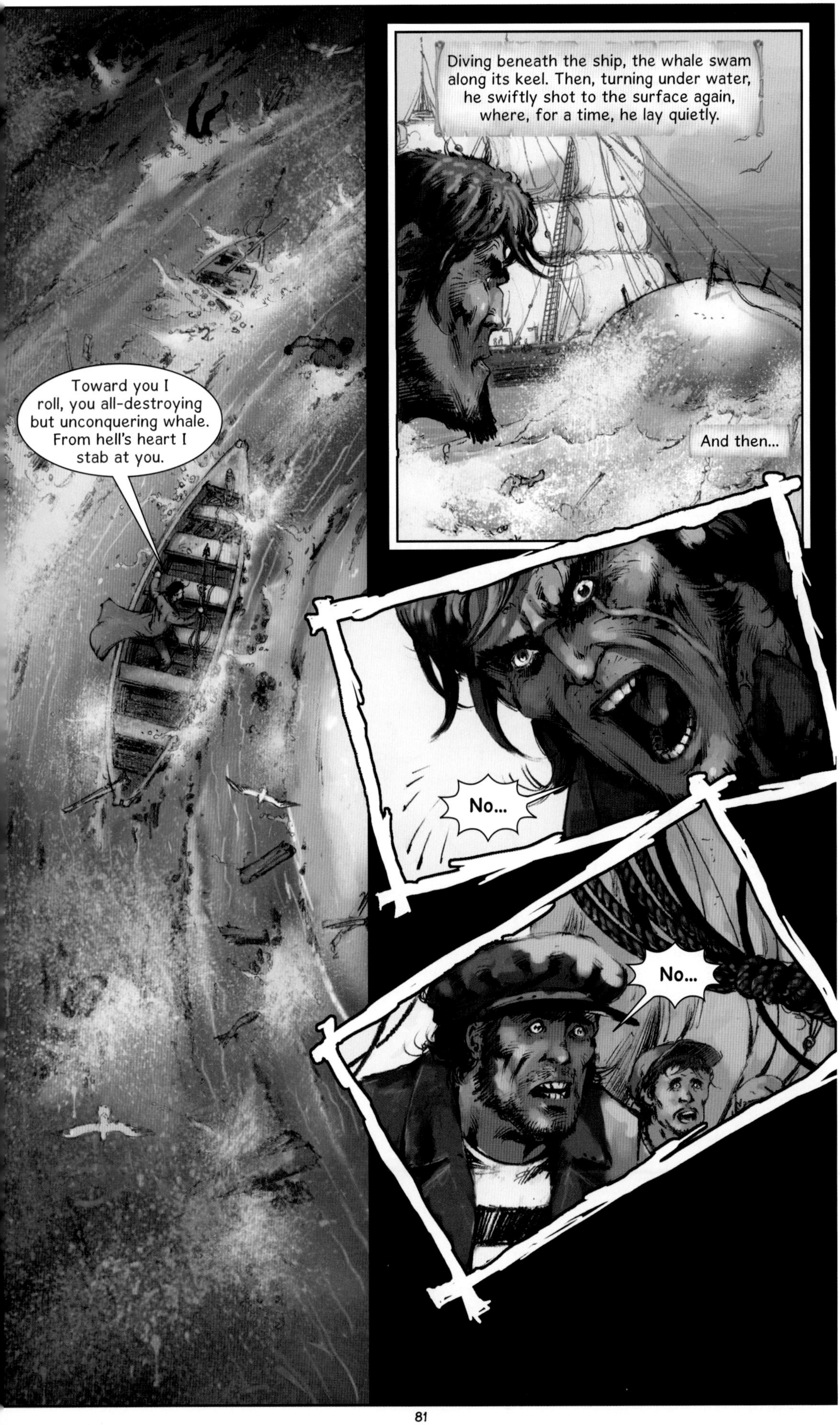

Toward you I roll, you all-destroying but unconquering whale. From hell's heart I stab at you.
Diving beneath the ship, the whale swam along its keel. Then, turning under water, he swiftly shot to the surface again, where, for a time, he lay quietly.
And then...
No...
No...

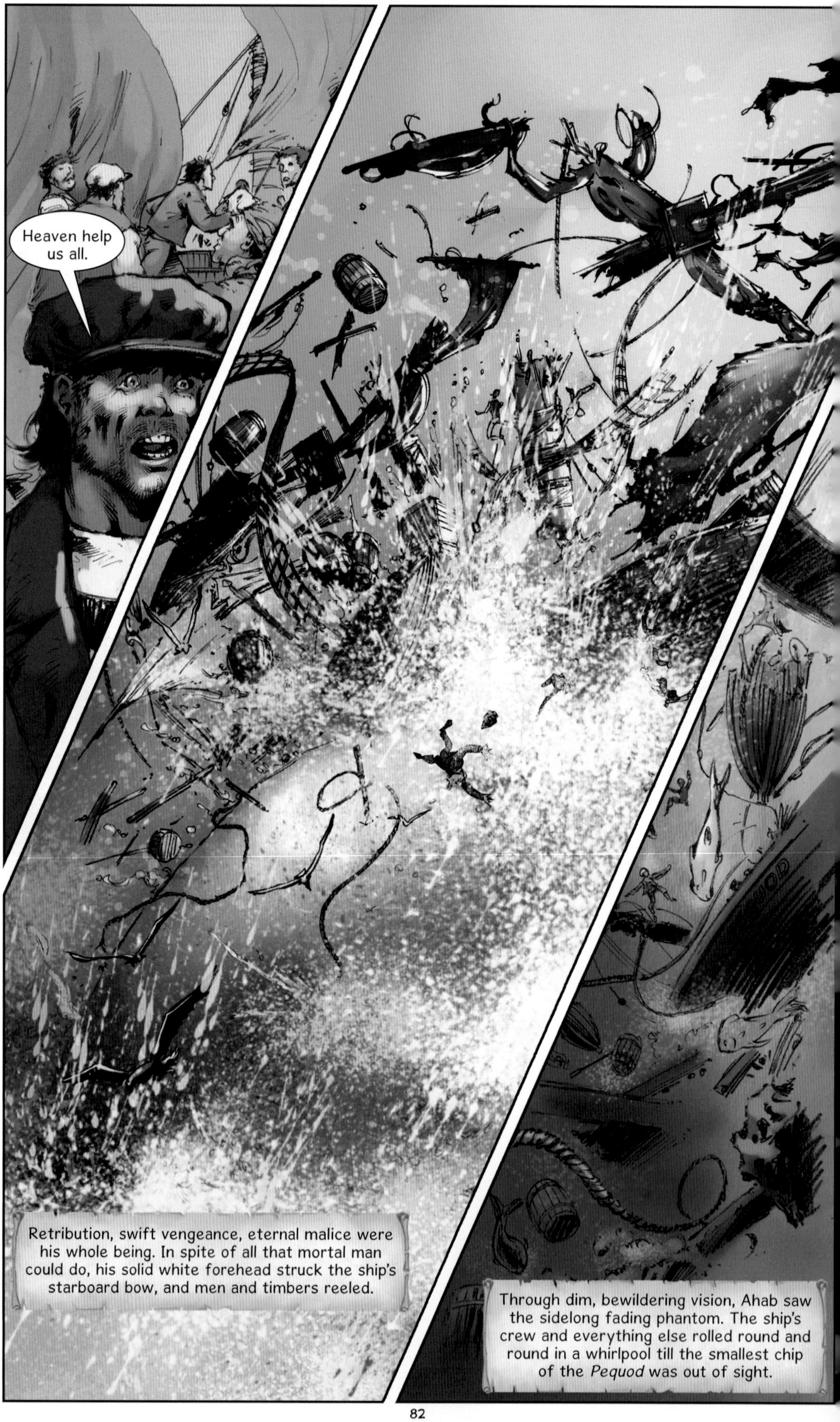
Heaven help us all.
Retribution, swift vengeance, eternal malice were his whole being. In spite of all that mortal man could do, his solid white forehead struck the ship's starboard bow, and men and timbers reeled.
Through dim, bewildering vision, Ahab saw the sidelong fading phantom. The ship's crew and everything else rolled round and round in a whirlpool till the smallest chip of the *Pequod* was out of sight.

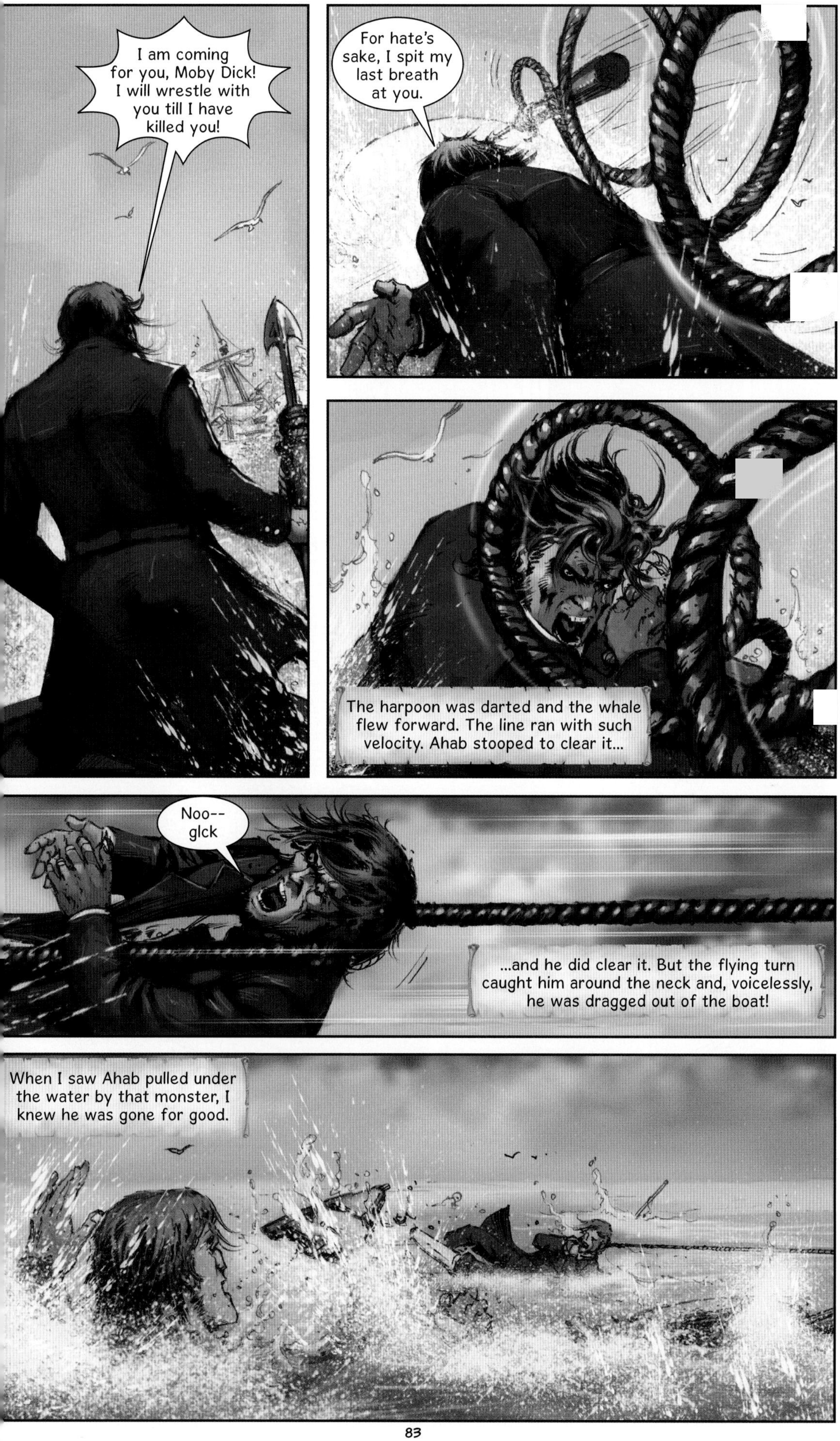

I am coming for you, Moby Dick! I will wrestle with you till I have killed you!
For hate's sake, I spit my last breath at you.
The harpoon was darted and the whale flew forward. The line ran with such velocity. Ahab stooped to clear it...
Noo-- glck
...and he did clear it. But the flying turn caught him around the neck and, voicelessly, he was dragged out of the boat!
When I saw Ahab pulled under the water by that monster, I knew he was gone for good.

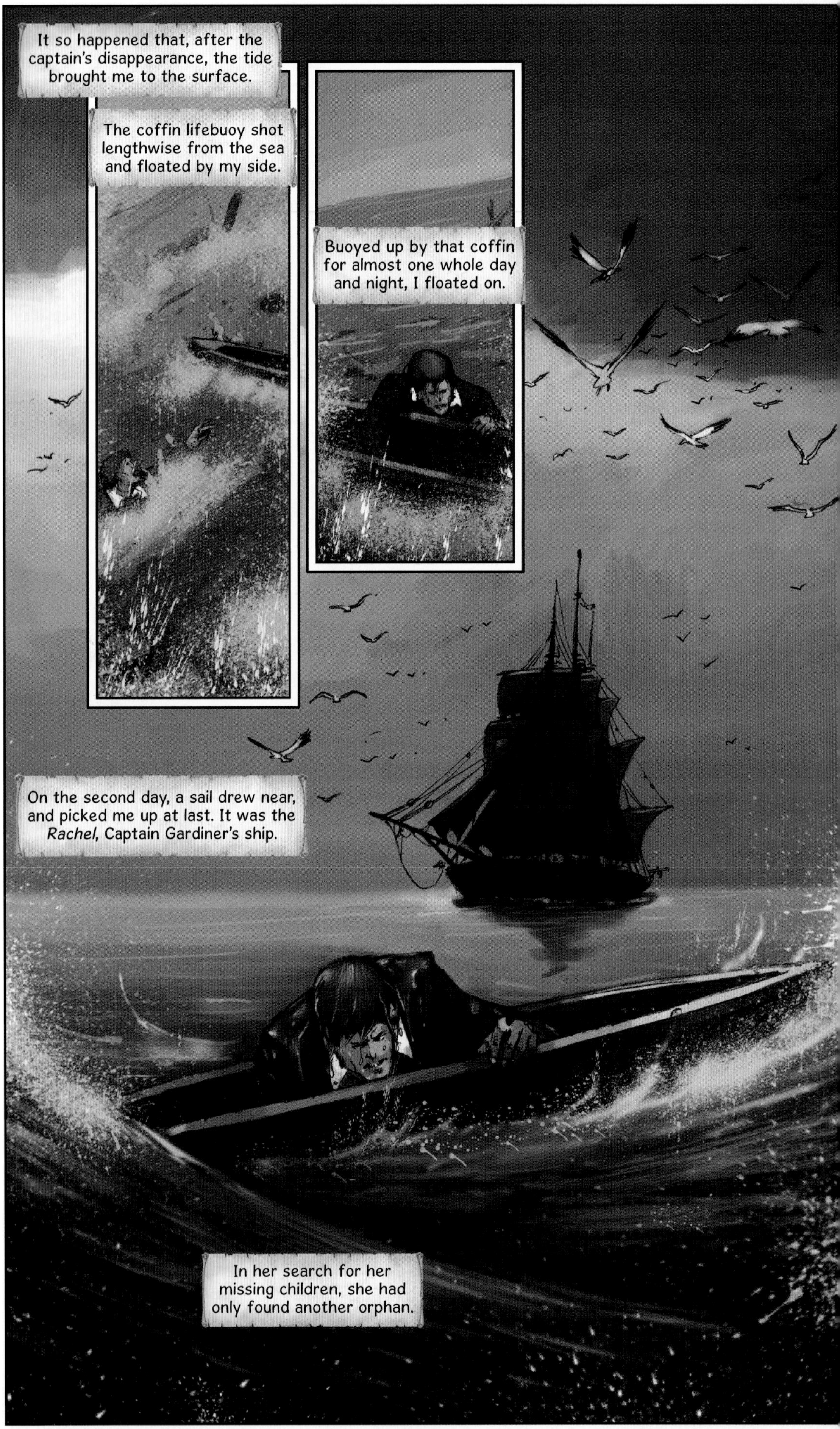
It so happened that, after the captain's disappearance, the tide brought me to the surface.
The coffin lifebuoy shot lengthwise from the sea and floated by my side.
Buoyed up by that coffin for almost one whole day and night, I floated on.
On the second day, a sail drew near, and picked me up at last. It was the *Rachel*, Captain Gardiner's ship.
In her search for her missing children, she had only found another orphan.

CAMPFIRE™

About Us

It is nighttime in the forest. The sky is black, studded with countless stars. A campfire is crackling, and the storytelling has begun—stories about love and wisdom, conflict and power, dreams and identity, courage and adventure, survival against all odds, and hope against all hope. In the warm, cheerful radiance of the campfire, the storyteller's audience is captivated, as in a trance. Even the trees and the earth and the animals of the forest seem to have fallen silent, bewitched.

Inspired by this enduring relationship between a campfire and gripping storytelling, we bring you four series of *Campfire Graphic Novels*:

Our *Classic* tales adapt timeless literature from some of the greatest writers ever.

Our *Mythology* series features epics, myths and legends from around the world, tales that transport readers to lands of mystery and magic.

Our *Biography* titles bring to life remarkable and inspiring figures from history.

Our *Original* line showcases brand new characters and stories from some of today's most talented graphic novelists and illustrators.

We hope you will gather around our campfire and discover the fascinating stories and characters inside our books.

WHALE HO!

SPERM WHALE

The sperm whale is the largest of all toothed whales. Usually gray or brown in color, it has a huge head which accounts for one-third of its body, and which contains more than a thousand liters of oily fluid called spermaceti. Weighing about nine kilograms, the sperm whale's brain is the largest of any living creature. It's even bigger than the brain of the giant blue whale! Interestingly, the sperm whale is also the deepest diving marine mammal, and is known to plunge to depths of up to 4,000 feet in search of its favorite food—the giant squid. During these dives, it often holds its breath for more than an hour! The sperm whale travels in groups called pods and the members of a pod communicate with each other by making loud clicking sounds.

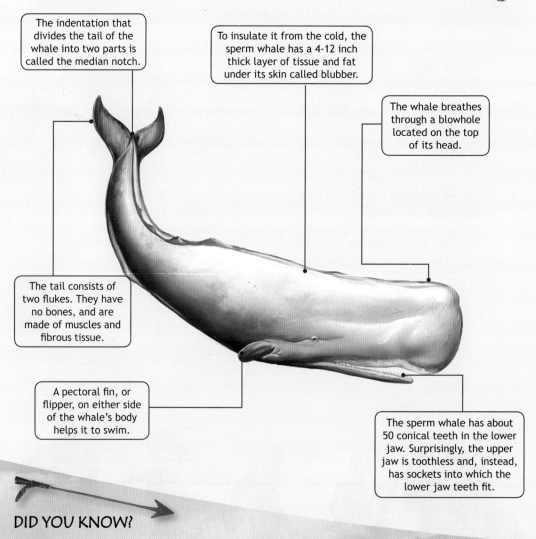

The indentation that divides the tail of the whale into two parts is called the median notch.

To insulate it from the cold, the sperm whale has a 4-12 inch thick layer of tissue and fat under its skin called blubber.

The whale breathes through a blowhole located on the top of its head.

The tail consists of two flukes. They have no bones, and are made of muscles and fibrous tissue.

A pectoral fin, or flipper, on either side of the whale's body helps it to swim.

The sperm whale has about 50 conical teeth in the lower jaw. Surprisingly, the upper jaw is toothless and, instead, has sockets into which the lower jaw teeth fit.

DID YOU KNOW?

The character of Moby Dick was supposedly inspired by a real-life whale named Mocha Dick. Mocha Dick was a huge white sperm whale that lived in the Pacific Ocean in the 19th century. Named after the island of Mocha near Chile, many accounts say that it killed more than 30 men and destroyed several ships! Like Moby Dick, it escaped countless attacks from whalers, and survived dozens of harpoons being thrown into its back. Mocha Dick was eventually killed in the 1830s.

THE 19th CENTURY WHALER

Whaling, or the hunting of whales, flourished in Britain and America during the 19th century. Oil, bones, and meat were all valuable commodities that were acquired by capturing whales. Sperm whales, in particular, were hunted for spermaceti, which was used in many things like lamp fuel, perfumes, and candles. The 19th-century whaler was a ship, especially designed for whaling. Not only did it carry the equipment for hunting and killing its prey, but also the facilities for processing, storing, and preserving it until its return to port. It was a large ship and was spacious enough to store provisions for long voyages as well as the yield from a hunt.

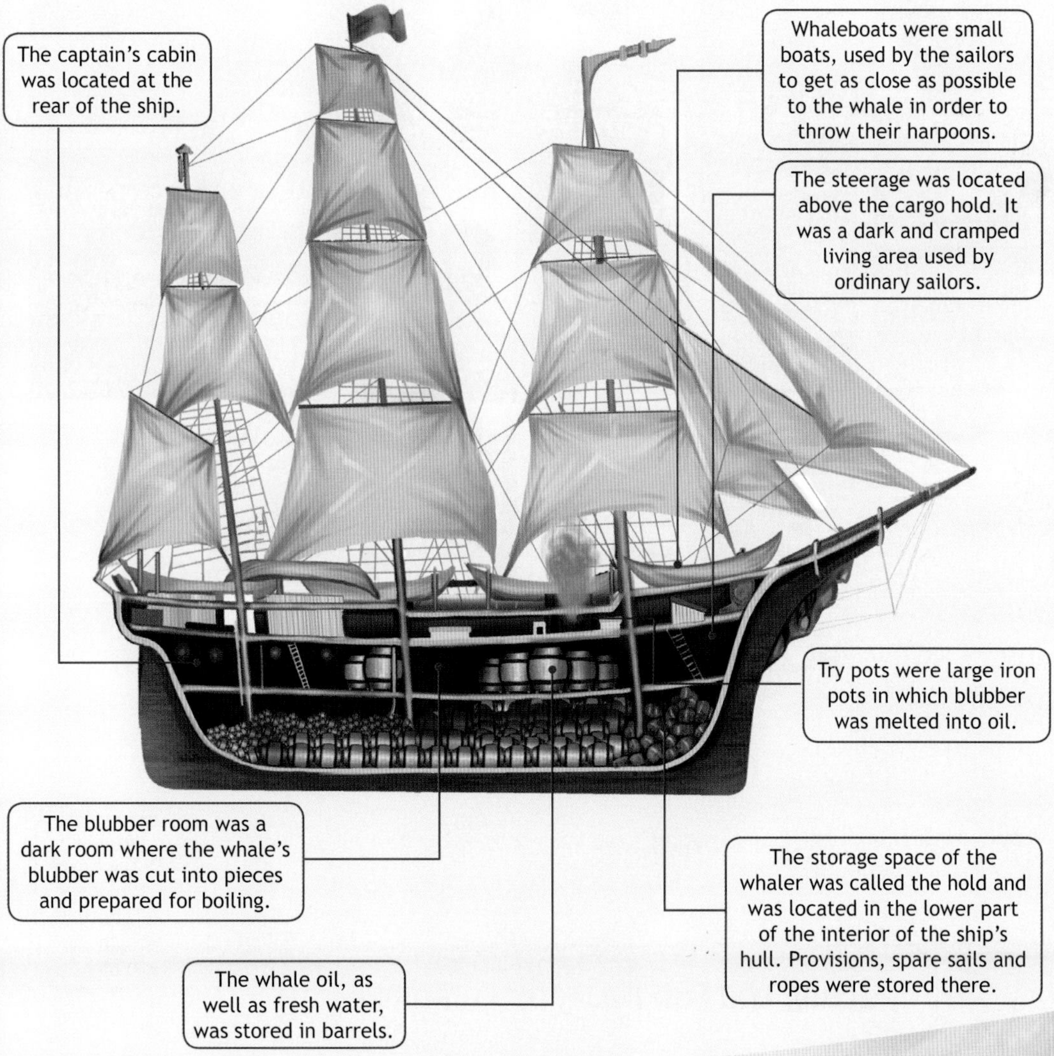

The captain's cabin was located at the rear of the ship.
Whaleboats were small boats, used by the sailors to get as close as possible to the whale in order to throw their harpoons.
The steerage was located above the cargo hold. It was a dark and cramped living area used by ordinary sailors.
Try pots were large iron pots in which blubber was melted into oil.
The blubber room was a dark room where the whale's blubber was cut into pieces and prepared for boiling.
The storage space of the whaler was called the hold and was located in the lower part of the interior of the ship's hull. Provisions, spare sails and ropes were stored there.
The whale oil, as well as fresh water, was stored in barrels.

DID YOU KNOW?

In their spare time, the crew of whalers carved beautiful designs on the teeth of sperm whales. This art was called scrimshaw. Figures were carved on the surface of a whale's tooth with a knife or needle, and then filled in with ink. Most sailors carved whaling scenes and their loved ones.

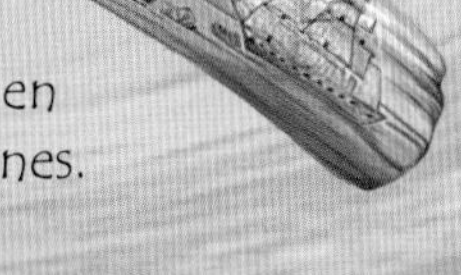